Readers love
BRAD BONEY

The Eskimo Slugger

"I really loved this book!! Brad has once again written a book that was thought-provoking, well written and one that just takes you on a sweet and tender love story."

—Love Bytes

"This is a very personal story. I didn't want to leave it… Hope is given body and soul here in this book."

—Prism Book Alliance

The Nothingness of Ben

"I would venture to say that *The Nothingness of Ben* is destined to be one of the top novels of 2013. Yes, dear reader—it is *that* good!"

—Joyfully Jay

"This is a book that will live in the hearts of readers for a very long time."

—All About Romance

The Return

"I liked the book… I laughed and cried. Fell a little in love with the guys. So, for me this was worth the read."

—Live Your Life, Buy the Book

"Without a doubt a well-written and engaging novel, especially if you are a music lover… This one is a must read for fans of the genre."

—MM Good Book Reviews

By BRAD BONEY

The Eskimo Slugger
The Nothingness of Ben
The Return
Yes

Published By DREAMSPINNER PRESS
http://www.dreamspinnerpress.com

YES

BRAD BONEY

Published by
DREAMSPINNER PRESS

5032 Capital Circle SW, Suite 2, PMB# 279, Tallahassee, FL 32305-7886 USA
http://www.dreamspinnerpress.com/

This is a work of fiction. Names, characters, places, and incidents either are the product of author imagination or are used fictitiously, and any resemblance to actual persons, living or dead, business establishments, events, or locales is entirely coincidental.

Yes
© 2015 Brad Boney.

Cover Art
© 2015 Alex Saskalidis.
Cover content is for illustrative purposes only and any person depicted on the cover is a model.

ISBN: 978-1-63216-841-2
Digital ISBN: 978-1-63216-842-9
Library of Congress Control Number: 2014920687
First Edition March 2015

Printed in the United States of America
∞
This paper meets the requirements of
ANSI/NISO Z39.48-1992 (Permanence of Paper).

"It takes a long time to become young."
—Pablo Picasso

CHAPTER ONE

IAN PARKER flushed the urinal and returned the toilet brush to its bucket. He knew there were better ways for a grown man to spend a Friday night, but he hated getting dinged on Yelp for not having clean bathrooms. He bent his knees, checked himself in the mirror, and fluffed his thinning hair. His beard looked a little scraggly, and he hadn't been to the gym in over a week. For a man on the brink of forty, he needed to do better.

Ian returned the cleaning supplies to the utility closet and then slipped behind the counter to check on Matthew, a college senior and his newest employee. Ian found him fumbling with the espresso machine while three people waited in line.

"Let me handle that," Ian said. "You take the orders. What is this supposed to be, anyway?"

"A single decaf soy latte, for here."

"Then why do you have the regular milk out?"

"I couldn't find the soy." Matthew turned to the first person in line and said, "Welcome to La Tazza Magica. What can I get for you this evening?"

Ian swapped milks and went to work. He placed a shot of decaf espresso into one of La Tazza's tall, stainless steel glasses and added the steamed soy milk. He set it on the counter, and a young woman stepped forward to claim it. She nodded to Ian, as if to say "Thanks for saving the day." Matthew relayed three more beverage orders, and Ian expedited them in quick succession.

As a young man in a Killers T-shirt picked up the last drink, Matthew turned to Ian and said, "Sorry about that, boss. I don't think the machine likes me."

"I should be the one apologizing. I'm sorry I snapped at you. I know the machine is temperamental, but it makes the best cup of

1

espresso in Austin. You'll get the hang of it eventually. Remember, when your line gets to three, call for help."

"I did, but you were cleaning the bathroom with the door closed. I don't think you heard me."

"Okay. Well, that's my mistake, then. No harm done. Could you bus and wash the dishes now?"

"Sure thing." Matthew pulled out his phone and scrolled through his notifications screen. Ian saw how many text messages he had, at least ten. On a good day, Ian felt lucky if he got one or two. Matthew plugged his phone into the sound system. "This is the new Dime Box album. I downloaded it this morning. Did you know the lead singer is gay?"

"No," Ian said. "What's his name?"

"Topher Manning." Matthew left the bar area and began collecting cups, plates, and glasses. Ian looked at the clock. Almost seven and a customer occupied every table, except for the large one in the corner with a "Reserved" sign on it. Ian did that for a freshman study group that came in every week. He scanned the room and thought about the day five years earlier when he bought the building that would become La Tazza Magica.

Located north of the UT campus on one of Austin's main thoroughfares, the former thrift shop proved to be the perfect size for a European-inspired café. With its vaulted twenty-foot tin ceiling and expansive windows, Ian transformed the space into a haven for students, writers, and the occasional chess player. In one corner, he set up a small living room with two identical black sofas facing each other and a red Queen Anne-style coffee table in between. In the opposite corner, he installed a dessert case and wooden bar, for an old-world pub feeling. A fifteen-foot wine rack stood like a tower behind the bar, and Ian suspended another rack from the ceiling for glasses and beer mugs.

He filled the central seating area with a variety of tables, both large and small, some regular height and others of the taller bistro style but all made of dark wood. He painted the plaster walls a deep mahogany and trimmed the windowpanes in black. He updated the electrical system and tripled the number of outlets, in order to accommodate laptop and phone chargers. He found a vintage corner bookcase at an antique fair and stocked it with classic literature and board games like Monopoly, Life, Risk, and Trivial Pursuit. He hung paintings of Italian cafés on the slivers of wall between the windows and surrounded the building with a U-shaped stone patio for outdoor seating.

For food, Ian designed a simple menu of sandwiches and salads, with an accent on seasonal, fresh, and local. He served wine, beer, and the best espresso in town. He named the place after his favorite café in Florence, La Tazza Fresca, but changed the adjective. Most nights he had a packed house, and at peak times, Ian would introduce strangers to each other and encourage them to share a table. He posted his prime directive on a sign above the east door:

Buy something
Stay as long as you want
Don't be a dick

The barista on duty always had the final say over music selection, but Ian encouraged an eclectic and low-key atmosphere. During job interviews he grilled potential candidates about their musical tastes, so as not to hire a Belieber or anyone with a Wagner obsession. What he ended up with surprised him—anything from Johnny Cash to Billie Holiday to Justin Timberlake to Mozart to the Carpenters to this new band called Dime Box.

The freshman study group burst through the east door and waved hello. They removed the "Reserved" sign and claimed their table. The same five students came in every Friday night, and Ian knew each of them by name—Jessica, Tyler, Ashley, Emily, and Quentin, the ringleader who had been coming into La Tazza since it opened.

"Hey, Ian," Quentin said as he approached the bar. "Nice tunes."

"You should tell Matthew. He's the DJ tonight."

"Thanks for saving the table."

"You're welcome, Q, as always. What's on the agenda tonight?"

"Econ and our Shakespeare survey course. Finals start in two weeks."

"You ready?"

"I'm a B minus student with an A plus personality. That's gotta count for something, right?" Quentin pulled out a credit card and set it on the bar. "Let's open a tab, since Ben still pays my American Express bill. How about five bottles of ice-cold Shiner Bock?"

"Nice try, buddy, but you're not twenty-one yet, and your brother will sue me if he finds out I'm serving booze to minors."

"Hey, it was worth a shot. Let's start with the usual, then."

"Skim lattes for Jessica and Ashley, a skim mocha for Emily, and straight espressos for you and Tyler."

"You're the man."

Ian swiped the credit card and handed it back to Quentin, then crossed to the machine and prepared the first drink. "Have you decided on a major yet?"

"No," Quentin said. "I have another year. I like my art classes, but it doesn't seem practical as a major. Ashley thinks I'd make a good counselor, but I hate listening to other people's problems. I'm way too self-absorbed for that."

Ian finished the second latte and started on the mocha. "I saw Ben on the news the other night. Something to do with a death penalty case?"

"He loves playing the big shot, doesn't he? Thirty years old and already arguing in front of the Texas Court of Appeals. Frankly I think they should fry the dude for what he did, but big brother says the state shouldn't be in the business of killing its own citizens."

"He's got a point." Ian finished the mocha and set it on the counter, then turned back to the machine to make the espressos. "How are Travis and your other brothers doing?"

"Jason's freaking a little because his boyfriend's moving to New York in the fall. And it's baseball season, so that's pretty much all Cade and Travis talk about. Speaking of Cade, we're having a huge blowout at the house for his sixteenth birthday. You should come by."

"When is it?"

"Memorial Day weekend. I can text you the details closer to the time."

Ian pulled out his phone, unlocked the welcome screen, and handed it to Quentin. "Put your number in there and then call yourself. That way you'll have mine. How are things with you and Ashley?"

"Awesome," Quentin said as he typed in his information. "She finally met my big gay family last week and loved them. She and Jason are going shopping tomorrow, and she wants Travis to teach her how to make chicken and dumplings." Quentin tapped the screen and put Ian's phone to his ear. After a few seconds, he said, "Hey, douchebag. Stop watching so much porn and get some studying done." He turned off the phone and handed it back.

Ian laughed as he put it into his pocket. He placed the five drinks on a tray and slid it across the bar. "There you go—two skim lattes, one skim mocha, and two espressos."

"Thank you, sir."

"Will the Walsh clan be joining us for Jeopardy Pursuit Night next month? You boys have a title to defend."

"We wouldn't miss it. All I have to do is whisper 'returning champion' into Ben's ear and he'll be there."

Quentin picked up the tray and carried the drinks to the group's corner table. The north door opened, and Bartley James, another of La Tazza's regulars, walked in. Bartley was Ian's customer crush, but with his all-American good looks and clean-cut appeal, he was also out of Ian's league—or at least that's what Ian believed. His nerves kicked into high gear as Bartley approached the counter.

"Hi, Ian. Can I get a double skim, please?"

"For here or to go?"

Bartley brushed a lock of golden-blond hair out of his eyes. "I need it to go tonight. I'm heading back to the office to finish the blueprints for the new house. We're breaking ground tomorrow."

"This the house you designed for the couple in Westlake?"

"One and the same. I've finally graduated from being an assistant to a full-fledged architect."

"Sounds like you'll need some food, then. Let me throw a sandwich together for you."

"I only brought in enough cash for the latte."

Ian turned to the espresso machine to make Bartley's double skim. "The sandwich is on the house. You're in here almost every day. It's the least I can do to help celebrate your big project."

"Well, thanks. I suppose food would be a good idea. I'm used to running on caffeine at times like this."

"You ever have our Pilgrim sandwich? I got the idea from a deli in P-town. You ever been there?"

"Provincetown? Mason and I went last summer, before everything fell…. Never mind. I need to stop…. What's on the sandwich?"

"Turkey, dressing, and homemade cranberry sauce. It's like Thanksgiving dinner."

"Sounds good," Bartley said. "But how do you get all that onto one sandwich?"

"Well, it can be a little messy, I admit, but it's bloody delicious."

"Bloody?"

Ian cringed. This was usually the part where he started blabbering about something of no importance. All his attempts to be cool around Bartley ultimately ended in failure. He knew he should shut up, but instead he launched into the inevitable explanation. "I've been watching this British soap called *Hollyoaks*. Twenty-three minutes a day, five days a week. Totally addictive, crazy show, and I'm not exaggerating. Half the characters belong in a mental institution. One of them named his kids Lucas and Leah. You know, after the *Star Wars* characters? There are these five insanely hot Roscoe brothers. The two things I've picked up are 'bloody' and 'sort it.'"

"What do you mean by 'sort it'?"

"Well, in Texas, when we have a problem, we fix it or handle it or deal with it. But in England, they sort it. I swear to God, they're constantly sorting things. And if you go to court, you don't testify, you give evidence."

"Hmm. What made you start watching a British soap opera?"

Ian finished the latte, handed it to Bartley, and then turned his attention to the sandwich. "It has a lot of gay characters. I'm a little obsessed with gay stories on television shows."

"Did you find it on BBC America or something?"

"No, YouTube. That's where all the good stuff is. People edit together the gay storylines from European soaps and add English subtitles. They're called 'trims.' Max and Iago from *El Cor de la Ciutat*. Lenny and Carsten from *Gute Zeiten, schlechte Zeiten*. Christian and Oliver from *Verbotene Liebe*."

Bartley laughed. "*Forbidden Love?*"

"Very good. Americans only know Brian and Justin from *Queer As Folk*, or Will and Sonny, of course, but there are all these other gay supercouples out there they've never even heard of, let alone seen. I recently lost an entire Saturday afternoon to Elias and Lari."

"Where are they from?"

"Finland. I can't pronounce the original title, but it translates as *Secret Lives*. Did you know people in Finland have saunas in their apartment buildings?"

"I didn't know that." Bartley took a sip of his latte. "You got any big plans for the weekend?"

"My friend Mark is taking me to Denver for my birthday."

"Today's your birthday?"

"No, tomorrow."

"Happy early birthday. How old?"

Ian hesitated as he spooned some dressing onto the sandwich. "Forty."

"Ouch. I'm coming up on thirty next year, and that's scary enough. I can't imagine what forty must feel like. Why Denver?"

"Mark is a big pothead. Sunday is April 20, and he wants to be there for the first legal 420 celebration and rally."

"So you're going somewhere for him on *your* birthday weekend?"

"I know. I do want to see what it's like at this stage, though, before it gets all commercialized."

"Do you smoke, yourself?"

Ian nodded. "Occasionally."

Matthew walked up to the counter with his busing tub. He grabbed two glasses and said, "I'm going into the back to start these."

Bartley smiled and said, "Hi, Matt."

"Hey, Mr. James."

Matthew turned away, and Ian tried not to laugh when he saw Bartley's ashen face. Once Matthew turned the corner, Ian said, "That's what forty feels like. I see you've already introduced yourself."

"Where did you find him, anyway?"

"He filled out an application like everyone else."

"And I suppose the fact that he looks like Andrew Garfield had nothing to do with why you hired him."

"Please," Ian said. "I'm old enough to be his father."

"I wasn't suggesting you want to sleep with him. I meant he's a good business decision. A lot of your young female customers will specifically choose this place over Starbucks because of him."

"And I hope a lot of the young male ones too. For his sake."

"Is he gay?"

Ian finished the sandwich and sliced it in half. "I asked him on the second day if he had a girlfriend—you know, almost in passing—and he said, 'Nope, I'm gay.' No hesitation whatsoever. It's a different world for these kids today. But if you plan on asking him out, stop calling him Matt. He hates that."

"Ask him out? No, that's not my plan. But why didn't he correct me?"

"Because people who work for tips aren't in the habit of contradicting customers." Ian wrapped the sandwich and handed it to Bartley. "That's four twenty-five for the latte." Bartley gave him a five dollar bill, and Ian noticed a large bandage on the inside of his right forearm. "What's that?"

Bartley sat the sandwich on the bar next to his double skim and peeled back the bandage. He displayed a fresh tattoo of a single Chinese symbol. "I just got it last night."

"What does it mean?" Ian asked.

YES

"Please don't take this the wrong way, but I'm keeping that a secret for now."

"No, that's cool. I totally understand. Every man should be entitled to a little mystery." Ian carefully examined the tattoo as he handed Bartley his change. "Where did you get it done?"

"The place over near Airport and Forty-Fifth Street." Bartley replaced the bandage and deposited the change directly into the tip jar. He picked up his sandwich and latte. After a brief hesitation, he said, "You know, we should get dinner sometime."

Ian felt his face get warm. Was Bartley asking him out?

"As friends."

Of course. As friends. In other words, no, Bartley was not asking him out. Not on a date, at least. They were going to be buddies. Wingmen. Bros. Ian plastered a smile on top of his disappointment and said, "I'd enjoy that."

"Excellent. Let's shoot for next week. Thanks again for the sandwich. I'll see you soon."

"Good luck with the groundbreaking tomorrow."

Bartley left the shop, and Ian cursed under his breath. He went into the back to relieve Matthew. "I'll finish the dishes," Ian told him. "You can go cover the register."

"You sure? I don't mind."

"I'm sure."

Matthew dried his hands with a towel. "Are you okay? You seem upset about something."

"I'm fine, but I'd rather have you up front. It's a good business decision. I'm trying to pull in the young and hip crowd, and no one thinks young and hip when they see me."

Matthew hung the towel on one of the hooks beside the dishwasher. "How old are you, anyway?"

"I'm glad you asked me that today. I'm thirty-nine."

"Why? What happens tomorrow?"

Ian removed some glasses from a rack and placed them on one of the metal shelves. "I turn forty."

"Forty's not that old."

9

"Thanks, but we both know you're only saying that because I'm your boss."

"No, I'm not." Matthew ignored Ian's instructions and began filling an empty rack with dirty cups and glasses. "Do you have a thing for Mr. James?"

Ian felt himself blushing and turned away. "Why would you ask that?"

"Because you don't exactly give free sandwiches to everyone. And I've noticed you get nervous around him."

"Whether or not I have a thing for Bartley is irrelevant. I'm too old for him."

"How do you know that?"

"I've seen the boys he brings in here," Ian said. "Bartley is out of my league."

"Have you ever asked him out?"

"No, but he just invited me to dinner. As friends."

"Oh." Matthew nodded. "So that's why you're upset. You want it to be more than friends."

"I didn't say that."

"You didn't have to. Do you mind if I offer a different perspective?"

"Sure. Why not? It's a two penny ante to play."

Matthew reached into his pocket, pulled out two pennies, and set them on the counter next to Ian. "Sometimes guys use the 'as friends' thing to ward off rejection. Test the waters, so to speak. You know, gauge interest. How long has he been coming in here?"

"He moved to the neighborhood with his boyfriend last year. He started coming in then."

"He has a boyfriend?"

"No, not anymore. They broke up last fall."

Matthew slid the rack of dirty cups and glasses into the dishwasher, closed the steel door, and pressed the red Start button. "And the boys he's brought in since then? They've been younger?"

"Your age."

"And how old was the ex-boyfriend?"

"In his thirties," Ian said.

"Well, that explains it. The twinks were rebound sex. He needed to prove he still has it, you know? But he wasn't serious about any of them. Now, suppose he wakes up one morning and he is serious. *About you*, for example. Put yourself in his shoes. He comes in here all the time and thinks you're a total stud. You're tall, handsome, well built—you've got that whole Al Parker, muscle daddy thing going on."

"How do you know who Al Parker is?"

"I watch a lot of vintage porn, but that's beside the point. Clearly you have a perception problem, boss. It sounds like you don't see yourself the way other people see you. Trust me, there's no reason why Bartley James wouldn't want to date you. The question is, would you want to date him? Sure, maybe you flirt around, but how does he know you don't do that with all the customers? How does he know you don't give them all free sandwiches? You see what I'm saying? You own the place where he gets his coffee. He doesn't want to make you uncomfortable if you're just being friendly, so he's keeping things on ice in case you're not interested. He's providing you with a graceful exit, which means he's at least an above-average guy. He probably thinks he has a better chance with you if the setting is low-key."

"Really?"

"Totally. You should definitely hang out with Mr. James and see where it goes."

"So you think he's into me?" Ian asked.

"Honestly, I don't know. All I'm saying is, you can't rule it out based on him asking you to dinner as friends. If he wants to jump your bones, something tells me he'll find a way to let you know."

"What does that mean?"

"Come on, boss." The green light on the dishwasher started to blink, and Matthew lifted the door and stepped away from the emerging steam. "You don't recognize a player when you see one? The dude's too perfect, with his Liam Hemsworth chin and his Chris Pine eyes. And the way he introduces himself? 'Hi, I'm James. Bartley James.' Ridiculous."

"I think it's charming."

"Of course you do." Matthew reached in and slid out the tray, then tapped it a few times to shake off the remaining droplets of water. "Look, I said he's above average, didn't I? But it wouldn't kill you to be a little wary. With guys like that, you can't believe everything that comes out of their mouths."

"Sounds like you had your heart broken pretty bad."

"This isn't about me."

"I was only welcoming you to the club." Ian removed several of the glasses from Matthew's clean rack and placed them on the middle shelf. "Did you call him Mr. James on purpose?"

"Maybe. He keeps calling me Matt."

"I told him to stop."

"Really? Thanks. That was nice of you." Matthew piled a few coffee cups and moved them to the top shelf. "Look, you guys would make a great couple. That's all I'm saying. He's not my type, but I can absolutely see why you have a thing for him."

Ian grumbled. "Even if you're right, there are still other reasons why it would never…. Forget it."

"What?"

"You're too young to understand."

"Wow," Matthew said. "You have no idea how offensive that is."

"I'm sorry. But there's no way you can understand regret."

"What could you possibly have to regret? You run your own business. That's the dream, dude."

"That's not the whole picture, *dude*." Ian wiped down the counter with one of the towels. "La Tazza is the one thing I've done right, but it can't erase the decade and a half that came before it. I was a mess, plain and simple. I took stupid risks and flushed what should have been the best fifteen years of my life down the toilet. I missed that crucial off-ramp to happiness, and now I can never go back and find it. I may be successful, but I'm also alone. Learn from my mistakes, Padawan. Make something of your life while you're still young enough to enjoy it."

"Would you go back?" Matthew said. "If someone gave you the chance?"

Ian chuckled. "Are you serious? In a heartbeat. I could reshape my whole life."

YES

Matthew looked unconvinced. He arranged the empty racks on top of the dishwasher and then leaned against the counter. He folded his hands across his chest and said, "I don't know. I think I might avoid certain mistakes, but then I'd end up making brand new ones. Rethinking the past is a pointless exercise."

"Maybe." Ian heard the west door open. "Someone just came in. Out to the front, please."

"Okay, I'm going. You should listen to me, though, about Mr. James. I'm pretty smart for a college student, even if I can't work an espresso machine."

"Yet," Ian said. "Give it time. You've only been at it for a few days. It's like driving a stick shift."

"Maybe that's my problem."

"You've never driven a manual transmission before?"

"Nope."

"Man, that's a shame."

Matthew turned to go but then stopped and said, "One last thing. Someone asked me yesterday what La Tazza Magica means. I felt like an idiot because I didn't have an answer for her."

"Your generation doesn't know how to use Google Translate?"

Matthew grinned. "I think she was just flirting with me."

"It's Italian for 'the magic cup.'"

"Oh, cool."

"I always wanted to open an enchanted coffee shop. Pretty stupid, huh?"

"Not at all. Look, you provide jobs for college students. I don't know if I'd call that enchanted, but it's definitely not stupid. If I haven't said thank you for hiring me, well, thanks."

"You're welcome. Now up front. And don't forget. Colleen's in charge this weekend while I'm gone. Whatever she says goes."

"Sure thing, boss." Matthew grinned. "Oh, and since I won't be seeing you tomorrow, happy birthday."

WHEN IAN got home after closing, he poured a glass of red wine and sat in his dark kitchen. He downloaded *John Denver's Greatest*

13

Hits and both Dime Box albums onto his phone for the plane ride. He glanced at the time. It was after midnight and officially his birthday. He got up and went to the counter. He had bought a six-pack of cupcakes as a treat, and he put one onto a plate. Ian rummaged through several drawers until he found a box of candles and some matches. He pressed one of the candles into the chocolate icing and lit it. The glow from the flame threw shadows around the kitchen as he sang "Happy Birthday" to himself. Then he closed his eyes and blew out the candle. Since no one could hear him, Ian didn't see any harm in saying it out loud.

"I wish I could go back and do it all over again."

CHAPTER TWO

THE NEXT morning at six, Ian stood at the foot of his driveway and waited for his best friend, Mark. A single piece of rolling luggage rested beside him. The sun wouldn't rise for another hour and a half, but the temperature had already climbed into the sixties. Spring in Austin could be unpredictable, but Ian never considered living anywhere else.

He pulled out his phone and swiped the screen. He opened up Grindr out of habit. No messages. He scrolled through the thumbnails of headless torsos and the occasional face pic. Barely anyone over thirty. What did he expect in a neighborhood so close to campus? A flash of headlights appeared at the end of the block, and Ian put his phone away. The car stopped in front of his house, and the trunk popped open. Ian laid his bag next to Mark's, slammed the trunk closed, and got into the passenger seat.

"Happy birthday, sunshine."

"Thanks," Ian said. "Although I don't see what there is to be happy about."

"You're not going to be grumpy all weekend, are you? Haven't you ever heard of aging gracefully?"

"I'm the birthday boy. If I want to be grumpy, that's my prerogative."

"Great. I can tell this is going to be a cheerful and upbeat two days." Mark put the car into drive and headed back to the main road. "I want to point out, however, that I wasn't grumpy on my fortieth birthday, last year."

"You had a hundred people at your party. What did you have to be grumpy about?"

"Well, maybe if you had something in your life other than that damn coffee shop, you'd have more friends than just me."

15

"I used to have lots of friends. It's not my fault everyone ended up married or in rehab. Besides, I'm supposed to have dinner with someone next week."

"A date?"

"Not exactly. The architect."

"He asked you out? Oh my God, why didn't you text me? That's huge!"

"He didn't ask me out. He said we should have dinner next week. As friends. We didn't even exchange phone numbers. Besides, you know it would never work."

"Why not? Friends is a good place to start."

"I don't want to talk about it."

"Fine. Forget about him, then. By this afternoon, we're going to be so Rocky Mountain high that nothing else will matter."

"You're right. I'm as ready as Freddie Roscoe. I even loaded up my phone with John Denver last night, so bring on the legal weed."

THEY ARRIVED at their hotel around noon and hit a gourmet burger joint for lunch. Although residents and tourists could now buy and possess a limited amount of marijuana in Colorado, they could not smoke it in public or even hotel rooms, making things difficult for tourists. Mark solved this problem by booking a room with a balcony, which still broke the law but greatly reduced the possibility of getting caught. After hitting a few shops and purchasing some samples, they went back to their room and spent the afternoon on what they dubbed, rather unimaginatively, Ian thought, the Mary Jane Terrace. As the sun set, they were joined by two young couples, one on each side of them, who had the same idea. They introduced themselves, but Ian forgot their names almost immediately. One of the women asked where they were from.

"Austin," Mark said.

"Oh, we love Austin. Don't we, Stephen?"

Her boyfriend or husband or whatever he was nodded. "Great music town."

"We were there last month for South by Southwest. Terrible tragedy. What possesses a young man to drive into a crowd of people like that? We're from Seattle, but our legal weed doesn't start until this summer. Stephen works for Microsoft. What do you two do for a living?"

"I own a café near the UT campus."

"And I'm a lawyer for the great state of Texas," Mark said. "I work in the attorney general's office. All the big cases."

Ian grinned, because Mark didn't work on any big cases for the attorney general's office. He reviewed tax code legislation for the state Senate. But Ian could play this game, especially when they were stoned. "Did I mention that Sandy stopped in Friday for a latte?"

"No," Mark said without missing a beat. "Is she filming *The Heat 2*?"

The woman sat forward in her chair. "Sandy?"

Mark turned to her. "Oh, sorry. Sandra Bullock. She lives in Austin, you know. Owns a restaurant and everything. She loves the chai lattes at Ian's shop."

"No shit?" Stephen said. "She was good in *Gravity*."

Mark leaned in and lowered his voice. "She *loathed* the director, but if you tell anyone I said that, I'll deny this conversation ever happened."

"Are you boys a couple?" the woman on the other side of them asked. The man sitting next to her looked too baked to participate in the conversation.

"No," Mark said. "Just friends. We know each other too well for anything more."

"Did you grow up together?"

"Not quite," Ian said. "We met in college, at UT. We lived in the same dorm."

The second woman nodded. "I see."

They were silent for several minutes. Then the first woman took a drag from her joint, blew out the smoke, and made a sweeping hand gesture toward the mountains. "Would you look at that fucking view?"

IAN AND Mark took a short nap and then went out for a late dinner. Afterward, they strolled the streets of Lower Downtown until they chanced upon a narrow alley. At the end of the alley stood a small shop with a blue neon sign over the door.

Enchantmints

"Let's check it out," Ian said.

They walked the short distance and stepped into the shop. Bars, chocolates, licorice, taffies, gumdrops, and marshmallow treats were stacked in glass cases, waiting to be purchased and devoured. A prominent placard on the wall informed them that all the goods were infused with THC, the buzz-worthy chemical in pot.

"It's like Willy Wonka for stoners," Mark whispered.

"As if Willy Wonka wasn't already for stoners."

The concept of candy edibles represented an excellent workaround to the "no smoking in public" problem. There were a few tables for sitting, but instead of espresso on the menu, the chalkboard above the cash register listed a variety of candy-flavored sodas and hot chocolates. Since he didn't see anyone, Ian yelled, "Hello?" A few moments later, a young man appeared from the rear of the store. He wore a black University of Colorado T-shirt and some puka shells around his neck. He had dirty-blond hair that fell into his eyes and an adorable, sheepish grin.

"Greetings, gentlemen. Welcome to Enchantmints. My name is Tad."

"Do you own this place?" Ian asked.

"No, I just work here. I can answer any questions, though. I'm *highly* familiar with the merchandise."

Mark stepped up to the counter. "What do you recommend?"

"Well, that depends on what you're trying to accomplish. The gumdrops are much more energetic than your average high, and they come in fourteen different flavors. Very good for daytime activities like sightseeing. If you have altitude sickness, try the marshmallow crispies. They're one of our best sellers. The peanut brittle is both delicious and powerful. Great for watching action movies but not romantic comedies or foreign flicks. Especially avoid anything French or starring Patrick Dempsey."

"Even his early stuff?" Ian said, playing along with Tad's shtick. "Like *Can't Buy Me Love*, or maybe *Loverboy*?"

"Especially not his early stuff. You might be able to get away with *Transformers*, because it's an action movie and has Shia LaBeouf as a bitter counterbalance, or possibly Dempsey's obscure guest appearance as Matthew the sportscaster on *Will & Grace*. But tread lightly with *W&G*, dude—that shit's like crack if you binge watch it. Now, if you'd rather kick it old school, you can't go wrong with an excellent Alice B. Toklas brownie, even though the original recipe actually belonged to a young painter named Brion Gysin. I made these myself from a Nestlé recipe I found online. Full disclosure—they're a heartbeat away from mushrooms. Perfect for camping in the mountains."

Ian squatted down and peered into one of the cases. Under a tiny glass dome sat a single chocolate kiss wrapped in gold foil. A small sign sat next to the dome.

Made with Manick Butter!

$100

Ian stood up. "What's Manick Butter?"

Tad got a sparkle in his eye. "That's one of Mrs. Brown's special editions."

"Who's Mrs. Brown?" Mark asked.

"No one really knows. She's kind of shrouded in mystery. Lives up on Curtis Street. Some people say she's a direct descendant of Molly Brown. But then I say, how do you explain the German accent? She bakes a lot of our specialty items and every once in a while does a limited run—four or five pieces with a totally unique high. Some have even called them magical. She gives each edition a distinctive name but never tells us what it means. For the big celebration this weekend, she only made one of these kisses. What is Manick Butter, you ask? The answer lies in the experience."

"Boy, oh boy," Mark said. "You're good. It better be pretty spectacular for a hundred bucks, though."

Tad nodded. "I agree it's a risk, but I envy the lucky bastard who has the balls to go for it. Mrs. Brown has a real Zen approach to these one-of-a-kind chocolates. When she brought it in yesterday, I said, 'Mrs. Brown, who's gonna pay a hundred bucks for a single kiss?' She looked me right in the eye and said, 'Vatch, my leetle Tad. Zee keess vill find zee right coostomer.' I've had a lot of tire kickers today, but no one's taken the plunge."

"I'll take it," Ian said.

"Are you crazy?" Mark exclaimed. "A hundred bucks for a single high? Don't you know when you're being Don Drapered? No offense, Tad."

"I take that as a compliment."

"The place is called Enchantmints," Ian said. "For one night, I want to have my delusion that something magical might happen to me, even if it's just a really sweet buzz."

Mark shook his head. "I'm not saying another word. Throw your money away if you want, but you're an idiot."

"I thought you weren't going to say another word." Ian turned back to Tad. "Could I have the kiss and two of the brownies, please?"

"You got it. Anything for you, sir?"

Mark nodded. "I'll take two of the marshmallow crispies, six gumdrops—I don't care what flavors, surprise me—and some of the peanut brittle."

Tad rang up their order. Ian's tab came to one hundred forty dollars and Mark's to ninety. They left the shop and returned to their hotel, where they ate some of the peanut brittle, watched *Olympus Has Fallen* on pay-per-view, and fell asleep.

THE NEXT day they celebrated April 20 with gumdrops and the big rally at the Civic Center. The festivities continued into the evening with brownies and marshmallow crispies, all of which were excellent in both flavor and stonage. By the time they woke up on Monday morning, all the candy had been eaten, except for Ian's chocolate kiss made with Manick Butter. He thought about it once or twice over the weekend, but the time never seemed right. In the taxi to the airport, he reached into his coat pocket and pulled out the small candy box. He removed the top and revealed the foil-wrapped kiss. "Look what I forgot."

"Your hundred-dollar high?" Mark said. "How could you forget that?"

"I don't know."

"Well, you might as well eat it now. You can't risk going through security with drugs."

"Technically, it's not pot."

"Are you ready to explain that to a TSA agent when his dog barks the alarm?"

Ian unwrapped the kiss. It hadn't melted in the slightest. "I don't really want to do this right before I get on a plane, but I also don't want to throw a hundred bucks away."

"Just eat the goddamned thing."

"You want half?"

Mark held up his hand. "No. I need to sober up. I haven't had a weekend like that since I was twenty-one."

Ian popped the kiss into his mouth and chewed. "Mmm, delicious. It's made with a rich dark chocolate. What if it melts my skin or something?"

"You should have thought of that before you ate it."

By the time they boarded the plane, Ian felt a little sleepy but not buzzed in the least. Mark inflated a neck pillow and covered his eyes with a mask. Once they reached cruising altitude, Ian put in his earbuds and listened to John Denver's "Leaving on a Jet Plane."

Then he too fell asleep.

IAN WOKE up when a flight attendant brushed his arm with the beverage cart. The music in his ears had changed to one of the new Dime Box songs he purchased on Friday night. He looked at Mark, who was out cold, and then checked the time on his phone. They had been in the air for almost an hour, and he still didn't feel stoned. He'd been bamboozled again. *What a waste of a hundred bucks*. Ian paused the music and stuffed the phone and earbuds into his pocket. He unbuckled his seat belt, stood up, and yanked at the waist of his jeans. He walked down the aisle to the rear of the plane, but the sign on the door of the bathroom read "Occupied." As Ian waited, a beautiful and buxom young woman came down the aisle and joined him in line. He saw several men turn and follow her with their gaze as she passed.

She smiled at Ian. "You waiting for the bathroom?"

"I am."

She tilted her head and said, "Me too."

Was she flirting with him?

"You live in Austin?" she asked.

Ian nodded.

"Go to UT?"

He looked over her head and down the aisle toward Mark, to see if he had put her up to this, but he remained sound asleep. "Do you mean as a professor?"

Her bright smile faded. "No, as a student, silly. Unless you're one of those supersmart freaks who graduated when he was twelve."

An elderly man exited the toilet. Ian aborted his bizarre conversation with the young woman and stepped inside. He hunched over and closed the door, then threw the latch into the occupied position. A soft overhead light came on. Ian looked down at the steel bowl. He opened his pants and took a long piss, then zipped up and pulled his belt tight.

Ian looked down and saw two more notches than usual. That struck him as odd. He had dropped a pound or two in the last few weeks but not two notches worth. He flushed the toilet and turned toward the tiny basin. He soaped up his hands and checked his eyes in the mirror. They didn't look bloodshot at—

Ian froze.

His eyes darted up and down his reflection. He immediately flashed back to the day, six years earlier, when he got hit by a car on his bike. He couldn't feel his legs or feet for almost two days. The paralysis turned out to be temporary, but it gave Ian plenty of time to ponder his future. As the car hit him, he remembered thinking, *This could change everything.* After that, he slammed against the pavement and blacked out.

Ian blinked and snapped back to reality. He stared at the mirror again but didn't recognize the person staring back at him. He reached out and touched the glass with his soapy finger. It wasn't just that he looked twenty pounds lighter.... He tilted his head forward and checked out his scalp. Where did that come from? He carefully pinched the bottom edge of his white T-shirt, lifted it up, and gasped at the flatness of his stomach. "What the fuck?" Ian let the T-shirt drop and spun around, as if he expected to find someone standing behind him. As the gravity of the situation dawned on him, Ian shook his head. No way. Things like this didn't happen in real life. He turned back to the basin and rinsed off his hands. He splashed some water on his face, rubbed his eyes, and checked the mirror again. He touched his cheekbones and scowled. His beard made him look like a hipster.

This could change everything.

"Don't panic," he said to his reflection.

Ian dried his hands and pressed them against the mirror to make sure it wasn't some kind of trick. No one could pull that off. Not on a commercial airline, at least. He poked around the corners near the ceiling and looked for a hidden camera. No, he had to be hallucinating, except he didn't feel stoned at all. Or was he so stoned that he didn't even realize how stoned he was? Then again, if this wasn't a hallucination—if it was really happening—that would explain why the young woman in the aisle mistook him for a student. Unless maybe she was part of the hallucination too.

Was he even on an airplane?

Ian lowered the lid of the toilet, sat down, and pulled his knees to his chest. It couldn't be a trick and it couldn't be real. Even though he didn't feel stoned, this had to be the effects of Manick Butter. His visions in the mirror and his conversation with the young woman were all part of a wild trip. He must have imagined her. No other logical explanation existed. He cursed his decision to eat the kiss before boarding a plane, but at the same time, he wasn't a novice at this kind of thing. Ian remembered the night he did too much GHB at a bathhouse in Fort Lauderdale, and another night he did too much ketamine at a circuit party in Houston. He looked around the compact bathroom. He felt comfortable enough. Maybe he could stay here for the rest of the flight and ride it out.

Someone knocked on the door and said, "Excuse me?"

Ian pulled his knees in closer. The voice belonged to the young woman waiting after him, which meant he hadn't imagined her. "Are you okay in there?"

"I'm fine," Ian said. "I'm sorry. I'll be out in a minute."

"Thank you. I really need to pee bad."

He couldn't stay in the bathroom any longer. It would only create a scene and draw attention, two things Ian needed to avoid. Despite his uncertainty, he eased his legs forward and stood up. He washed his hands again and tried to avoid looking at himself in the mirror. He had no idea how to proceed. "You can get through this," Ian told himself, but he needed an anchor.

Mark.

He had to keep it together for sixty seconds and get back to his seat next to Mark. Then everything would be okay. Ian dried his hands and took a deep breath. He opened the door and practically knocked over the young woman waiting in line. He apologized and hurried past her down the aisle. He took his seat next to Mark, shook him, and lifted his sleep mask.

"Wake up," Ian said. "I'm having a really bad trip."

Mark opened his eyes and recoiled. "What the fuck, man? Who in the hell are you?"

"What are you talking about?"

Mark shook off his nap and looked around. "You must have overshot your row or something. Someone else is sitting there. What's your seat number? Do you have your boarding pass?"

"It's me. Ian."

"Ian?" Mark glanced up and down the aisle. "Okay. If you say so. There's no point in getting into an argument about it." With a look of subdued terror on his face, Mark reached up and pushed the flight attendant button.

"What are you doing?" Ian said. "Don't you recognize me? I thought I was hallucinating. Tell me I'm hallucinating."

YES

Mark removed the pillow from around his neck and swiped off his mask. "Let's let the flight attendant handle this, okay? I don't want any trouble. Please, whatever you're doing, you don't have to go through with it. Think about prison at your age. Have you ever seen *Turned Out*? Or *Oz*? Sure, I know it looks hot when it's Chris Meloni, but this isn't fiction, young man. You're on a real plane, and I'm a real person. These things have consequences, and there's no point in ruining your life before it's even begun. I'm sure your cause—whatever it is, religious or otherwise—I'm sure it's a worthy one. Have you been wronged by the American political system? Well, take a number and get in line. But you have to ask yourself, is this kind of criminal behavior worth what comes after? Have you thought about being thrown into solitary confinement? Because you seem to have anger issues. I know I just met you, but it doesn't take a degree in psychology to figure that out. It makes me wonder, have you asked yourself the hard questions? We always have options."

"Mark, it's me. Can't…? Look, I'm wearing Ian's clothes."

"And that's supposed to convince me? You're wearing jeans and a plain white T-shirt. If they belong to Ian, then what have you done with him? What's your angle here, kid? Why do you insist on pretending you're Ian Parker?"

"I'm not pretending."

"Then prove it," Mark said.

"I can… I can tell you things I know about you, like your favorite TV show is *RuPaul's Drag Race*. You're obsessed with Robbie Rogers, which I totally don't get. And you have a dog named Kitty."

"Practically anyone who follows me on Instagram could know those things. Have you been stalking me? Does this involve sexual blackmail? Because let me tell you right now, I—"

"We met at Jester Hall twenty-two years ago. You live on West Thirty-Ninth Street between Avenue B and Avenue C. You used to have a boyfriend named Troy, but I called him Sparky for no other reason than I thought it suited him better than Troy."

Mark paused, and it looked like maybe Ian had convinced him. But then Mark shook his head and said, "Still not conclusive. Are

25

you al-Qaeda? Or maybe NSA? It's so hard to tell the difference these days. Or a spy? No, you're too young to be a spy. What am I saying? They have spies who are kids now. There's a whole movie franchise built around them. What have you done with my friend? Did you lock him in the bathroom? Is that what you did? Because if you've hurt him in any way, I swear I'll—"

"I am your friend. Why can't you look at me and see that?" Ian glanced down the aisle and saw a female flight attendant heading their way. He had to think of something fast. He turned to Mark and whispered, "Okay. I didn't want to go there, but could practically anyone else know you have a thing for twincest porn? Maybe Elijah and Milo Peters? Or the two brothers from Brazil?"

Mark's jaw dropped.

"I thought that would do the trick."

The flight attendant appeared next to their seats. "Can I help you gentlemen?"

Mark looked at Ian and then at her. "I'm sorry. I must have hit the wrong button. I meant to turn on the reading light."

"That's not a problem," she said cheerfully. "It happens all the time." She turned on Mark's light and then walked away toward the front of the cabin.

Mark reached out and touched Ian's face. "Am I dreaming?"

"I don't think so," Ian said as he slapped Mark's hand away. "Stop touching my face."

"Look at me."

Ian turned and stared at his friend. They gazed into each other's eyes for several moments and then started laughing.

"Oh my God," Mark said. "It really is you. How is that even—?"

"Do I look like I did in college? I mean, am I actually young again?"

Mark nodded.

"I went to the bathroom and saw myself in the mirror. I thought it must be the Manick Butter kiss—that I was hallucinating. But if you see it too, then I don't know what's going on. Mark, I'm scared. What if none of this is real? What if I'm on some kind of extreme *Jacob's Ladder* trip? Then again, what if it *is* real, like a quirk of the universe or something?"

"Why would it be happening to you now?"

Ian remembered his birthday wish, but instead of telling Mark about it, he answered, "I don't know."

"Well, we can't be sure that anything is happening until we get home."

"What are you talking about?"

They were interrupted by the voice of the pilot. "Hello, folks. We've begun our descent into Austin, and it looks like we'll be pulling into the gate about ten minutes ahead of schedule. The weather report shows sunny skies with a temperature of seventy-eight degrees. We want to thank you for flying United today—we know you have a choice. Flight attendants, please prepare the cabin for arrival. We'll be on the ground shortly."

Mark pulled his messenger bag from underneath the seat in front of him and packed away his pillow and mask. "Let's stay calm and not make a scene. There's got to be a logical explanation for this. Once we land, we'll go back to your house and do a test."

"What kind of test?"

"Shush. Lower your voice. If anyone finds out about this, you'll be dragged off screaming to some laboratory in Virginia. Don't say anything more until we get back to your place."

"But—"

"Silence," Mark said. "I need to concentrate."

Ian extended his arms. "Would you look at my skin? There are no age spots, and those droopy little blobs around my elbows are gone."

CHAPTER THREE

THE PLANE landed in Austin, and they caught a shuttle bus to Mark's car. He drove them to Ian's house in silence, and they went inside. Ian parked his luggage in the hallway next to the door and then led Mark into the kitchen. "Do you want something to drink? Or smoke?"

"No, thanks. I'll be right back."

Ian got two bottles of water from the fridge and sat on one of the stools next to the kitchen island. Mark returned from the living room with Ian's antique copy of *Alice's Adventures in Wonderland*, by Lewis Carroll.

"Really?" Ian said. "Don't you think the comparison is a little heavy-handed?"

"That's not what this is about. It just happened to be the first book I grabbed. I want you to read it."

"Now?"

"Out loud," Mark replied. "This is the test I was talking about. Read a couple of sentences."

"Why?"

"I saw it on *Teen Wolf*. Stiles said you can't read when you're dreaming. We need to eliminate the possibility that this is a hallucination."

"So that's your first move? You're taking a cue from an MTV show about werewolves? What happened to a logical explanation?"

"Just read, please."

Mark handed the book to Ian, and he opened it. "Holy shit. I don't even need glasses for this." Then he read out loud, "'I could tell you my adventures—beginning from this morning,' said Alice a little timidly, 'but it's no use going back to yesterday, because I was a different person then.'"

Mark grabbed the book and skimmed over the page. "You did it. This isn't a dream, Ian. Or a hallucination."

"So it's real. Then what's the next step?"

"We need pictures."

"Why?"

"To figure out how old you are. Where are your pre-phone photographs?"

"In the guest room closet. There's a shoe box full. But I didn't have a beard back then."

"Then I'll have to imagine you without one."

Ian retrieved the box and spilled the photos onto the kitchen countertop. Mark rummaged through the pile and occasionally held one up to compare it to Ian's face. Finally he found a match. "I took this at my twenty-second birthday party."

"Which means I was twenty-one," Ian said.

Mark looked him over carefully. "Your hair's the same—everything except the beard. You're twenty pounds lighter, just like you were back then." Mark stared in disbelief. "It had to be the kiss. Manick Butter isn't a high. You're literally half your age. It's like that movie *Big*—only gay and in reverse."

"What?"

"You know. The one with Tom Hanks, about a boy who becomes a man overnight. Then there's *13 Going on 30*, about a girl who becomes Jennifer Garner overnight. Although technically that's a time-travel story, because everyone else around her grows up too."

"Are you saying I'm trapped in a body-swap comedy?"

"No. This is different from *Freaky Friday*. There's no swapping going on here. You're still you."

"But *Big* and *13 Going on 30* are about people getting older. Does it ever go in the other direction?"

"*17 Again.*"

"Ah, the one with Matthew Perry."

"Chandler Bing himself," Mark said. "Thirty-seven-year-old Mike O'Donnell makes a wish with a mysterious high school janitor. Later that night, when he's driving home, Mike sees the janitor about to jump off a bridge. Mike tries to save him, but then the janitor disappears and Mike falls into the river, where he's magically transformed into a teenager who looks like Zac Efron."

"I never bought that part. Not the 'Mike becoming seventeen again.' I had no problems with that. But there is no universe in which Matthew Perry ever looked like Zac Efron." Ian put his head in his hands. "I can't believe this. Then again, I guess I shouldn't be surprised."

"What are you talking about?" Mark asked.

"You said Mike O'Donnell made a wish. Well, so did I. On my birthday cupcake. I wished that I could go back and do it all over again, and now this is my chance. I put myself out there. I took the plunge and bought the kiss, and look what happened."

"We should call the store and report it."

"Why?" Ian protested. "Aren't you listening to me? I did this. Me and Mrs. Brown. What are we going to report? That my wish came true? That Tad should have charged me a million bucks instead of a measly hundred?"

Mark walked out of the kitchen. "Where are you going?" Ian asked as he followed him to the hall closet. Mark reached up and pulled the Scrabble box off the top shelf. He took it back to the kitchen, sat down on his stool, and removed the lid.

"Why do you want to play Scrabble at a time like this?"

"I don't want to play Scrabble. It's an anagram."

"What's an anagram?" Ian asked.

"A word or phrase formed from another by scrambling—"

"No, you idiot. I know what an anagram is. I meant, what word or phrase are you talking about?"

Mark placed the board in the middle of the counter and dumped the letters out. "Manick Butter. Tad said Mrs. Brown gives each special edition a distinctive name, but she never tells them what it means."

"So?"

"So, then it must mean *something*. Manick Butter. Why does it have a 'k' in it?"

"I don't know. Marketing I guess, or maybe it's somebody's name. Why does it matter?"

"The '*k*' in Manick is there for a reason. I'm sure of it. I bet the anagram doesn't work without it. So you can either stand there and argue with me or help me figure out what it means."

"Okay, okay." Ian sat down, and they spelled it out on the Scrabble board.

MANICK BUTTER

"Now," Mark said, "we have to rearrange the letters until they form something different."

"Like what?"

"Hell if I know. It should be fairly obvious, once we figure it out."

They slid the letters around the board, but nothing took shape. Then Mark got a lead.

AMBIENT TRUCK

"Ambient Truck?" Ian said. "I don't think that's it." Ian rearranged the letters again.

A CRUMB KITTEN

Followed by Mark's second attempt.

MARTIN BUCKET

"It doesn't make any sense," Mark said. He rubbed his face and then played with the letters again. "I know it's in there somewhere."

"Again, I'm going to ask, why does it matter?"

Mark sighed and shook his head. Then his eyes lit up and he screamed, "Oh my God, that's it!" He unscrambled the letters and lined them up into three words. He turned the board toward Ian, who looked down in utter amazement. Using the same letters as Manick Butter, Mark had spelled:

TURN BACK TIME

"No way," Ian muttered.

"Mrs. Brown knew exactly what she was doing. *Zee keess vill find zee right coostomer.*"

Ian sat back. He ran his fingers through his lush head of hair. His stomach growled, and he said, "I'm hungry." He got up and went to the pantry. He pulled a bag of chocolate fudge cookies from the middle shelf and then grabbed a pair of scissors from the knife block. He cut the bag open, popped a cookie into his mouth, and chewed. His phone rang in his pocket.

"Who's that?" Mark asked.

Ian pulled it out. "No one. It's just the alarm for my meds." As soon as Ian said the words, Mark jumped off his stool. Ian dropped the bag of cookies onto the linoleum floor and felt goose bumps race up his arms and neck. He could hear his heart pounding in his chest as he said, "Do you think…? It would only make sense, right?"

"What time is it?" Mark asked.

"Four o'clock."

"The clinic is open for another hour. The results take like twenty minutes."

"Let's go."

Without bothering to pick up the bag of cookies, they ran outside and jumped into Mark's car. He drove to the public health clinic as fast as he could. Ian signed in with the receptionist and paid the twenty-dollar fee. Five minutes later a young man called Ian into a small room and pricked his finger with a tiny needle.

"That's it?" Ian asked.

"That's it," the nurse said. "Since we're not busy, it should only take about ten minutes. You can go back to the waiting room, and we'll call your number when we have the results."

Ian paced the small lobby until Mark ordered him to sit down and try to relax. Ten minutes stretched into fifteen, and then a woman in her fifties opened the door and called number twenty-one. As Ian approached her, she said, "Your father can come along if you want."

Ian laughed and turned to Mark. "You coming, Dad?"

They followed the woman into a small office and sat down. She took a seat next to a tiny desk and smiled. "The news is good. Your test came back negative."

Ian closed his eyes and almost started to cry.

"Was this a routine visit, or did you engage in some risky behavior?" the woman asked. "You seem a little overwhelmed by the results."

Ian couldn't answer.

"It's complicated," Mark said.

They left the clinic and returned to Mark's car. They sat in silence for a moment. Ian couldn't breathe, so he pressed a button on the door handle and lowered the window. The cool, moist breeze calmed him down. The biggest mistake of his life had just been erased. He pinched his arm until it hurt. He had never allowed himself to dream of a cure. He had never imagined a day when he could go on a date without the pressure of disclosure. Ian handled the medical part of the disease without much fuss. He took his meds and maintained an undetectable viral load and never got sick. His doctor told him he'd better plan for his retirement, because he'd probably live a full life. But every time he met someone new, someone he really liked, or even if he just wanted to get laid, he had to disclose his status. That part Ian hated.

When he first tested positive ten years earlier, some of the negative guys he met were okay with it, but then the "DDF" and "I'm clean, UB2" hookup culture changed all that. Disclosure became a brutal gauntlet that almost always ended in rejection. Ian heard "no" so many times that he adopted the word as his protective mantra. *No, I need to work. No, I'm too tired to go out. No, I'd rather not get my heart broken again.* Eventually he traded sex and romance for PornHub and unhealthy crushes on men like Bartley James. He kept up appearances, went to the gym, ate right, and pretended to care. But if anyone had bothered to look closely, they would have seen that Ian had become a supporting character in his own life.

"What's going through your head?" Mark asked.

"I'm not dirty anymore."

"Ian, you were never—"

"You don't know anything about it, so don't pretend or preach to me. I've always felt like damaged goods. I made the stupidest mistake of my life ten years ago, and I've been paying the price ever since. But this… whatever it is. This thing that happened to me—it's a clean slate."

"So… what? You're going to start over now?"

"Why not? I'm still Ian Parker. I own my house and La Tazza. I can figure out a way to make this work."

33

"It's not right, Ian. The world doesn't work that way."

"Are you suggesting I call Tad and ask him to reverse this? You'd rather I go back to being a lonely, middle-aged, HIV-positive gay man who hasn't gotten a Grindr message in months? Do you know I wasn't planning to have dinner with the architect, even as friends? I had about six excuses lined up for how to get out of it. I'm sick and tired of being rejected because of my HIV status, and now I don't have to worry about that. Ever again."

"What about your family?"

"I don't know. I'll figure something out."

"What if it's only temporary?"

"Then I'll enjoy it for as long as it lasts. Look, I understand if you're not on board. I know the world doesn't work this way, but I don't care. I'm done. HIV has exhausted me, and I want it off my back, even if it's only for a little while."

"Okay. You're right, I don't know how it feels. I can't blame you. But I also can't shake this feeling, like Guinan in 'Yesterday's Enterprise.'"

"Who's that?" Ian asked.

"Whoopi Goldberg's character on *Star Trek: The Next Generation*. She's the bartender in Ten Forward. When a previous version of the Enterprise travels through time and changes the course of history, Guinan's the only one who senses something's wrong. Whoopi always knows the score. What if what happened to you isn't some kind of wish fulfillment? What if it's a rip in the space-time continuum—or worse, black magic? You have no idea what you're dealing with here."

"I don't care. I'll move to another city if I have to. Hell, I'll move to another country. But I won't need to do either of those things if you help me. What did Matthew Perry do when he became Zac Efron?"

"Don't you remember?" Mark said. "His friend Ned pretended to be his father, and they enrolled him in high school."

"Well, that's a ridiculous plot line. I'm too old for high school, and there's no way I'm going back to college. Have you seen the price of tuition these days?"

"You don't have to go back to college. It's possible for you to keep running La Tazza, but you'll need a cover story."

"Does that mean you'll help me?"

Mark gripped the steering wheel. "If you're determined to do this, then I want to be a part of it."

"Okay," Ian said. "Thank you. Then let's go back to my place and figure out a plan."

THEIR FIRST decisions involved the basics of Ian's cover story. How could he explain to his employees that he woke up two decades younger? The answer, of course, was that he couldn't. He would have to become someone else.

"It's not that simple," Mark said as they sat at Ian's kitchen island and smoked a bowl. "Do you know what's happening to me right now, by the way?"

Ian blew out some smoke. "What?"

"I'm sitting here looking at you, the college Ian with a beard, and it feels like we're hitting the bong in my dorm room. I should be jealous because you're so young, but the fact that you look twenty-one years old makes me *feel* twenty-one years old."

Ian giggled. "Excellent. It feels good, doesn't it?"

"It does."

Ian lifted up his T-shirt. "Did you see my abs?"

"You always had a naturally trim stomach."

"Not after I turned thirty-five, I didn't. Wait until I get this body to a gym. I didn't even start working out until after I tested positive. Imagine what I can do now."

"Not you. You can't be Ian Parker anymore."

"Then we need to come up with a new identity."

Mark shook his head. "It's not that simple. Any story we concoct needs to answer two fundamental questions."

"What are those?"

"One, who are you? And two, where did Ian go?"

"Oh, shit. I forgot about that second part."

"That's why I'm here. If you shaved the beard, you wouldn't look like Ian at all. Well, I take that back. There'd be enough of a resemblance to suggest that your new identity should involve a relative. You could be Ian's long-lost son, conceived during one of his youthful and drunken attempts to prove his nonexistent heterosexuality."

"That wouldn't explain why Ian disappeared."

"Good point."

"How about a brother?" Ian said.

"Born twenty years apart? Possible, but not plausible. We need to keep it simple. That's the key." Then Mark's eyes widened. "I've got it. Not a son, not a brother, but a brother's son. You can be Ian's nephew."

"But my brother Jeff's son is ten years old."

"So? Nobody here knows that. Jeff is older than you are. Were. It's perfectly reasonable that he'd have a twenty-one-year-old son, and it's also perfectly reasonable that there'd be a family resemblance. What's his son's name again?"

"Ryan."

"Then that's it. You're now Ryan Parker, Ian's nephew from San Diego. The best cover stories always contain a kernel of truth. You do have a brother named Jeff, and Jeff does have a son named Ryan."

"Okay, then what happens to Ian when Ryan shows up?"

"We need to connect the two threads. Something came up with one of Ian's parents. His mother got sick, and he had to go home for a while, so Ryan comes to house sit and run La Tazza in Ian's absence. It's his way of helping out."

"That could work. Ryan would have to be gay too, though."

"Even better. Ryan came out to Ian at sixteen. Ian helped him tell Jeff. The two of you have always been close, and that's why Ian trusts Ryan to run La Tazza."

"Ian would at least call Colleen and tell her what's going on. Does my voice sound different?"

"Try a little deeper."

Ian took a breath and dropped his diaphragm. "How about now?"

"Perfect. She won't suspect a thing, and if she does, just tell her you have a cold. Say you got a call while you were in Denver and you had to catch a plane straight to Phoenix. You don't know when you'll be back, but Ryan will pay all the bills and sign all the checks. How long has Colleen worked there?"

"Two years."

"Then tell her Ryan lived with you three summers ago and worked at La Tazza for extra money. That will explain why he knows what he's doing."

"You're good," Ian said.

"Don't you know it. I can't believe I'm the sidekick, though. I was supposed to be the leading man if something like this ever happened."

"Sorry about that. What about my driver's license?"

"You'll need to get a fake one."

"How?"

"I'll take care of it." Ian started to say something, but Mark stopped him. "Don't ask. You want to maintain plausible deniability. Your ATM card and all your credit cards will still work. Your signature hasn't changed." Mark snapped his fingers. "I just thought of something. Ryan will need a phone."

"Awesome. I'm going to get a Samsung this time. Matthew at work has one, and it's so cool. I need to go clothes shopping too. My pants don't fit."

"Okay, then. Let's do a little test run."

"What do you mean?"

"What's your name?" Mark asked.

"Ryan Parker."

"What's your middle name?"

"Charles."

"When's your birthday?"

"April 19, 1993."

"Don't use Ian's birthday," Mark said.

"Okay. May 19, 1993."

"Tell me about your childhood."

"I was born and raised in San Diego, California. My parents are Jeff and Amber Parker."

"I will never get over the fact that your brother married a woman named Amber. I have three words for you. 'Above the Clouds.' Genius."

Ian reached out and smacked Mark on the head. "I'm Ryan now, remember?"

"Oh, right. Sorry, I forgot. Keep going?"

"I grew up surfing."

"Have you ever been surfing?"

"No, but he's from San Diego. I want his biography to have some classic California elements. I'm trying to build an archetypal character here."

Mark patted him on the hand. "Oh, honey. Don't you know what happens when you try to build an archetypal character? Nine times out of ten, you wind up with a twenty-story cliché."

"No one's ever going to ask me to go surfing in Austin."

"Fine, but from now on, keep it within the realm of your experience. Otherwise you're just begging to screw up. And if someone suspects you're not who you say you are, things could get very ugly, very quickly. Capisce?"

"Now who's the cliché?"

"When did you realize you were gay?"

"Two months after my fourteenth birthday. I fell in love with my best friend, Moondoggie."

Mark bowed his head and groaned. "No. You cannot use the character from *Gidget*. I won't allow it."

"What should I call him, then?"

"Cleveland."

"That's a city."

"It's the name of the guy's crush in *The Mysteries of Pittsburgh*. Your pop culture references need to be a little more obscure."

"Who remembers *Gidget*? It's totally obscure."

"I said no, and that's my final answer."

"I have a question," Ian said. "If the guy's name is Cleveland, then why did Michael Chabon call the book *The Mysteries of Pittsburgh*?"

Mark sighed in exasperation. "Would you keep going, please? I don't have all night."

"Okay. I fell in love with my best friend, Cleveland."

"Was he your first?"

"No. We never did it. A year later, I lost my virginity to Casper Middleton."

"Sprinkle your vocabulary with the occasional 'dude.'"

"I lost my virginity to Casper Middleton, dude."

"He sounds like a cricket player, not a surfer."

"He played on the varsity lacrosse team."

"What position?" Mark asked.

"Goalie. I fucked him in the boys' locker room after a match. Dude."

"Fine, but remember, not everything has to be a scene from a William Higgins movie."

"I'll be okay. I can make it up as I go along."

"Just don't contradict yourself. Remember, keep it simple. No elaborate backstories." Mark went through a mental checklist. "You have keys, transportation, and access to money. You should stay off the road until I get your new ID. Call Colleen tomorrow and tell her you're in Phoenix taking care of Phyllis, but then give Ryan a couple of days to show up. That will make it more realistic, and it'll give us time to go over your story. It's best if you stay inside."

"I can't go to the gym?" Ian asked.

"Okay. But your gym is open twenty-four hours a day, so pick a time when no one else is there. I'll bring in food and anything else you need."

"How long do I have to live like a prisoner?"

"Ryan can arrive on Thursday."

"That's three days away. Why can't I go outside?"

Mark threw up his hands, as if the answer was obvious. "Because Ryan's story is going to be that he flew in on Thursday. What if Ryan meets his new coworkers on Friday and one of them says, 'Gee, that's funny, because I just saw you at the Hancock H-E-B three days ago.' How are you going to explain that?"

"Okay, I get it. I'll stay in the house."

"If you want this to work, you must think it through and always be four steps ahead. Otherwise it's certain to blow up in your face."

"I said, I get it."

"I'm going home, then. Will you be okay by yourself?"

"I'll be fine. I'll probably take a shower and order a pizza. I'm still hungry."

Mark got up from the table. "I'll call you tomorrow morning. Don't do anything stupid."

Ian grinned. "Maybe you should define 'stupid.'"

CHAPTER FOUR

AFTER MARK left, Ian went into his bedroom and undressed. He inspected his new body in the full-length mirror. All the artificial gym muscle he'd packed onto his torso in the last ten years was gone, replaced by a more natural tone enhanced only by running and tennis. His cock looked the same—that hadn't changed much. The gray in his pubes had disappeared. *Want to know how old someone is? Check out their skin.* His looked flawless. The partying and drugs he would do in his late twenties had yet to take their toll. Ian flexed his arms. *If I had known I was this hot the first time around, I wouldn't have been so desperate.* The duality of his situation unnerved him. He looked twenty-one years old, but his memories of the previous two decades remained intact. He remembered getting fired from his first office job. He remembered the day he tested positive. He remembered when Adam Reynolds broke his heart. Both times.

Ian headed for the bathroom and shaved off his beard. He showered and stood in front of the sink. The transformation was remarkable, as if a Titan man had been replaced by a Corbin Fisher boy. He grabbed his phone and took some selfies. He uploaded the best one to his Grindr profile and changed his age and screen name. It would take at least a couple of hours for his new pic to be approved, so he got dressed and returned to the living room. Ian ordered a pizza online and then checked his DVR. He had several episodes of *Scandal* backed up, so he started one and stretched out on the sofa. Toward the end of the show, the doorbell rang.

Ian paused the DVR, got up, and answered the door. A good-looking young man about his age stood on the porch, holding a pizza and a twelve-ounce bottle of Dr Pepper. He had dark buzzed hair and gray eyes and wore a pair of faded brown shorts with a red Papa

John's T-shirt. "Come on in," Ian said. "I need to get some cash out of my other pants."

The pizza boy stepped into the foyer. Ian went back to the bedroom and rummaged through his jeans. He pulled out two twenty-dollar bills and returned to the living room.

"Nice place you got here," the young man said with a heavy Texas drawl. "You live with your folks?"

The time for Ryan's debut had arrived.

"No, I'm house-sitting for my uncle. I'm from San Diego. I just got here today."

"Right on. Never been outside of Texas myself. Anyway, it's eighteen eighty-nine."

Ryan handed him the two twenty-dollar bills. "Can you break one of these for me?"

"No problemo."

The pizza boy handed Ryan the box and cold plastic bottle. Ryan set them on the coffee table and said, "You know what? Never mind. Keep it. I've had a good day."

"Are you sure? That's more than a twenty dollar tip."

"I'm sure. My uncle left me some cash to live on, so why not be generous with it, right? You can take your girlfriend out for a drink or something."

The pizza boy blushed. "I'm not much into…. You know…. Chicks."

"No kidding? Me neither."

"Really? I just moved to Austin and don't know hardly nobody. My name's Sam, by the way. Sam White."

"I'm Ryan Parker."

They shook hands.

"I have two more deliveries in the car, so I gotta run. Would you maybe like to hang out sometime? Since we're both new to town and all?"

Ryan smiled. This kind of thing never happened to Ian. "Sure. I feel guilty enjoying this place all by myself. My uncle has a Ping-Pong table and a Jacuzzi in the backyard."

"Right on. Can I get your number?" Sam pulled out his phone and handed it to Ryan. It was the kind of cheap flip phone Ian hadn't seen in years. He used the arrow keys to navigate through the awkward menus, added his name, and then....

"Shit," Ryan said.

"What's the matter?"

Ryan didn't have a phone yet, so he keyed in Ian's number instead. Mark wasn't going to be happy about that. He would say the separation between Ian and Ryan needed to stay clean from the beginning and that exceptions would only trip him up in the end. But since it didn't technically qualify as stupid in Ian's book, he went ahead and did it anyway.

"Nothing's the matter," Ryan said. "I just realized I forgot to pack my charger. No big deal. I can pick one up in the morning." He handed the phone back to Sam. "Text me sometime."

"I'll do that."

"Cool. Well, thanks for the pizza."

"You're welcome. Thanks for the tip. That's gonna come in mighty handy this week. I'll text you real soon."

Ian ate his dinner and watched a second episode of *Scandal*. Afterward, he stowed the remaining slices in the fridge and went to the bedroom to check his phone. He deleted a couple of junk e-mails and read a text from Colleen. Ian decided to put that call off. Then he opened up Grindr.

"Whoa."

Sixteen messages.

Ian thumbed through the profiles. His policy had always been to respond to everyone, but clearly that wasn't going to be possible. He zeroed in on the hottest guy with a face pic, HydeParkBttm.

Online
2 miles away
22 years old
6'1" 190 lbs
White
Muscular

Dating

Grindr Tribes
Jock, Discreet

Headline
be true

About
wanna spend the night, don't bring pajamas

Looking For
Right Now

Ian tapped through to the message screen and read:

HydeParkBttm: hey stud

Ian typed back.

RynPrkr: hey

About thirty seconds later, the next message came through.

HydeParkBttm: whats up
RynPrkr: nada u?
HydeParkBttm: horny u looking?
RynPrkr: might be
HydeParkBttm: ic how hung?
RynPrkr: 7.5c
HydeParkBttm: u know how to use it?
RynPrkr: only one way to find out
HydeParkBttm: so u are looking...?

Ian sent him an old picture of his hard dick.

*HydeParkBttm: nice! i love it when a young guy
like you pounds my hole*

HydeParkBttm sent a series of ass pics.

*RynPrkr: looks good
HydeParkBttm: u clean? bb?*

Ian sat down on the bed. He wanted to get laid, but not by guys like this.

*RynPrkr: i'm hiv neg... but if you're implying
that poz guys are dirty then no i'm not looking...
at least not for you
HydeParkBttm: what's ur problem dude?
RynPrkr: guys like you are my problem... and no,
i don't bareback*

Ian closed the message screen, blocked HydeParkBttm, and browsed his other fifteen options. A cute geeky kid caught his eye. Ian had seen his profile over the past few months but never dreamed he'd get a chance to chat with the guy. His screen name was Frodo, and from his pic at least, he even looked a little bit like Elijah Wood. Ian glanced through the rest of the profile.

Online
800 feet away
27 years old
5'9" 145 lbs
White
Toned
Single

Grindr Tribes
Geek

Headline
Looking for my Samwise.

About
Out of my mind and into the light.

Looking For
Chat, Dates, Friends, Relationship

Ian continued to the message screen.

> *Frodo: Does that stand for Ryan Parker?*

Ian noted the complete sentence with proper capitalization and punctuation. He typed back:

> *RynPrkr: You're cute AND smart.*

Ian waited for over a minute but got no response. He returned to the home screen and checked Frodo's status. The green light indicated he was still online, but another minute went by and still nothing. Ian almost gave up and closed the app, but then an alert sounded. He tapped through to the message screen.

> *Frodo: Haha! Thanks. I'm Jeremy.*
> *RynPrkr: Hi, Jeremy.*
> *Frodo: You're pretty cute yourself. Am I too old for you?*

Ian almost choked on the question until he remembered Ryan was several years younger than this kid.

> *RynPrkr: Not at all.*
> *Frodo: I've never seen you on here before. You visiting?*

*RynPrkr: House-sitting for my uncle. Looks like
you're close. You want to hang out?
Frodo: Well, I'm not usually into hookups, but
I'll make an exception. Do you mind if I ask your
status?*

Nice. Straightforward, polite, no stigma.

RynPrkr: I'm negative.

When Ian saw the words on the screen, they felt like a lie. But
they weren't, and he had the test results to prove it.

*Frodo: Me too. Are you cool with keeping it
safe? Maybe some kissing and a little oral, if we
click.
RynPrkr: Sounds perfect. You want to host or
travel?
Frodo: Travel if that's okay.
RynPrkr: That works. Here's the address. It
should be just down the street from you.*

Twenty minutes later Jeremy knocked on the front door. He
had dark brown hair and eyes and wore a black T-shirt that read:
"One does not simply Telnet into Mordor." He had a cute smile and
a shy charm that Ian found incredibly sexy. They introduced
themselves, and Jeremy stepped into the living room.

"This is a great house. Your uncle must do pretty well for
himself."

"He owns a coffee shop over on Guadalupe," Ryan said.

"Cool. Which one?"

"La Tazza Magica."

"Oh, I've been there. They have an excellent mocha latte."

"It's the Italian chocolate he uses. I'd offer you a beer, but my
uncle didn't leave any in the fridge."

"That's okay," Jeremy said as he looked through the sliding glass doors and into the backyard. "Is that a Ping-Pong table?"

"It sure is. Do you play?"

"I used to, in high school. We had a table in our rec room."

"Let's take it for a spin."

They went outside, and Ryan pulled two paddles and a ball from the shed. Ian loved any kind of tennis—table or hard court—but his speed and reflexes had deteriorated over the years. Jeremy served the ball, and Ryan returned it with a lightning-quick backhand shot. The ball skimmed the table and then flew into the grass.

"Come on," Jeremy said as he retrieved the ball. "You didn't tell me you were a pro."

"I'm not a pro. I just play a lot."

"Great. Why do I have the feeling I'm about to get my ass kicked?"

And that's pretty much how it went. After his 21-6 win, Ryan peeled off his tank top and asked, "You want to get in the Jacuzzi?"

"You have all the luxuries, don't you?"

"Courtesy of my uncle." They removed the cover on the aboveground hot tub, and then Ryan turned the knob to start the jets. He dropped his shorts and said, "It takes a few minutes for the water to warm up."

Jeremy toed off his sneakers, undressed, and threw his clothes into a pile on the grass. He brushed his floppy bangs out of his eyes. Ryan stared down at the massive uncut cock dangling between Jeremy's legs. He dropped to his knees and took it into his mouth. Jeremy braced himself against the edge of the Jacuzzi and moaned. Ryan sucked his dick until it got nice and hard. Then he stood up and they kissed. Ryan stepped to the side and dipped his hand into the water to check the temperature. "It's ready."

"Good thing your uncle put up a privacy fence."

They climbed in, and Ryan sat down. Jeremy straddled him and rubbed their cocks together while they made out. It felt so sweet and innocent that Ian started to laugh.

"What's so funny?"

"Nothing," Ryan said. "You're just really cute."

"Me? Come on. We both know you're the hot one in this tub."

"You underestimate your appeal."

"I wish more guys shared your opinion. Sit up on the ledge so I can suck your dick."

Ryan did as instructed. Jeremy gave a world-class blow job with a lot of tongue swirl. Ryan closed his eyes, and it all came flooding back. Ian had a frustrating sex life in college because he always came too fast, and now it appeared the second time around would be no different. Ryan felt his balls tighten, and he stopped Jeremy.

"Was it that bad?"

"No," Ryan said. "You give an excellent blow job. But we need to switch, or else this will be one of those annoying thirty-second clips on XVideos."

"You're close?"

"I'm twenty-one, remember? I come quickly but often."

Jeremy sat on the ledge, and Ryan returned the favor, looking up into Jeremy's eyes as he sucked. Jeremy ran his fingers through Ryan's hair and grinned. He threw back his head and thrust his hips. Ryan deep-throated Jeremy's cock, a technique Ian had not yet mastered twenty years ago. He ran his fingers up Jeremy's legs, then cupped his balls with one hand and stroked his cock with the other. Jeremy stood up on the seat and fucked Ryan's face. He must have gotten close too, because he stopped and said, "Let's switch again."

"Why don't we go inside?" Ryan said.

"Even better."

They exited the Jacuzzi, gathered up their clothes, and went into the house. Ryan grabbed a towel from the bathroom, and they dried each other off. Then he led Jeremy into the bedroom. Ryan dropped the towel on the floor, and they jumped onto the bed. They made out some more and ended up in a sixty-nine position, which brought them both to the brink of orgasm within a matter of minutes. Ryan stroked Jeremy's cock until he shot a healthy load all over Ryan's chest.

"I want you to come on my face," Jeremy said.

Ryan knelt on the bed and obliged. After a few seconds of recovery, he retrieved the towel from the floor and offered one end to Jeremy. As they wiped away the semen, Ryan asked, "You hungry?"

"I'm always hungry after sex."

"I have some cold pizza."

"That would hit the spot."

Ryan put on his shorts and Jeremy his jeans. They went into the kitchen shirtless, and Ryan pulled the pizza from the fridge. He opened the box and set it on the kitchen island. They sat on the stools and each took a slice.

"Best after-sex food ever," Ryan said. "Do you have a house in the neighborhood?"

"No, I wish. I still live in an apartment."

"What do you do for a living?"

"I teach algebra and calculus at one of the local high schools."

"Ah," Ryan said. "No wonder you still live in an apartment."

"Don't get me started. When did you get into town?"

"Today. You're my first Austin conquest, if you don't count the pizza boy."

"You had sex with the pizza boy?" Jeremy asked.

"No, but he asked for my number, and I gave it to him."

"I could never do something like that. I'd be too embarrassed. How many messages did you get on Grindr?"

"Sixteen."

Jeremy shook his head. "Jesus."

"It's the fresh-meat syndrome. Give it a few weeks and I'll be just another tired face."

"I doubt that. How long you house-sitting for?"

Ryan held up his hand and chewed, which bought Ian enough time to organize his thoughts. He swallowed and said, "Undetermined. My uncle is in Phoenix with my dad, taking care of my grandmother. My dad can work from anywhere and my mom can take care of our house, but my Uncle Ian doesn't have anyone to watch this place or La Tazza. So I offered to do it for him."

"That was nice of you."

"Not really," Ryan said. "I love this town. I spent a summer here after I graduated from high school. I've been dying to come back anyway."

"Where are you from?"

"San Diego."

"Ah," Jeremy said. "I've been many times but never ventured much beyond the convention center. Heard the beaches are nice, though."

"Amazing beaches. I started surfing before I started walking."

"Wow. Can you teach me?"

"Sorry, I don't think Lake Travis has the waves for it."

"Is San Diego pretty gay?" Jeremy asked.

"It's super gay. Hillcrest is what they call the gayborhood, but it also has some of the best restaurants in the country. You have to try the OMG French Toast at Snooze."

"Do you look like your uncle?"

"I don't think so," Ryan said. "I suppose there's some family resemblance. Why?"

"Does he have a beard?"

"How did you know that?"

"I think I've seen him on Grindr," Jeremy said. "You two have similar eyes."

"You're very observant. I came out to him when I was sixteen, and he helped me tell my dad. We've been pretty close ever since. He never had too much luck in the boyfriend department, unfortunately."

"Nice guys always finish last."

Ryan shook his head. "I refuse to believe that."

"You're optimistic. That's how it should be at your age, I suppose."

"At my age? You're only twenty-seven, Jeremy. That's a little too young to be jaded."

"Maybe you're right. So why aren't you in school? Since you're free to take a gig of undetermined length in the middle of April, I assume you're not enrolled anywhere."

"No, I'm done with school for now, unless it's the school of life. I did a year at UC San Diego. That was plenty."

"So, now what?" Jeremy asked.

"No idea. I'm here for a little while at least, so we'll see what Austin has to offer." Ian knew he needed a simple story that would explain why Ryan had the financial resources to do whatever he pleased. "My parents are kind of loaded."

"Ah. So are mine, but they cut me off two years ago, when I turned twenty-five."

"That sucks," Ryan said. "I try not to be a brat about it, but they're not pushing me to grow up yet. I think my dad sees a lot of Ian when he looks at me, and I'm not even talking about the gay part. Ian never fit into the corporate world either. He wandered aimlessly for years before he bought La Tazza. I'd like to do something like that. Be my own boss. I enjoy building things. I've thought about becoming a carpenter and selling handmade furniture. Only this time, I'm not going to wind up alone."

"This time?"

Ryan choked on a piece of pizza. "Oh. Did I say that? Sorry, must be the jet lag." He got off his stool and pulled a bottle of water from the fridge. He held it up and asked, "You want one?"

"Sure."

He handed it to Jeremy and pulled another for himself. Ryan sat back down and took a drink. "I take it you're a Tolkien fan?"

Jeremy laughed. "Pretty obvious from my profile, huh?"

"And your T-shirt. But you could have liked the movies and never read the books."

"Oh, I've read the books. Several times. And seen the movies too."

"What did you think of them?" Ryan asked.

"Jackson did a great job, for the most part. 'The Scouring of the Shire' is my favorite chapter. It's the ultimate payoff for me, when they return all grown up and kick some major hobbit ass. I was kind of disappointed when it got cut from the last film. I understood why, but still."

"Sean Astin ruined the whole thing for me. He sucked so bad it made my teeth hurt, and he got worse with each movie."

"Have you seen *The Hobbit*?"

Ryan nodded. "It's criminal—a step away from fan fiction—like a train wreck I couldn't stop watching. That poor little story is going to collapse under the weight of all the bullshit Jackson keeps piling on top of it."

"I agree," Jeremy said. "When Legolas showed up in the second film, I almost gagged on my popcorn."

"So you're looking for your Samwise?"

Jeremy chewed on his crust. "I guess. I don't know what to put on those profiles, but I figured I might as well be myself. I'm a math geek, I play Dungeons & Dragons, and my favorite TV show is *Arrow*."

"Stephen Amell? What's not to like? I hated Grant Gustin on *Glee*, but I love him as the Flash. I take it your familiarity with the San Diego Convention Center means you go to Comic-Con every year?"

"Guilty. I've never met another gamer I wanted to date, but I figured with a headline like 'Looking for my Samwise' I might at least meet a guy who likes guys like me."

"How's that working out?" Ryan asked.

"Terrible. Most of the messages I get are from old pervs who want to fuck me or flakes collecting dick pics. It seems like every other conversation starts with barebacking or PNP. Even the guys with 'no hookups' in their profile message me for a hookup."

"What was that other thing you wrote?"

"Oh. 'Out of my mind and into the light.' I don't know where that came from. I think I read it on someone else's profile. I thought a quote from *The Lord of the Rings* would be a bridge too far."

"So you went with something that sounds like Marianne Williamson instead?"

"I don't know who that is," Jeremy said. "I'm a very cerebral person, and I have this idea that the right guy would get me out of my head."

"You should change it to 'Out of my mind and into my pants, where you'll find my nine-inch dick.' I bet that would get you some attention."

"Maybe. But not the kind of attention I'm looking for."

"Have you dated anyone recently?" Ryan asked.

"No, not since I moved here. Bars aren't my scene, and I seem to disappear on sites like Manhunt or Adam4Adam. Grindr is the only place I actually meet guys, and even then it's rare and generally leads to nothing."

"You need to find a nice boy and settle down."

"Do you have someone in mind?"

Ryan grinned and changed the subject. "How long have you lived in Austin?"

"Two years. I went to school at SMU and then taught in Dallas before I moved here."

"You didn't like the Big D?"

"No," Jeremy said. "It's too big for me, and the gay guys there are horrible to each other. Austin is more laid back and the perfect size."

"It's getting bigger every day. Have you heard the joke about the gay pickup lines in Texas?"

"No. Tell me."

"You always know what city you're in by going to a gay bar and listening to the pickup lines. In Houston, it's 'Do you want to go home?' In Austin, it's 'Do you want to get high?' And in Dallas, it's 'Why'd you wear *that*?'"

Jeremy laughed. "You pretty much nailed it. Who told you that one?"

"My uncle." Ryan swallowed the last of his pizza and wiped his face with a napkin. "You want to spend the night?"

Jeremy looked surprised. "Really?"

"What's wrong?"

"I don't know. Hookups usually end after someone comes. I've never had pizza afterward, let alone been invited to spend the night."

"Maybe you're hooking up with the wrong guys."

"Maybe," Jeremy said. "I have to be at school at seven in the morning, so tonight's probably not a good time."

"You're right. I forgot tomorrow is Tuesday and people have to work. I'm starting at La Tazza this weekend, so you should stop by if you want."

"I'll definitely do that. It was cool to meet you, Ryan. Knowing that guys like you exist gives me hope."

"I enjoyed meeting you too, and you're welcome to try and redeem yourself at the Ping-Pong table anytime."

"Thanks, I'll probably take you up on that. I just need to grab my shirt and shoes from the bedroom and I'll get out of your hair."

Jeremy finished dressing, and they said good-bye at the front door. Ian went into the kitchen and grabbed the bag of semi-crushed cookies from the pantry. He poured himself a glass of milk and returned to the living room. He flipped through his DVR menu, but nothing caught his eye. Sleep would be impossible. He ate a cookie and washed it down with a swig of milk.

This is the single greatest thing that's ever happened to me.

CHAPTER FIVE

IAN HAD no intention of allowing Mark, who still used an iPhone 4, to pick out Ryan's most important accessory. So the next morning, in direct defiance of Mark's orders, he headed to a shopping center after the morning rush. An hour later, Ryan emerged from the Best Buy with a brand new Samsung Galaxy S5, which had only been on the market for less than a month. He couldn't wait to show it to Matthew. The Best Buy happened to be located next to a GAP, and since Ryan needed new clothes, he went in and bought a pair of skinny jeans and a few shirts.

When he got home, he started a load of laundry and then used Ian's phone to call Colleen. He lowered his voice and launched into the story about his ailing mom. He tried to sound distraught as he laid out his abrupt change of plans. Her concern made him feel bad, since his mother was probably playing golf or drinking mai tais with her friends. He told her about Ryan's imminent arrival and emphasized she wouldn't have to take on any additional responsibility. She assured him she could handle things for the next few days and looked forward to meeting his nephew.

In the evening, Mark came by with some pad Thai and a yellow curry from Titaya's. Ian pulled some plates from the cupboard and opened a bottle of wine. As they sat at the kitchen island and ate dinner, Ian and Mark worked on expanding Ryan's biography, including where he went to high school (Saint Augustine) and who he asked to the senior prom (no one—he went stag).

Ian took a sip of wine and grimaced. He went to the sink and poured the wine down the drain. He rinsed out the glass and then refilled it with milk. "Shouldn't Ryan have a Facebook profile?"

"No," Mark said.

"What do you mean, 'No'?"

"How stupid would that look? He wouldn't have any history or friends."

"Oh," Ian said. "You're right. I hadn't thought about that."

"Are you starting to appreciate the complex nature of this endeavor?"

"A little. But everyone's on Facebook. How am I going to explain that?"

"Go in the opposite direction. Make Ryan an outlier and a rebel. He used to be on Facebook, but then he quit—he shut the whole thing down and deleted all his photos. There's a twenty-something kid in my office who told me he did the same thing. It's considered badass."

Ian raised his middle finger. "Fuck you, Facebook."

"Exactly. Fuck you, Facebook. Fuck you, Twitter. Fuck you, Instagram. Ryan is the first wave of a new generation—one that will unplug from social media."

"I can sell that. And now that I think about it, the less of an online footprint he has, the better."

"The fewer public lies he tells, definitely the better. Remember the prime directive."

"Keep it simple," Ian said.

"You'll need an e-mail address, though."

"That's easy enough."

Mark picked up a shrimp with his chopsticks and popped it into his mouth. "Keep Ian's phone in the house. Only make calls on it from here. I can just picture a scene at La Tazza, where Colleen calls Ian and a phone in your backpack starts to ring."

"Good point." Ian told Mark about the pizza boy and Jeremy and driving to get Ryan's phone. He told the whole truth, because withholding information from Mark, who he trusted more than anyone in the world, would only make things worse in the long run. As Ian suspected, Mark expressed concern about giving Ian's number to Sam, but he reacted to the hookup with Jeremy in a surprisingly upbeat manner.

"You should do more of that," Mark said. "Hookups are a great way to rehearse, and they're like disposable razors. Use 'em and toss 'em. The more you practice being Ryan, the more convincing you'll be when you start at La Tazza on Friday."

"Use 'em and toss 'em? You are so cold sometimes."

"Look, this is one situation where the fast-food nature of the hookup scene works in your favor. Chances are you'll never see any of those men again, so if you screw up, who cares? No real harm done. Embrace it. And I don't think I need to tell you to play safe, do I?"

Ian spooned some more pad Thai onto his plate. "No, you don't need to tell me. But Jeremy seems to have quelled my thirst for Grindr hookups."

"That didn't take long. By the way, I should have your new ID by Thursday, but until then, stay off the road. Unless it's on a bicycle. Honestly, who knows what would have happened if a policeman had pulled you over this morning."

"I was careful."

"Careful has nothing to do with it. Haven't I told you police officers pull people over because they're bored? They don't need a reason, or if they do, they'll make one up."

"Nothing happened, but okay, I'll stay off the road."

Mark poured some curry sauce on his rice. "Have you decided if Ryan is a top or a bottom?"

"Can't he be both?"

"No. I liked the story about the goalie. Ryan should be a top, like a young Topher DiMaggio."

"Topher DiMaggio's not young anymore?"

"God, no. He's almost thirty."

Ian rolled his eyes. "He bottomed once. I saw it."

"One of the worst scenes ever filmed. The pained expression on his face?"

"That's the only thing that made it hot."

"Ugh. You would say that."

Ian started picking around the curry bowl to find the remaining shrimp. "But I used to enjoy bottoming back in the day."

"And how long has it been since someone fucked you?"

"Years."

"See? You have the maturity of a good top inside the body of a twink. Use it to your advantage."

Ian shook his chopsticks at Mark. "Don't call me that."

"What? A good top?"

"No, a twink."

Mark waved his hand. "Please. You should be thanking the Lord someone's calling you a twink. Look at you. Don't make me slap you upside the head. Being a young top would work with Ryan's whole outlier persona. The mental picture of him fucking the lacrosse goalie in the boys' locker room? Hot."

"That is so disturbing," Ian said.

"It would give his character a little edge, if you really commit."

"He's not a part in a play."

"Maybe not, but you should approach him like one."

Ian grabbed a fork from the drawer to clean up the last of the rice. Mark finished his glass of wine and pushed his plate away. He went to the fridge for a bottle of water, then sat back down and said, "You'd better think carefully about these next few days, because the choices you make will affect the rest of Ryan's life." Mark took a long pause. "You do understand how this will eventually have to go down, don't you? I know I haven't spelled it out for you yet, but tell me you see what's coming twelve moves ahead."

Ian felt sick. "What are you talking about?"

"I know you want to go back and do it all over again, but this cover story still gives you an out. Everyone thinks Ian is alive and well in Arizona. He could conceivably come back at any time."

"How?"

"I don't know. We haven't even looked into it. We could call Tad. Maybe this isn't permanent, or maybe Mrs. Brown can come up with a remedy and reverse it."

"I told you, I don't want to do that."

"You don't want to do that *now*, but things can change. The way I see it, you can play out this cover story for maybe three months, tops. After that, the separation between Ian and Ryan will become untenable. People won't understand why Ian never visits.

They'll keep asking when he's coming back. You won't be able to sustain his absence forever."

"What are you suggesting?"

"Ian will have to…."

"What? Die?"

Mark laid his chopsticks down.

"That's crazy," Ian said.

"If you see another option, I'm all ears. My way, Ian has an accident in Phoenix, leaves La Tazza to Ryan, and you continue with his life."

"Isn't that illegal? Faking your own death?"

"Not per se. I looked it up. There's the potential for fraud down the line, since you'll be impersonating your nephew, but I can help with that."

"My family would have to be in on it."

Mark looked like he was thinking it over. "You're probably right. You'd have to change your will and leave everything to the real Ryan Parker, but Jeff would have to know the truth, in order to protect your assets."

"How do I convince them?"

"We'll figure that out when the time comes," Mark said. "They don't have any plans to visit in the next three months, do they?"

"No, but you know my family. My parents especially love to surprise me."

"Then you should call and tell them you're going on a European vacation or something."

Ian reached for the wine bottle and refilled Mark's glass. "That's a little extreme, don't you think?"

"Not at all. Until you decide to fully commit to a future as Ryan Parker, your family is your greatest liability. Keep them away, whatever it takes."

"God, this is complicated."

Mark took a gulp of wine. "Imagine where you'd be if I wasn't here."

Ian stacked their plates and carried them to the sink. "Why can't Ian move to Belize or Thailand? Death is so permanent."

"What happens when Ryan gets married? His uncle doesn't even bother to show up for his wedding, like Sonny's brothers on *Days*? Where were they when he married Will? They were nowhere to be found, that's where. Have you ever heard of anything so preposterous in all your life?"

"Can we get back to me, please?"

"At a certain point, you'll have no other choice but to kill Ian off. How do you think I'm going to feel? I'm losing my best friend."

"No, you're not." Ian left the dishes in the sink and returned to his stool. "Just because I'm starting over, it doesn't mean I've forgotten all the hangovers we nursed together."

"Things may be the same privately, but in public? You'll be Ryan. People will think I'm pathetic if I hang out with a twenty-one-year-old all the time."

"That's nonsense. You and Ryan could get to know each other and become good friends, especially if you were his dead uncle's BFF. Transgenerational friendships are very common in the gay community. What do you care if a handful of assholes think it's weird?"

"You have no idea what's going to happen when you start hanging out with people your own age."

"I have some idea. I know I'm not going to turn into a total dick."

"Fine. Forget I said anything. How are you doing otherwise?"

Ian shrugged and finished his glass of milk. "I can't believe Friday is three days away. I'm ready to get this show on the road."

CHAPTER SIX

MARK CAME over for dinner again the following night, and Ian ate the entire meal in character as Ryan. They continued to expand Ryan's biography and even layered in a few contradictions to make his personality more three dimensional. Mark suggested that Ryan's tastes should occasionally diverge from Ian's, in order to avoid raising any eyebrows. They decided, therefore, that Ryan loved crime procedurals, hated *American Hustle*, and thought the ending of *The Sopranos* was brilliant.

On Thursday, Mark arrived with Ryan's new ID, and Ian prepared to play him around the clock. He called Colleen from Ryan's phone and introduced himself. He told her he'd just arrived in Austin and that he'd be at La Tazza bright and early the next day. He also mentioned that his uncle had told him so many nice things about her.

As he shaved in the mirror on Friday morning, Ian noticed that Ryan's reflection was becoming more familiar with each passing day. He got dressed and rode his bike the short distance to La Tazza. When he arrived, he entered through the east door. No one had turned on the music yet. When he saw Colleen cleaning the espresso machine, Ryan took a deep breath and walked up to the bar. "I'm looking for Colleen."

"That's me. Are you Ian's nephew?"

He nodded. "I'm Ryan."

"Sorry to hear about your grandmother. Must be bad if Ian had to fly straight from Denver."

"She had emergency surgery, but she's stable now. My grandfather's going to need help while she recovers, though, so Uncle Ian may be gone awhile."

Colleen laughed. "Uncle Ian. That's cute. He is kind of everyone's favorite uncle, isn't he?" She stepped away from the machine and put her hands on the bar. "So how does all this break down? Are you running the place now?"

"Well, give me a day to get up to speed, but after that I'll be able to take over."

Colleen looked relieved. "Damn, I'm glad to hear that. I'm a grad student, and I have a huge seminar paper due next week. My only responsibility here has been to run things when Ian's gone, but that's about all I can handle."

"If you can finish your shift today, I can give you the rest of the weekend off. How's that?"

Colleen took a sip of her latte. "I like you already, but there's no way you can learn everything in one day."

"Didn't my uncle tell you I used to work here?"

"No, I guess he left that part out."

"Three years ago," Ryan said.

"Ah. Must have been before my time."

"I lived with him for the summer. I know this place up, down, and sideways. And now that I'm old enough to serve alcohol, I can finally work alone. I'll handle the vendors, place the orders, pay the bills, and make up the schedules too."

"How's your latte art?" Colleen asked.

"Can I show you?"

"Be my guest."

Ryan walked around and slipped behind the bar. He made a cup of espresso and poured in the steamed milk, leaving a classic tulip design on the surface.

"Very nice," Colleen said.

"I learned from the master."

"You've obviously used that machine before. It can be a real bitch sometimes, but your uncle refuses to buy a modern one."

"He says it—"

"I know. I know. It makes the best cup of espresso in Austin. I've heard it a million times, but look around. Do you think people come here for the espresso? No, they don't. Your uncle charges three sixty-five for a single latte. You know how much Epoch and Flightpath charge?"

"No."

"Three dollars. How does he get away with that?"

Ryan shrugged, but Ian found this new side of Colleen fascinating.

"I'll tell you how he gets away with it, and I'll tell you in one word. Atmosphere. Do you know some people believe this place is actually enchanted? Students tell me they do better on their tests when they study here. And see that guy over on the sofa?" Colleen nodded toward Dean, a retired CEO who now fancied himself an author of historical fiction. "He wrote two novels in his study at home and got nothing but rejection. A year ago he started coming here to write, and yesterday he told me his third book got picked up by a small press in New York. They're going to give him a profile on Amazon and everything."

Ian wanted to walk right over and say congratulations. He'd been encouraging Dean for months to submit his manuscript to one of the niche publishing houses, and now it had finally paid off. But of course, Dean had never met Ryan.

"So you're saying my uncle could buy a new machine, make all the employees happy, and not lose any customers?"

Colleen winked at him. "You catch on quick."

RYAN WORKED the day shift with Colleen, and he pretended not to know certain things to make his training more believable. He started to get excited as afternoon approached. Matthew would be in at four, and Ian wondered how he would interact with Ryan. Now that they were the same age, Ian thought they might become friends, especially since Matthew didn't technically work for Ryan. And what would the freshman study group think of Ian's nephew from California? Would Quentin invite him to a party or maybe just to hang out?

The person Ian most wanted to see, however, was Bartley James. As Ryan, Ian now believed he stood a chance at something more than friendship with the studly architect. He sat smack in the middle of Bartley's dating demo, and there would be no awkward disclosures of HIV.

At about five minutes 'til four, Ian heard Colleen talking to someone in the back. He took a step closer and recognized Matthew's voice. A few moments later, they came up front, and Colleen introduced him.

"Ryan Parker. Nice to meet you."

They shook hands.

"Matthew Butler. Sorry about your grandma. Nice of you to cover for your uncle, though."

Ryan shrugged. "I didn't have a job anyway."

Colleen gathered her book bag and coat from behind the bar. "Can you boys hold down the fort if I leave you alone for the night?"

"We'll be fine," Ryan said. "I have a set of keys and I'll open tomorrow morning at eight. Spend the rest of the weekend writing your seminar paper."

"Are you sure? You have my cell number in case anything happens."

"I'm sure."

"I'm working on Sunday too," Matthew said. "I might be able to answer some questions and help him a little."

Colleen laughed. "You've been here all of two weeks. You haven't even figured out the machine yet."

Matthew grinned. "Hey, but the customers love me, right?"

"And that's all that matters." Colleen waved to them as she walked toward the door. "Don't call me unless the place is on fire."

She left them alone with a spattering of students, most of whom were only drinking the free water. "This is kind of a slow time of day," Matthew said. "Things usually pick up around four thirty or five."

With no customers to serve, they sat on stools behind the bar and waited. Ryan pulled out his phone and launched the home screen.

"What?" Matthew said. "Is that the new S5?"

"I just bought it a few days ago."

"Can I take a look?"

"Sure." Ryan handed him the phone.

"This is sweet," Matthew said as he thumbed around. "Why don't you have any contacts?"

Ian had already thought of that. "I haven't transferred them over from my iPhone yet."

"You can do that right on the Samsung website, you know? You plug in your iPhone, the website grabs all your compatible content, and then you plug this in and everything loads. Text messages, photos, contacts—you name it. I never owned an iPhone, but I watched my friend Cecilia do it. You're gonna love the bigger screen. And did you know it automatically scrolls while you read?"

"No way."

"I'm not shitting you, dude." Matthew handed the phone back to Ryan and looked down. "Why are you wearing your uncle's shoes?"

Ian had *not* already thought of that. Ryan bought new jeans and shirts but forgot about footwear. In the fraction of an instant, he decided he shouldn't try to convince Matthew that the shoes didn't belong to Ian. "How did you know they were his?"

"The laces. Those are very distinctive laces, and I remember noticing them the day I started here."

"I forgot to pack a good pair of shoes for being on my feet all day. I only wear flip-flops at home and didn't even think about it. Since Uncle Ian and I wear the same size shoe, I asked him if I could borrow something from his closet."

"That's weird, though. He always wears those shoes. I might even guess they're his favorite pair. It's hard to believe he went to Denver without them."

"Maybe he has more than one pair. Some people do that, you know, when they find shoes they really like."

"Maybe," Matthew said. Then he stared at Ryan for a moment. "There's definitely a family resemblance."

"I've heard that before."

"But it's not like anyone's going to mix you two up. You're a twink and he's a daddy. Not like he isn't a hot daddy…. I mean—I didn't mean I think your uncle is hot. But some guys are into the whole daddy thing, and if that's the case, then he would be considered pretty…. Never mind."

"Are you…?"

"Into the whole daddy thing?"

"No," Ryan said. "Are you gay?"

"Oh. I guess I didn't establish that, did I? Is that a problem?"

"No. I'm gay too."

"Really? Does your uncle know?"

"He was the first person I came out to. He helped with my parents, and I even spent a summer here. That's how I know how to work the machine."

"You already know how to work that piece of shit?"

Ian was certainly learning a lot about his employees. "It's not that tough. It just takes a little patience and finesse."

"That's what everyone says. I shouldn't complain. Any other boss would have fired me by now, but your uncle is pretty cool."

"You think so?"

"Absolutely. He knows I'm gay, and I know he's gay, but he's never said anything even remotely creepy to me. A lot of guys his age can be total pervs. You know what I mean."

"Spend five minutes on Grindr."

"Right?" Matthew said. "Dude, I had to get rid of it. Seriously. I had to delete it from my phone. Guys would send me pictures of their junk, from out of the blue. No, 'Hi, what's up?' Just, 'Here's my junk.' And some nasty looking dicks too. The last time I got on, I had something like twenty messages. Everything from 'let's fuck' to 'you're a stuck-up asshole.' Do people really expect me to answer every single message?"

"No response is a response."

"Exactly. And half the time the app didn't even work, so I finally deleted it."

"Congratulations, you're Grindr-free. I'm Facebook-free."

"Really? Now that takes balls."

"What kind of guys do you like?" Ryan asked.

"I don't have a type, per se. If the attraction is mutual, I don't give a shit if anyone else thinks he's hot. Though I guess I do gravitate toward guys my age. And it helps if he's a top, or at least mostly a top."

Ryan smiled. *That's new information.*

"What about you?" Matthew asked.

"I like older men, but not daddies. More like the older brother type. Clean cut. Dreamy. The kind of guy who could whisk me off to Mykonos or Saint-Tropez."

"Sugar daddy, eh?"

"No, nothing like that. I can pay my own way."

Matthew laughed and slapped Ryan on the back. "I know your type, Parker. You're looking for a Madison Avenue penthouse with Gucci sheets on the bed."

"Is it wrong to like nice things?"

"No, not at all," Matthew said. "Anything else you want to add about your dream man?"

"Oh, it helps if he's a bottom, or at least mostly a bottom."

"Really? Well now, it's hard to find a young guy who knows what he's doing in the top department."

"I've been having sex since I was fifteen," Ryan said. "I fucked Casper Middleton in the boys' locker room after a lacrosse match."

"What position did you play?"

"I was an attacker. He was the goalie, and a senior."

"How old are you, anyway?"

"Twenty-one."

Matthew grinned. "Well, I'm twenty-two, so I guess that technically qualifies me as the older-brother type."

Ryan felt his face turn red, but before he could react, the west door opened and a large group walked in.

Matthew jumped off his stool. "Since you know how to work the machine, how about I take the orders. I'm good at that part." Over the next two hours, Ryan and Matthew developed a shorthand and a rhythm together. They flirted with the girls and joked with the guys (or sometimes vice versa) and never got a single order wrong. Around six o'clock Ian realized he needed to save the corner table for the freshman study group. It didn't seem realistic that Ian would remember to tell Ryan about such a small detail, so he went to the bathroom and called Mark.

"Can you go to my house and text me from Ian's phone? Use your key to get in. The phone's on the charger next to my bed. The password is 3946. I put Ryan in my contacts. Text him to save the corner table for Quentin's study group."

"I'm on it," Mark said. "How's it going?"

"So far, so good. Matthew noticed I'm wearing Ian's shoes. I think I covered okay, though."

"Damn. Shoes, of course. Why didn't I think of that? Those laces are very distinctive. That boy has the eyes of a hawk. You need to be careful around him."

"I got it under control."

"Okay. Give me a few minutes to get over to your house."

Ryan returned to the bar and purposefully sat his phone on the counter next to the register, where Matthew could see it. About ten minutes later, a text came through. Matthew fell right into the trap and glanced down. "Hey, look. You got a text from Uncle Ian. How cute."

"Why does everyone think it's cute that I call him Uncle Ian?" Ryan picked up his phone and opened the text. He showed it to Matthew and asked, "Do you know what this means?"

"Oh shit," Matthew said. "I forgot all about that." He grabbed the red "Reserved" sign from under the bar and went into the seating area. A young woman was studying at the large corner table, so Matthew charmed her into moving and then slapped the sign on top. He smiled and walked back to the bar.

"What was that all about?" Ryan asked.

"Your uncle reserves the corner table for a freshman study group every Friday night."

"Who's Quentin?"

"One of the students in the group. Don't ask me why your uncle feels obligated to kiss his ass. Text him back and tell him I took care of everything. And tell him I'm sorry about his mom."

Ryan typed in the response, and Ian thought, *Kiss his ass? Is that what everyone thinks I'm doing?*

An hour later, Quentin and his gang arrived. As soon as they saw Ryan behind the bar instead of Ian, they whispered under their breath and glanced sideways at each other. Ian reminded himself that Ryan didn't know any of them, and they obviously didn't know him.

Quentin walked up to the bar.

"Can I help you?" Ryan asked.

He got no response. Quentin just stared at him. Ryan stared back and tried to remain calm.

"Do you want to see a menu?"

"Where's Ian?" Quentin asked.

"He's in Phoenix. My grandma had emergency surgery, so he's helping my grandpa take care of her."

"Who are you?"

Ryan laughed. "Sorry, I'm his nephew. I offered to help out while he's in Arizona. I'm watching his house too."

"Ah. I could never imagine Ian as a young man, but he probably looked a lot like you."

"I've been told there's a certain family resemblance around the eyes."

"If you want to see a family resemblance, I'll drag my three brothers in here and show you a textbook case."

"Your name's Quentin, right?"

"How did you know that?"

Ryan grinned and took out his phone. He showed Quentin the text from Ian. "My uncle messaged me earlier about your table."

"Oh. Well, okay. That was nice of him. I see you got an S5. That's a sweet phone. What's your name?"

"Ryan."

Quentin reached out and shook his hand, then nodded his head toward Matthew, who had finished busing tables on the other side of the room. "What's it like working with Harry Styles, over there?"

Ryan laughed. "He's nice."

"If you ask me, a person who's that good looking should at least have the decency to be a moron."

"He seems pretty bright to me."

"Figures."

"Would you like to order?"

"Oh, right." Quentin looked over at his friends, then turned back. He took a credit card out of his pocket and handed it to Ryan. "I'll take two skim lattes, a skim mocha, and two espressos."

Ryan took the card, swiped it, and handed it back to Quentin. He stepped over to the machine and churned out the five drinks like a pro. He set them on a tray and pushed it across the bar.

"Looks like you've done that before," Quentin said.

"For an entire summer three years ago."

"Really? You mean at another coffee shop?"

"No," Ryan said. "Here at La Tazza."

Quentin looked confused but didn't press it any further. "Okay. If you talk to your uncle, tell him I hope his mom gets better real soon. Phoenix you said, right?"

"Right."

"And you're from…?"

"San Diego."

"Really? California. Nice beaches."

"You've been?"

"Last year," Quentin said. "Anyway, thanks for the excellent service."

He walked away, and Ryan took a deep breath.

Matthew came up behind him and said, "That kid's a real smartass, isn't he?"

"Why do you say that?"

"He called me Harry last week, and I don't look anything like Prince Harry. I'm not even a ginger."

"I think he meant another Harry," Ryan said.

"Which one? Potter? I do not look like—"

"No, Styles."

"Who's that?"

"The lead singer of One Direction."

"The boy band?" Matthew asked.

"I think he meant it as a compliment."

"Somehow I doubt that. If he listens to One Direction, then he's got shit for taste on top of being a smartass. Rock, paper, scissors to see who washes glasses?"

71

"Sure."

They pounded their fists against their palms three times, and Ryan formed a rock.

Matthew extended two fingers and said, "Terrific." He picked up the tub filled with cups and glasses. "I'll be in the back if you need help. Just give me a holler."

"Will do."

Matthew disappeared into the rear of the café, and Ryan sat down on one of the stools behind the bar. With no one in line to order, he took out his phone and opened his YouTube app. He started to watch an episode of *Hollyoaks*, but he barely got past the opening credits when Bartley walked through the north door. Ryan looked up and smiled. He would only get one chance to make a first impression. *Play it cool.* Ryan stood up and shoved the phone into his pocket. Bartley approached the bar, looking seriously hot in jeans and a plain white T-shirt.

God, I want to marry you.

"Welcome to La Tazza Magica. Can I take your order?"

"Are you Ian's nephew?"

"I'm Ryan. And you are…?"

"Sorry." He offered his hand. "I'm James. Bartley James."

Ryan shook it. "I like your tattoo. What does it mean?"

"Don't take this the wrong way, but I'm kind of keeping that a secret for now. I just got it last week."

"Oh, cool. Are you the architect?"

"Ian told you about me?"

"He said something about dinner plans with an architect named Bartley and that he didn't have your number. He's sorry he stood you up. How do you know who I am?"

"I'm a regular here," Bartley said. "I noticed your uncle went AWOL earlier in the week, so I asked Colleen if she knew anything. She told me about his mom and that his nephew would be flying in from San Diego to help out. You're the new guy behind the counter, so I figured you must be him. I can definitely see a resemblance around the eyes. So how's your grandma doing?"

"She's stable now. My grandpa's old too, so he can't do everything by himself until she's up and about."

"Were you raised in San Diego?"

"Born and bred," Ryan said.

"Do you surf?"

"I do. That's the first thing I miss whenever I leave California. Do you surf?"

"I did for a few years in college. I went to undergrad at Cal Poly."

"Sweet. I love San Luis Obispo." Ryan figured he had to ask questions to which Ian already knew the answers. "Where'd you go to grad school?"

Rice.

"Rice."

"I did a year at UC San Diego."

"You make it sound like you were in the slammer."

"That's pretty much how it felt," Ryan said. "I'm not cut out for college. I want to do something with my hands, so I'm looking for a carpentry class while I'm in town."

"I know a guy who makes his own furniture, if you want me to talk to him. He has a small storefront in South Austin, and I think he even teaches a workshop or something. If you're interested."

Ryan interpreted Bartley's eagerness to help as an encouraging sign. "That would be fantastic. Thank you."

"How long will Ian be gone?"

"Hard to say. A few weeks, maybe all summer. This is kind of an open-ended gig."

Bartley didn't mask his disappointment.

"Are you okay?" Ryan said.

"I was just looking forward to our dinner, that's all. Your uncle seems like a good guy, and I could use one of those in my life right now."

Ryan saw his opening and said, "I know I'm no replacement, but...."

"What?"

"Maybe I could treat you to dinner in exchange for a guided tour of downtown? Next week sometime. Unless.... Were you two going on a date?"

"No. It was just as friends."

"Then I'm sure he wouldn't mind. I haven't been to Austin in a while and would appreciate someone showing me around the city."

Bartley hesitated but then said, "Sure, I'd be happy to. But would you mind giving me Ian's number? I'd really like to talk to him."

Ryan wasn't crazy about the idea, but it made no sense that he would say no. He pulled out his phone, unlocked it, and handed it to Bartley. "He's in my contacts. Why don't you put your number in there while you're at it?"

Bartley took the phone and pulled out his own. He tapped back and forth between the two devices. "Why do you only have three contacts?"

"It's a new phone. I haven't transferred everything over yet."

Matthew came out from the back and said, "Hey, Mr. James."

Bartley looked up. "Hi, Matthew." He handed the phone to Ryan. "Give me a call this weekend, and we'll set something up."

"I'll do that. Did you want something to drink?"

"I think that's why I came in here. A double-skim latte to go, please."

Ryan made the drink as Matthew hovered over him. When Ryan finished, he set the paper cup on the bar. "That will be four twenty-five." Bartley paid with cash, left his customary seventy-five cent tip, and exited the shop.

Matthew immediately turned on Ryan. "Did you just ask Bartley James out on a date?"

"Why? What's wrong?"

"Do you even know he's your uncle's crush?"

Ian had not foreseen this complication. "I didn't know that," Ryan said, "but I wasn't asking him out on a date. I was giving him Uncle Ian's phone number."

"Then why did he tell you to give him a call this weekend to set something up?"

"Because Uncle Ian said I should ask Bartley to show me around town. So I did."

"Well, when he said that, I don't think Ian meant for the tour to include Bartley's bedroom."

"What are you talking about?"

"Come on, Ryan. Look at you. You're practically salivating."

"Don't be ridiculous. It's totally innocent."

Matthew scoffed. "Dude, you just told me what your type is. Older brother? The kind of guy who could whisk you off to Monte Carlo? In other words, Bartley James."

"First of all, don't 'dude' me. And second of all, it was Saint-Tropez, not Monte Carlo."

"Same difference. Look, we both know that Bartley's the kind of guy you're into. But if you sleep with him, you'll be stabbing your uncle in the back. He and I talked about this last week. Bartley had just asked him out, and he was upset that it was only as friends."

"Okay," Ryan said. "I didn't know that. But I haven't done anything wrong. Uncle Ian said Bartley is a cool guy and he knows the city really well. All I did was offer to buy him dinner in exchange for a guided tour of downtown. I haven't stabbed anyone in the back."

"Fine. But you'd better be careful. He's a player. I'm sure of it. If he tries anything, just—"

"I can take care of myself."

"That's what I'm afraid of," Matthew said under his breath.

"What are you implying?"

"We both know that everything's 'totally innocent' until it's not. See that sign above the door? *Don't be a dick.* Words to live by."

Ryan looked at the clock. "I need to take a piss." He walked away and into the restroom. Ian pulled out Ryan's phone and called Mark.

"Is everything okay?"

"I don't know," Ian said. "Everything I say has the potential to blow up in my face."

"It's not as easy as they make it look in the movies, is it?"

"No. It's not. Can you come over when I get off work? We need to talk."

CHAPTER SEVEN

"IF THERE'S one thing I'd like to get out of this reboot, other than the chance to correct every mistake I've ever made in my life, it's the chance to date Bartley James." Ian was sitting in his kitchen with Mark shortly after midnight. Mark had a glass of wine in front of him and Ian a glass of milk.

"Who's Bartley James?" Mark asked.

"The architect."

"Ah, I see. Okay, continue."

"As Ryan I'm in his target demo and I'm HIV negative. Win, win. But Matthew figured out that Ian had a crush on Bartley before we went to Denver, so now Ryan can't pursue him without Matthew thinking he's a total douchebag."

"You're going to have to repeat that about four more times before it makes any sense at all."

Ian took a drink of milk and swallowed. "The night before we went to Denver, Matthew asked if I was into Bartley."

"And who's Matthew again?"

"The new guy at work. A senior at UT. I hired him about two weeks ago."

"Okay. So how did he know you liked Barkley?"

"It's *Bartley*. He saw me give him a free sandwich and he could tell by the way I acted around him."

"Was this before or after Bartley asked you to dinner as friends?"

"Immediately after. So this evening, Bartley comes into La Tazza. He and Ryan seem to hit it off. He even offers to help me find a carpentry class."

"I didn't know you wanted to be a carpenter."

"Neither did I. I've only been thinking about it for a few months. Anyway, when I tell Bartley that Ian may be gone all summer, he looks disappointed. I see an opening and offer to treat him to dinner in exchange for showing me around town. We trade phone numbers, and as Matthew walks up to the counter, Bartley says, 'Give me a call this weekend and we'll set something up.'"

"I see where this is going."

"Bartley leaves, and Matthew turns on me. 'Did you just ask Bartley out on a date?' and 'Don't you know that's your uncle's crush?' and 'If you sleep with him you'll be stabbing Ian in the back.' I mean, what a drama queen. He could tell Ryan liked Bartley too. He's got some sixth sense or something."

"What did you say?"

"I claimed ignorance and innocence. I told him I didn't know Ian liked Bartley. I told him it wasn't a date and that Ian said I should ask Bartley to show me around. Matthew was like, 'Everything is innocent until it's not.' Now, if I try to date Bartley, Matthew's going to think I'm a dick."

"So?"

"So I'm not a dick. I'm Ian. I can't stab myself in the back."

"But he doesn't know that."

Ian shook his head. "You're being absolutely no help."

"If you're so enamored with this Bartley character, then why have you been hooking up with guys on Grindr and giving your number to the pizza boy?"

"Oh, give me a break. That happened on the first night. You, of all people, will not slut-shame me for going a little crazy, especially considering what my life's been like the past few years."

"You're right. I'm sorry."

"Besides, it was *one* guy on Grindr."

"Admit it. You liked the attention."

"That's irrelevant. I'm talking about me and Bartley now. What if we were supposed to meet ten years ago? What if something happened and we got blown off course? He went to grad school, and I went to Hawaii and let that guy fuck me without a condom. Maybe

Manick Butter is the universe's way of hitting the reset button and fixing my mistakes."

Mark took a sip from his glass of wine. "Okay, here's what you do. Tell Matthew you talked to Ian. You asked if he liked Bartley, and Ian said no."

"But Matthew knows that's not true."

"And he's right. Look, go back to being Ian for a minute and let's play this out."

"What do you mean?"

"Before all this happened, you were a forty-year-old man with a ten-year-old nephew named Ryan. I've seen you with that kid. You love him to death, and you'd do anything for him. Am I right?"

Ian hunched forward. "You're right."

"So imagine it's ten years from now, and the real Ryan grows up to be a fine young man who also happens to be gay. He comes to visit and hits it off with someone you have a crush on. You've never been on a date with this guy. You have no claim on him whatsoever. All you have is your fantasy. What would you do?"

"That's easy. I'd put Ryan first, step aside, and encourage him to ask the guy out on a date."

"Exactly. And when you tell Matthew that…."

"He's going to figure out why Ian said he doesn't like Bartley."

"Bingo. It's a perfect setup. There's no way he can judge you if you've told Ian everything and have his blessing. In the meantime, stick to your story that it's not a date and find a way to diffuse Matthew's sixth sense. The best way to throw a dog off the scent is to give him another scent."

"Distract him from me and Bartley?"

"Preferably with someone else."

"Hmm. That could work."

"How did the rest of your day go?" Mark asked.

"Fine. Something was off with Quentin Walsh."

"Is he any relation to Ben Walsh?"

"They're brothers. How do you know who Ben Walsh is?"

Mark laughed. "Every lawyer in Texas knows who Ben Walsh is. Have you met him?"

Ian nodded. "I knew their father. He started coming into La Tazza the week it opened. Brought the whole family. Except for Ben, of course. He's only been back in Austin for about three years. He and his boyfriend, Travis, and his brothers come in for Jeopardy Pursuit Night every month. They've won the last three in a row."

"Why am I only hearing about this now?"

"I didn't think it was important. Besides, you hate Jeopardy Pursuit Night."

"It never occurred to you that I might want to meet Ben Walsh?" Mark asked. "He's like a frigging rock star among lawyers."

"I'm sorry. I didn't know that."

"So what does his brother have to do with this?"

"Quentin's part of a freshman study group that comes in every Friday evening. I reserve a table for them. When Quentin met Ryan tonight, he gave him this strange look at the end of the conversation. I have no idea what it was about."

"When is Jeopardy Pursuit Night again?"

"The second Thursday of every month," Ian said. "You're not going to show up just to meet Ben Walsh, are you?"

"I never said I hated Jeopardy Pursuit Night."

"You said it was suburban."

"Which is true," Mark admitted.

"You said it with disdain."

"Don't editorialize. So you've met Travis too? What's he like?"

"Very sweet. He and the youngest brother handle all the sports questions."

"So everything went okay with Colleen?"

"Perfect. She's off all weekend to write a seminar paper. I'm opening in the morning, so I need to get some sleep. Thanks for coming over, though. You know I couldn't do this without you."

"I know that." Mark stood up. "Are you working all day?"

"I'm working all weekend. You should drop in at some point to say hi to Ryan. Certainly they've met before, but we want to get their friendship off the ground."

"Okay, I'll do that. It won't be until Sunday, though."

MARK LEFT the house, and Ian went into the bedroom. He checked Ian's phone and found a voice message from an unknown number.

Hey, Ian. This is Bartley. I hope you don't mind, but your nephew gave me your number. I wanted to call and say sorry about your mother. Ryan told me you might be gone for a while, so looks like we'll have to postpone our dinner. I was kind of.... Never mind. Anyway, Ryan suggested I show him around a little. I wanted to talk to you and see if that's okay. So... give me a call when you get a chance. I'll talk to you later.

Ian saved Bartley's number to his contacts but decided it was too late to call him back.

RYAN OPENED La Tazza at eight the next morning. Teresa, the barista on duty, had little to say, and Ryan spent most of the morning in the office, paying bills and logging purchase orders. With Colleen gone and the door closed, he dropped the training act and did things in Ian's efficient manner.

Since Ian could only call Bartley from the house, he took a break around two o'clock and went home. He sat down on his bed with Ian's phone. He practiced lowering his voice and then dialed Bartley's number. It rang three times.

"Hello."

"Hi, Bartley. This is Ian."

"Hey, Ian. I'm glad you called me back. How's your mom doing?"

"Better. Looks like it's going to be a slow recovery, though."

"I'm sorry to hear that."

"It's okay," Ian said. "I'm glad I can be here to help. Ryan's certainly saving my ass."

"I met him last night. Seems like a good kid. But can I ask you a question?"

"Sure."

"Is he straight?"

Ian was dumbfounded. How did he get through that whole conversation with Bartley without establishing Ryan's sexual orientation?

"No. Ryan is gay."

"Okay," Bartley said. "That makes more sense. When I met him, I just assumed he was straight. But then he suggested we have dinner, and I wasn't so sure. He also asked me to show him around town. Are you okay with that?"

"Why wouldn't I be? It's not like you and I were going on a date or anything."

"I know. I just thought.... Never mind. I didn't want you to hear about it and think I was moving in on your nephew."

"Bartley, he's twenty-one years old. He's an adult. I want him to meet someone nice and dependable, and if that someone turns out to be you, even better. At least I know you're a good guy."

"Hold on a second. I think there's been a misunderstanding. I'm not interested in asking Ryan on a date. I'm showing him around a bit. As a favor to you."

Ian didn't like the sound of that at all. "Okay, if you say so. But Ryan and I have been close since he came out, and you're exactly his type. You should give him a chance."

"Oh. Well, he seems like a nice guy. It's just.... He's a little young, and—"

"I thought you liked younger guys," Ian said.

"Why would you think that?"

"Because of all the dates you've brought into La Tazza."

"Dates? I haven't brought any dates into La Tazza."

"Come on, Bartley. I've seen you with at least three college guys."

"Those weren't dates. I mentor three architecture students from UT. We meet every other month or so to talk about their career options. You thought I've been dating college boys this whole time?"

"I didn't know."

"Well, I haven't. In fact, I haven't dated anyone since Mason and I broke up."

"I'm sorry. It's none of my business. But I hope you'll give Ryan a chance and show him around. He doesn't know anyone, and he's way more mature than most guys his age."

"I would be happy to show him around," Bartley said. "Look, you sound a little stressed out, so I'm going to let you go. I just wanted to make sure everything's cool."

"I appreciate the call. Really, I do. But you're right—I'm a little stressed out. Living with my father and brother again hasn't been an easy situation."

"I can only imagine. You're doing the right thing, though."

"I suppose."

"Rain check?"

Ian was confused. "For what?"

"Our dinner. When you get back?"

"Oh. Sure," Ian said. "Rain check. Definitely."

Ian ended the call. He sat on the bed and stared at the wall. A little young? How could he have been wrong about that? An alert sounded on his phone. Ian looked down and saw a text from another unknown number. He opened it and read:

hey ryan, this is sam, the pizza guy... what up?

Ryan: *hey sam... heading back to work... gonna be there all weekend*

Sam: *you wanna hang out some night next week? i'm free tues and wed*

Ian knew Matthew usually worked at four on Wednesdays, and he saw an opportunity to throw him off the scent.

Ryan: *wed is cool... can we meet at la tazza magica at 5? it's a coffee shop... i'm working there while i'm in town*

Sam: *sure... don't know where but I can figure it out*

Ryan: *sweet... c u then*

He added Sam to his contacts and returned to La Tazza. Matthew had the day off, and Bartley didn't come in for a latte. Timothy replaced Teresa at four, and by ten things were slow enough that Ryan let Timothy go home.

Around ten thirty, a young man walked through the east door and up to the bar. He wore slim-cut jeans, a white shirt, a dark blue silk tie, and a light blue checked double-breasted blazer, with a black messenger bag flung over his left shoulder. He had jet-black hair, green eyes, and pale skin. Ian would have used the term *pretty* to describe him, had it not been for the sonorous tone of his voice.

"Hello. My name is Alexander Marlow."

Ryan reached out and shook his hand. "I'm Ryan Parker."

"Would it be possible to speak with Ian Parker?"

Alexander Marlow possessed a rich, masculine, and utterly seductive voice. Every word he spoke reverberated like a cello in the lowest part of its register. Ian could think of only one other person with that kind of deep bass voice—Lance Alexander, the porn star.

"Has my inquiry offended you in some manner?"

"Sorry," Ryan said as he snapped out of his thoughts. "No, I wasn't offended. It's just… my uncle is in Phoenix. I'm Ian's nephew. I'm running things while he's out of town."

"I see." Alexander Marlow sighed. "I know what you're thinking. I've witnessed that exact expression several times in the past year alone."

"What expression?"

"You associate the sound of my voice with that of one Lance Alexander, an actor currently employed in the gay pornographic film industry. Am I correct?"

"How did you know that?"

"You would not be the first person to make the comparison, nor, I suspect, will you be the last. It's not as if I harbor any objection. On the contrary, I find Mr. Alexander, with whom I also share a name, to be quite attractive. And I find his voice both harmonically resonant as well as aurally pleasing."

"Have you ever watched any of his scenes?"

"No, I admit I have not. I did watch a short interview with him on the YouTube machine, out of curiosity. I fear he has a rather simple disposition."

"Are you trying to say he's stupid?"

Alexander Marlow smiled but remained silent.

"What did you want to talk to my uncle about?"

"I have been tasked with the organization of a social custom known as happy hour. A group of architecture students wish to celebrate their graduation. Ergo, I find myself scouting possible locations. Bartley James suggested I speak with Mr. Parker. Mr. James is one of our mentors, and my working assumption is that he purchases a caffeinated beverage at this location on a daily, or at least semidaily, basis. Thus, he's formed a bond with the owner, in this case your uncle, which naturally led Bartley to recommend La Tazza Magica to me."

"You use a lot of words."

"I am aware of that fact, and yet I find there is virtually nothing I can do to control the number of words I use to express myself. If you added or subtracted even one, I would cease to be me."

"Okay, it wasn't meant as an insult."

"Nor was it taken as one."

"How big is your group?"

"The count currently stands at forty-two, which Douglas Adams famously posited as the meaning of life. Personally, however, I do not believe there is any relationship between the two data points. Regardless of this fact, you should prepare for a variance of plus or minus two percent. One must always consider the possibility that a stray parent will show up unexpectedly. Or, as in my case, not."

"What night?" Ryan asked.

"Friday, May 16."

"That's right during graduation."

"Congratulations. You have correctly placed the date within the context of the academic calendar."

Ryan decided to ignore the snark. "Hmm. Well, we'd have to close to accommodate that many people, but since Bartley's involved, you can put us down as interested and available."

"Thank you. This establishment would be quite agreeable, since the location is able to accommodate participants with varying transportation resources."

"So you're an architecture student?"

"Affirmative, but unfortunately my days in the ivory tower of academia will soon be little more than a distant memory. And since I have yet to secure employment in my chosen field, I shall find myself working side by side with my mother, come September."

"What does she do?"

"Private investigation."

"Sounds interesting."

"I fear, Mr. Parker, that you have watched too many television programs. More often than not, the reality of investigating the personal lives of strangers involves the pursuit of cheating husbands and wives. I would think it both true and fair to say that nothing is less interesting, or more common, than infidelity."

"You might be right. What are you doing until September?"

"I will be attending the six-week Career Discovery Program at Harvard University's School of Design, after which I shall travel to South America in an attempt to retrace the footsteps of one Ernesto Guevara, commonly known as Che, and the odyssey he chronicled in *The Motorcycle Diaries*."

"Do you realize that trip took him nine months and covered about five thousand miles?"

Alexander Marlow sighed. "I do realize the facts as you have presented them. However, my father was born and raised in Argentina, and since I never had the opportunity to make his acquaintance, the journey is largely symbolic."

"Well, I wish you all good fortune. I liked the movie. Gael Garcia Bernal is a total stud."

"I agree. He is a fine example of the male specimen."

"Would you like a latte?"

"No, though I do thank you for the offer. I have never put any kind of stimulant into my body."

"Not even a cup of coffee?"

"That is correct. I have yet to drink alcohol or smoke a cigarette or even take an aspirin."

"No kind of drug? Ever?"

"No kind, ever. There can be little debate over the fact that drugs cloud one's judgment and impair one's ability to process information."

"That's kind of the point."

"Then it is a point lost on me. As I said, I am quite grateful for the offer, but filtered water, preferably from a natural spring, is the only beverage I drink."

"Not even orange juice?"

"Why drink the juice and throw out the fruit? I cannot support a concept that reduces the nutritional value of food and, at the same time, creates unnecessary waste."

Ryan laughed. "Okay, then. I'll mark the date on the calendar, and you give us a call about a week ahead of time to iron out the details. You can get our number off the website."

"I find your plan satisfactory. I was not looking forward to this transaction in the slightest, Mr. Parker, but you have managed to make it almost enjoyable, and I hope you accept that in the complimentary manner with which it was intended. I wouldn't last five minutes in your line of work."

"That's why Hillary said it takes a village."

"Actually she was talking about raising children. Nonetheless your point is well taken, even if it would have been better articulated by a phrase such as, 'different strokes for different folks.' Something to consider for next time."

Ryan noticed a few beads of sweat on Alexander's brow. "Are you nervous?"

Alexander took a handkerchief from his bag and wiped his forehead. "Ryan," he said, "I have long been aware of the fact that people do not like me. I have been called pretentious and cartoonish to my face, so I can only imagine what goes on behind my back. One of my professors even called me a stereotype, although he never made clear exactly which stereotype I represent. What am I supposed to do about that? I talk the way I talk. I speak what is on my mind. How do I change those things? I bear no animus toward others, and yet I do not seem to fit into the world. And because of that, to answer your question, I am always nervous."

Ryan wanted to give him a hug. "I like you, Alexander. Sure, you're an odd duck, but this is La Tazza Magica. It's like the Island of Misfit Toys."

"I am unaware of such an island."

"You've never seen *Rudolph the Red-Nosed Reindeer?*"

Alexander's blank expression answered for him.

"We're gonna have to fix that," Ryan said. "But my point is, you fit in here just fine. There's no reason to be nervous around the likes of me."

"Thank you. I find your attitude to be a rare one indeed. Your uncle must think very highly of you, seeing as he placed his business into your young, yet clearly capable, hands."

"Just because we're young doesn't mean we can't be responsible, right?"

"I couldn't agree more. If everyone over thirty would simply get out of the way, I believe we could solve most of the world's problems in the span of a few years. And now, in keeping with the Italian theme of your uncle's café, I will say *buona sera* to you, Ryan Parker."

They shook hands.

"Buona sera, Alexander Marlow."

IAN GOT home after midnight, but at least he didn't have to open until nine the next morning. He poured himself a glass of milk and called Mark.

"How was your day?"

"I talked to Bartley. As Ian. He left a message on my phone, so I thought it'd be good to call him back and encourage him to go out with Ryan."

"How did that go?"

"He said Ryan's a little young."

"Young? I thought you said he liked young."

"I guess I was wrong. The guys I've seen him with were just architecture students from UT. He's a mentor there."

"So what kind of guys does he like?"

"I don't know. He didn't say." Ian pulled a box of donuts from the pantry and ate one.

"Well," Mark said, "what are you going to do now?"

"We all have a type and we all have exceptions to it," Ian said with his mouth full. "Ryan will have to be an exception. He probably doesn't like young guys because of the immaturity factor. But I'm forty inside, so that should work to my advantage."

"You hope."

Ian took a drink of milk. "He said he wasn't interested in a date with Ryan, but that can change."

"When are you going to call him?"

"Tomorrow. I'm going to suggest dinner on Friday."

"Maybe at Sandy's restaurant?"

"Maybe."

"I'm planning to stop in tomorrow and say hi," Mark said. "So, I've met Ryan before?"

"Don't you think? You've been friends with Ian for over twenty years. You've met the real Ryan, and certainly you would have met the fake Ryan when he stayed here three summers ago."

"You're right. We might actually have spent a fair amount of time together."

"Matthew's working with me in the morning. You should drop by then. Ask me about Sam."

"Who's Sam?" Mark asked.

"The pizza boy. I'm meeting him on Wednesday, to throw Matthew off the scent."

"Ah, okay. I'll be sure to mention him."

CHAPTER EIGHT

OF ALL the shifts at La Tazza, Sunday mornings were the slowest. Ryan arrived just before nine and Matthew about five minutes later. They prepped the counter in silence for a few moments. Then Matthew said, "I'm sorry I jumped down your throat on Friday."

Ryan opened the cash register and stocked it with ones. "It's okay. I think you're wrong, though."

"About what?"

"I talked to Uncle Ian and asked him if he liked Bartley."

Matthew slipped a pair of wine glasses into the rack above the bar. "So he told you, right?"

"No. He said he and Bartley are just friends and I should ask him out on a date if I want."

"That's not possible."

"You can call and talk to him yourself."

"But he told me—" Matthew paused, and his whole body language changed. "Oh, I get it."

Ryan closed the register drawer and turned to Matthew. "Get what?"

"Your uncle's stepping aside so you can have Bartley. Of course, that's the kind of guy he is. It doesn't mean you have to go through with it, though. Don't get me wrong, I think it's cool what he's doing. But it would be even cooler if you stepped aside for him."

RYAN SPENT the next hour scheduling shifts for the week ahead. When he went out to check on Matthew, Ryan found him working on his laptop behind the bar. Ian made it clear to all his employees that they were free to do their homework on the job, so long as there were no customers in line.

"Watching porn?" Ryan asked.

Matthew looked up and smiled. "Close."

"Really? I don't know what my uncle would say about that."

"I'm not watching porn. I'm writing a paper about it."

Ryan laughed. "For what class?"

"Performance Studies. It's an upper-level course in the drama department."

"But you're a music major."

Matthew looked surprised. "How did you know that?"

Shit. Ryan had screwed up again. "I.... Um, Uncle Ian must have said something."

"He mentioned me?"

"Sure. We went over all the employees. He told me you just started a couple of weeks ago, and that you're a music major, and that you don't know how to drive a stick shift."

"That's what he said?"

"Is there something you wanted to add? I can teach you, if you want."

"To drive a stick?" Matthew asked.

"It's not that tough, really. So what's this class about?"

"We study types of performance that don't necessarily happen in a theater."

"Like parades or flash mobs?" Ryan asked.

"Exactly. My final paper is about the relationship between porn and the real sex lives of gay men."

"You should talk to Uncle Ian's friend Mark. Have you ever met him?"

"No, not yet."

"He's stopping by this morning to say hi. I've heard he's an expert. I guess you've watched a lot yourself?"

"Hey, I had to do my research. Did you know they actually showed porn in movie theaters back in the '70s and early '80s?"

"I didn't know that," Ryan said, even though Ian did.

"It's true. Every breakthrough in technology has brought us closer and closer to our porn. It went from the movie theater to the

VCR to our phone. When you have sex, do you mimic what you see in the porn you watch?"

"No comment."

"Coward. The unexamined life is not worth living, dude."

The west door opened and Mark walked in. Ryan smiled and gave him a hug. "Hey, Uncle Mark. Were your ears burning? I was just telling Matthew about you."

Mark pulled away and looked unsure. "Why?"

"He's doing a paper on gay porn, and I told him you're an expert."

Mark extended his hand and introduced himself to Matthew. "I would rather that not be the first thing you learn about me, but I have seen a lot."

"I think it's cool," Matthew said. "Pull up a stool. I'd love to pick your brain."

"What do you want to drink?" Ryan asked.

"A cappuccino, please." Ryan ducked behind the bar and began to prepare the drink. Mark sat down and said, "When did you start working here, Matthew?"

"The beginning of April. How long have you known Ian?"

"Twenty years," Mark said. "Since college. Did Ryan tell you about his big date on Wednesday?"

"No. You have a date with Bartley already?"

Ryan poured milk foam into a cup of espresso. "No, I have a date with the pizza boy."

Matthew chuckled. "The pizza boy? Are you kidding me?"

"What's wrong?" Ryan said. "You're doing a paper on gay porn and you have a problem with me picking up the pizza boy? I'm sorry, but that's a highly regarded subgenre in and of itself. *The Pizza Boy: He Delivers* is an all-time classic."

Matthew took the cappuccino from Ryan and set it down in front of Mark. "Here you go. I take it you get free stuff?"

"I'd better. Has that changed, Ryan?"

"No, it hasn't."

"What's your paper about?" Mark asked Matthew.

"I'm looking at how porn influenced the sex lives of gay men. I'm starting with the '70s, when it mostly reflected what gay guys were doing in their bedrooms. There were no LGBT film festivals back then, so if you were a gay filmmaker interested in gay movies, you made gay porn. Since so many of the films from the '70s look like home movies, I have to assume that's how guys were fucking in real life."

"That's a big assumption," Mark said. "But I see your point. Nobody expected a gay porno to make money, so people could do what they wanted. Gay sex, as opposed to sex between two men, was still in its infancy. The concepts of top and bottom didn't even exist yet. It would never have occurred to Al Parker not to get…. Are you two okay having a frank discussion about this with a man twice your age?"

Ryan and Matthew looked at each other and shrugged. "It's fine with me," Matthew said.

"Me too. We're both legal."

"Okay." Mark took a sip of his cappuccino. "It would never have occurred to Al Parker not to get fucked in his films."

"But that all changed in the '80s," Matthew said, "with total tops like Jeff Stryker. And thanks to the VCR, guys could watch porn in their living rooms."

"Finally," Mark said. "VCR porn was the first viable gay market."

Matthew continued. "That's when the movies stopped reflecting real sex and started shaping it instead, because the studios realized they could make a shitload of money off this fantasy of 'the guy who never gets fucked.' Capitalism is responsible for an entire generation of gay men who are ashamed of bottoming. By 1990, taking a dick up your ass was considered a sign of weakness."

Mark flinched and said, "I don't know if 'weakness' is the right word, but it was definitely a sign of submission to a more powerful masculine figure."

"That's what I meant. Everyone bottomed for Jeff Stryker because he was the highest-paid star. Money talked."

"Did he ever get fucked on film?" Ryan asked.

"No," Mark said. "I remember when I first saw *Stryker Force*. At the end, he fucks Steve Hammond, another total top. One of the hottest scenes I've ever seen, because nothing beats the moment when a top flips. Except later I found out Steve Hammond used a stunt butt. You can only imagine my disappointment."

"If you ask me," Matthew said, "the '90s were a terrible decade. All the fun got sucked out of porn. The guys were buffed and waxed and bore no resemblance to men in real life. It was like the Disney version of gay sex."

"Until 1998," Mark said.

"What happened in 1998?" Ryan asked.

Matthew and Mark answered together: "Treasure Island Media."

"Paul Morris threw away the condoms and brought real sex back to porn," Matthew said.

Mark took another sip of his cappuccino. "He broke all the rules, and men who enjoyed recreational sex devoured his stuff. For years, you couldn't go to a sex party in this town without seeing *Dawson's 20 Load Weekend* in the background."

"Morris is a real interesting character, though. The dude's got a lot to say about representing male sexuality."

Mark nodded. "There are very few porn directors who have a distinctive visual style. The minute you see one of his movies, you know it's Treasure Island. Joe Gage is the same way."

"And William Higgins," Matthew said.

"You know your vintage?" Mark asked.

"You bet. It's all available online now. Colt's stuff was very distinctive too. And Bel Ami. Even Fratmen, with its glossy trademark look and no soundtrack."

Ryan sat down on a stool next to Matthew. "What about the Internet? That changed everything."

"Of course," Mark said. "Nothing has done more to reshape sex and porn than streaming video. It's created a demand that gay performers can't possibly fill. A lot of guys criticize the gay-for-pay industry, but they don't realize that if a site posts just one update a week, they literally run out of gay guys after six months. Our demand for new content created the Corbin Fisher/Sean Cody/Randy Blue triumvirate, and its sameness is mind-numbing."

"Maybe," Matthew said. "But there's a massive amount of porn produced on this planet every day, and you have to admit, it's pretty diverse. I watched a video last week—Superman getting fucked by a purple kryptonite dildo. I kid you not. There's Asian porn, black porn, black on white porn, Latino, blatino, you name it. There's a whole category just for Brazil."

"That may be true, but the popular performers, all the household names, are still white."

"Like who?"

Mark rattled off a list: "Colby Keller, Johnny Rapid, Zeb Atlas, Phenix Saint, Marcus Mojo, Kris Evans, Jake Bass, Paddy O'Brian, Christian Wilde, Spencer Reed, Brent Corrigan, Connor Maguire, Ricky Sinz, Tommy Defendi."

"That's a good list," Matthew said. "Though Spencer Reed looks bored with it all lately. And Matthew Rush is a household name who's not white."

"Okay, I'll concede that Matthew Rush is an exception."

"Colby Keller is arguably the greatest porn star of his generation, but truth be told, I don't watch his stuff anymore."

Ryan nodded. "Me neither."

"Why not?" Mark asked.

"I'm over him," Matthew said. "I'm pretty much the same way with Johnny Rapid and Christian Wilde. I can only jack off to the same guy so many times, no matter how hot he is."

Mark raised his eyebrows. "Did you see Christian Wilde bottom for Austin Wilde?"

"Okay," Matthew admitted. "I did watch that. But the volume of available porn has trained me to seek out constant variety. My argument in the paper is that my generation is going to have a big problem with monogamy because of that."

Mark laughed. "Blame it on the porn."

"I didn't say I personally have a problem with monogamy."

"What class is this paper for?" Mark asked.

"Performance Studies."

"Oh. Well then, I'd question the whole premise of your paper. What if all sex is performed, and there's no such thing as 'real sex'?"

Matthew looked confused. "I'm not sure what you mean."

Mark explained himself. "You've created an artificial division between porn and the real sex lives of gay men. But what if real sex is as much a performance as porn? Don't you feel it when you start having sex? We throw a switch in our brains. Our partner expects something from us. We're called upon to perform. When our dicks go soft, we call it 'performance anxiety.' We go to a theater to see a play, and at the same time we refer to sex as 'playing.' Some people create elaborate scenes, with props and costumes and special lighting effects. Sex parties are basically improvisational performances. Even when you're just having sex with your boyfriend, there's a button you turn on and off. You still play a character who's slightly different from your authentic self. I would argue that all sex is performed."

Matthew shook his head. "Shit. That's a great idea, but now I have to start all over."

"No, you don't. Just reframe your observations and use the word 'postmodern' a lot. And quote Marx when you discuss the effects of capitalism. I guarantee it'll get you an A. Do you have a favorite porn movie?"

"Wow," Matthew said. "Of all time? That's tough. There's a guy on GayForIt from Vienna. His name is Andy. He's posted about 500 vintage films. The one that always sticks in my head is *My Man Mickey*."

Mark snapped his fingers. "That's a great flick."

"What's it about?" Ryan said.

"One pair of friends meets another pair of friends. Couple A drugs couple B and then basically date rapes them once they pass out."

"And you liked this movie?" Ryan asked.

"Let him finish," Mark said.

"It's a classic revenge story with an almost Tarantino-esque flair. Couple B wakes up and finds the half-empty bottle that A used to drug them, because they left it behind by mistake. Then slowly couple B remembers what happened. One of them says, and I kid you not, 'They done raped us.' So they decide to turn the tables. They track down the other two guys and slip the leftover drug into their beer. Not only do they fuck them when they pass out, but they call a couple of their friends over to help."

"Okay," Ryan said. "I have to see this. But why is it called *My Man Mickey*?"

"A Mickey Finn is slang for a drugged drink," Matthew said. "You know, like slipping someone a mickey. Now, what's your favorite vintage?"

Ryan thought it over. "Probably *Crossroads*. Danny Sommers and… I don't remember the other guy's name."

"Chuck Barron," Mark said.

"The whole movie is just the two of them. Danny is a closeted military guy, and Chuck is married to Danny's high school sweetheart. It's a friends-to-lovers story, lots of dialogue, more like a one-act play with sex than your typical porno. I'll never forget the last scene, when Danny says, 'Careful there, lover boy, you almost bit my lip.' And Chuck says, 'I'm not a boy, but I am your lover.' They're really sweet together. What about you, Mark?"

Ian, of course, already knew the answer.

"*Fratrimony*. Another two-person movie. Tim Lowe and Butch Taylor play brothers who fall in love. Unbelievably hot."

Matthew slapped his hand onto the bar. "Why is porn at its most awesome when it deals with taboo subjects like date rape and incest?"

"Because it's an outlet," Mark said. "Like Mardi Gras or Vegas. It's the place where we release our id so that we don't rape people or sleep with our brothers in real life. There's a sick bastard in all of us, and sometimes he needs a little room to breathe. Think about everything you see in porn that we consider despicable in real life— sexual harassment in the workplace, guys molesting their sleeping roommates, priests fucking altar boys, guards fucking prisoners, doctors fucking patients, teachers fucking students, coaches fucking players. If you took the Jerry Sandusky story and cast it with eighteen-year-olds, gay guys would watch that as porn. And I've barely scratched the surface. Have you ever seen the movie where

96

the father takes his son to the XXX arcade and teaches him how to use a glory hole? Good God, who thought that up? There are gay guys recruiting straight guys, soldiers kidnapping men to use them as sex slaves, frat boys hazing pledges by fucking them, massage therapists seducing their clients—"

"Tyler Saint," Ryan said.

Matthew nodded. "The hardest working man in show business."

"All those things make for hot porn," Mark said.

"But what does that say about us?" Ryan asked.

Mark shook his head. "I don't know and I don't care."

"I think I care," Matthew said.

"And that's why you're writing the paper," Mark said. "Who are your nominees for greatest porn star of all time?"

"Wait," Ryan said. "First, I want to hear who turns you off. What we don't like is as interesting as what we do."

Mark finished his cappuccino and wiped his mouth with a paper napkin. "Fair point. Personally, I'm not a Brett Everett fan. I know people love the lips, but not me. I can't watch Bel Ami anymore, and I'm almost there with the whole Sean Cody genre. Always the same couch. Always the same bed."

"Dean Monroe," Matthew said.

"What?" Ryan asked. "Dean Monroe is totally hot."

"I know. It's a completely random and unjustified loathing, but I can't watch anything with Dean Monroe in it. The voice and that accent don't match the rest of the package. What about you, Ryan?"

"Nothing with Zeb Atlas. Or Trystan Bull. I never watch twink porn, and I hate Bel Ami—the way Czech guys kiss freaks me out. It's like they're sword fighting with their tongues. I'm completely over Treasure Island and their meth-head aesthetic. And I want to stab my eyes out every time I see Jake Cruise molesting another hot guy on PornHub."

Matthew laughed. "You're funny, Parker. So can we move on to greatest porn star of all time?"

"Why don't we do vintage and present day?" Ryan suggested.

"Good idea," Matthew said as he tapped his hands together in thought. "Okay. Jeff Stryker for vintage and Colby Keller for present day, even though I don't watch him fuck anymore. And I hope someone else is going to say Al Parker for vintage."

"Parker is my second choice too," Mark said. "But my first is Joey Stefano. It's hard to argue with Stryker, but I could make a strong case for Stefano. He was really the first bottom to become a superstar. As for present day, I'm going with Johnny Rapid. I can't stand that a straight man is the face of gay porn, but Johnny Rapid defines ubiquitous."

"For present day," Ryan said, "I think you're both right—it's a tossup between Keller and Rapid. Although Brent Corrigan does have more Twitter followers than any other gay porn star. But I'm going off the grid with a personal favorite—Kodi from Broke Straight Boys."

Matthew and Mark both laughed. "He's dreamy in a nasty way," Matthew said. "I like Bobby Owen too. Did Kodi and Bobby ever do a scene together?"

"Never," Ryan said. "And for vintage, I pick my namesake, Ryan Idol."

Matthew made a sour face. "Ugh. He represents everything that's bad about gay porn."

"Are you telling me you wouldn't let him fuck you in his prime?" Ryan asked.

"Of course I would. Don't be ridiculous. I can't stand Cody Cummings either, but I'd still let him fuck me."

"At least you're honest," Mark said. "That's one of the differences between men of your age and men of my age."

"You wouldn't have sex with Cody Cummings?"

Mark shook his head. "No. At a certain point, you lose the ability to have sex with men who make your skin crawl. It's called maturity."

"Ouch," Matthew said.

"I'm kidding."

"No, you're not."

"You're right, I'm not. But don't take it personally."

A group of students entered through the east door. "Time to wrap this discussion up," Ryan said. "I don't think Uncle Ian would want us subjecting his customers to our ramblings about gay pornography."

Mark got off his stool. "I need to run anyway."

Matthew stopped him. "Wait a minute. I'm putting together a team for Jeopardy Pursuit Night next month. Would you like to join?"

Mark looked at Ryan and smiled. "I would be delighted. You can get my number from your coworker, here. Ryan, call me if you need anything."

"I will, Uncle Mark."

Matthew laughed. "Can I call you Uncle Mark too?"

Mark paused, almost said something, but then turned around and exited through the west door.

RYAN AND Matthew served a steady stream of customers through the rest of the morning and into the afternoon. Around two o'clock, Ryan took advantage of a lull in business and stepped onto the patio to take a break. He pulled out his phone and dialed Bartley's number.

"Hi, Ryan."

"Hey, Bartley. I was calling about dinner next week. Did you talk to my uncle?"

"He said it was fine. I'd be happy to show you around."

"Great. How about Friday night? I was thinking dinner at Bess Bistro, and then maybe you could give me a walking tour of downtown, if you're up for it."

"Bess Bistro? You know that's Sandra Bullock's restaurant, right?"

"Actually I had no idea. Mark suggested it."

"Who's Mark?"

"Uncle Ian's best friend. He's kind of like my second uncle in Austin."

"He's Ian's boyfriend?"

"No, Ian doesn't have a boyfriend. He and Mark have known each other since college. I got to know Mark when I stayed here three summers ago."

"You've lived in Austin before?"

"Right after I graduated from high school. Mark's a funny guy. I'm surprised you haven't met him."

"Does he come into La Tazza a lot?"

"No, he actually avoids it as much as possible, but he stopped by this morning to say hi. I asked him for a restaurant rec, and he said Bess Bistro."

"It sounds like a nice evening," Bartley said. "But why do you need a tour of downtown if you've lived in Austin before?"

"I was hoping for some architectural insight. I figured you must know a few facts about the buildings down there, right?"

"The most interesting one is actually the capitol, but I'll give it some thought and see what I can come up with."

"Any conflicts on Friday?" Ryan asked.

"No, none. Can I meet you at La Tazza?"

Ryan did not want Matthew serving as an audience.

"I'm not working that night. I can pick you up."

"No," Bartley said. "Let me. We may end up doing a driving tour instead. Text me your address. I'll make a reservation for seven and pick you up at six thirty."

"Perfect. I'll see you then."

Ryan went back inside and ducked behind the bar. Matthew stared at him. "You talked to Bartley, didn't you?"

"How did you know that?" Ryan said.

"Because you got that glowy look."

"You're delusional."

"Oh, right. You've got Monte Carlo written all over your face."

"How many times do I have to tell you? It's Saint-Tropez."

"Whatever. Why can't you keep your hands off the one guy Ian has a crush on?"

"It's not a date. And besides, I have Uncle Ian's blessing."

"There are plenty of other eligible young men who would be happy to show you around Austin."

"Are you jealous?"

Matthew sneered. "Of Bartley James? You've got to be kidding. All I'm saying is, you could do better *and* be nice to your uncle at the same time. Bartley's not the right guy for you, Parker."

"And who is? You?"

"Maybe."

Ryan opened his mouth, but words failed him. Was Matthew joking around? They both turned away and fumbled for something to clean. Matthew collected some stray glasses sitting on the bar and piled them into a busing tub.

"What do I have to do to get a latte around here?"

Ryan turned around and saw Jeremy standing at the bar.

"Jeremy. Wow, it's great to see you."

"You said you'd be working all weekend and I should stop by. So here I am. Stopping by."

"Right. Of course." Ryan looked at Matthew, who raised one eyebrow. "I'm going to take a break."

"You just took a break," Matthew said.

"Then I'm going to take another one. Nobody's in line, dude."

Matthew looked at Jeremy. "Sure. Take a break. I'll hold down the fort."

"You want a single or a double?" Ryan asked.

"A single's fine," Jeremy said. "But can you make it with soy milk, please?"

"No problem. Why don't you grab a table, and I'll be right out with the drink."

Jeremy nodded and selected one of the smaller tables in the far corner.

"Who's that bozo?" Matthew asked.

Ryan turned toward the espresso machine and began to prepare Jeremy's latte. "He's not a bozo. He's a very sweet guy who deserves way better than what I'm about to give him."

"Where'd you meet him?"

"Grindr."

"How many guys are you juggling?" Matthew asked. "Three? You got Bartley, the pizza dude, and now fanboy Jeremy over there?

Did you see his T-shirt? When are they going to accept that *Firefly* got canceled because nobody watched it?"

"He's going to make someone a great boyfriend someday."

"But that someone's not going to be you?"

"No," Ryan said. "We just didn't click that way."

"You did make plans with Bartley, though, didn't you?"

"We're getting together on Friday. So what?"

"Why don't you just admit it? You like him."

Ryan stopped heating the milk and set the steel pitcher on the counter. "Okay, I admit it. I like him. But I told you, I have Uncle Ian's blessing. He's not interested."

"He only said that because he's putting you first. So why don't you put him first? He needs this more than you do, Ryan. I talked to him the day before he went to Denver, and he sounded pretty down in the dumps. If only you could see him and Bartley together. It's so obvious they're made for each other, but for some reason they haven't figured it out yet."

Ryan picked up the pitcher of milk and finished Jeremy's latte. "Why don't we ever talk about your love life?"

"Because I'm single and don't have a crush on my uncle's boyfriend."

"Boyfriend?" Ryan shook his head. "They've never even— forget it. Look, if this is the part where we lay our true feelings on the table, then why don't you admit that your problem with me and Bartley has nothing to do with my uncle?"

"I… I was joking when I said maybe."

"Oh, right. If you want to play it that way, fine. But you're a senior in college, not high school. If you like somebody, just tell them. And for the record, I'm not juggling the pizza boy either. He's new in town and needs friends. I told Mark it was a date so that you'd see us together and get off my back about Bartley."

"And why would you go to such lengths to get me off your back? Because you know I'm right. You should find someone else to show you around town and let Ian have his chance with Bartley."

"I've already made plans."

"Then cancel them. You're going to come around eventually, Ryan. You're going to change your mind between now and Friday. I have to believe that. Otherwise...." Ryan turned away, and Matthew said, "Never mind. Let Jeremy down easy, will you? Rejection sucks."

Ryan carried Jeremy's drink to his table and took a seat. "Here you go. It's on the house."

"Another one of your uncle's perks?"

"Something like that."

"Thanks," Jeremy said as he took a sip. "Who's your friend behind the bar?"

"Matthew? Just one of the guys who works here."

"He likes you."

"I think he's confused."

"Confused?"

Ryan had no further comment.

Jeremy took another drink. "I had a good time the other night."

"Me too."

"Would you like a repeat?"

Ryan bit his lip and lowered his head.

"Oh," Jeremy said.

"I'm sorry, but I'm interested in someone else right now."

"Matthew the barista?"

"No. The guy's name is Bartley. I met him on Friday. We're going to have dinner this week."

"I should have known someone would snatch you up."

"I wouldn't go that far, but I wanted to be honest. You're a great guy, Jeremy, and I'd like us to be friends, if that's possible. Do you have room in your life for one of those?"

"I've got nothing but room," Jeremy said. "I don't know what happened to me. I had tons of friends in Dallas, but it's been hard meeting people here. I love Austin, but the only buddies I have are the guys I game with, and they're all straight. No one on Grindr wants anything other than sex. Well, except you."

"You should hang out here more often. Matthew's okay, most of the time, and there are some really cute boys who come in here."

"I noticed."

Ryan turned and saw Matthew's line had grown to four. "Come over and sit at the bar. I need to help with these customers."

They vacated their table, and Ryan worked with Matthew to complete the orders. When the next lull came, Ryan introduced Jeremy to Matthew. Somehow the three of them got back to the topic of Matthew's porn paper, which interested Jeremy to no end.

"I was a math major, and trust me, we never got to write term papers about porn."

"What do you do now?" Matthew asked.

"I teach high school."

"Oh, cool. Which one?"

"Harvest Island Academy."

"No way. That's where I went."

"You grew up in Austin?" Ryan asked.

"Not exactly. We moved here when I was fifteen, right after my dad died."

"Oh," Jeremy said.

Ryan touched Matthew on the shoulder. "I'm sorry."

"It's all good. It was just me and my mom after that. I went to the Island on a music scholarship."

"Do you play an instrument?" Jeremy asked.

"The violin."

"Has Ryan told you anything about this Bartley guy he's interested in?"

Matthew snickered. "So he told you about Mr. Monte Carlo, did he?"

"We're not talking about Bartley," Ryan insisted.

Jeremy ignored him and continued. "What's he like?"

"Older," Matthew said. "Late twenties. Handsome. Successful. Slick. Some would even say slippery. The kind of guy who always gets what he wants."

"Ah," Jeremy said. "Not my type at all."

"What is your type?" Ryan asked.

"I don't know. The type who wants to go out with me?"

Ryan shook his head. "Come on. We all have a certain kind of guy that makes us weak in the knees."

"What kind of porn do you watch?" Matthew asked. "That will tell us everything we need to know."

"I don't want to say. It might come off as offensive."

"Let me guess," Matthew said. "Jewish guys submitting to German dudes?"

Jeremy laughed. "No, it's nothing quite that offensive. Maybe 'offensive' isn't even the right word. I like working-class men. You know, construction workers, mechanics, delivery guys, that sort of thing. In other words, the opposite of Bartley."

"So you have a white-trash fetish?" Matthew said.

Jeremy turned red. "I don't know if I'd put it quite like—"

"Okay, then. Say you get a message on Adam4Adam—because let's face it, no one pays the Manhunt membership fee anymore—and some smoking hot dude gives you his address. Now, what if that address turns out to be a trailer park? Would that A, make your dick soft, or B, make your dick hard?"

"B."

"Then 'white-trash fetish' is exactly how I'd put it. Nothing offensive about what you're into."

"But I'm not working class. My family is filthy rich."

"Oh," Matthew said. "I get it. You're into that whole upstairs, downstairs thing. You're like a Maurice in search of a Scudder."

"Not really. I said my family's rich, not that I am. I'm actually poor at the moment."

Matthew smiled. "No offense, dude, but I doubt you've ever seen poor in your life."

"I was just—"

"No, no, my bad. I'm sorry. I shouldn't throw my issues at other people. We're good, really."

Matthew presented his fist.

Jeremy grinned and bumped it.

They continued talking for another thirty minutes or so, and then Jeremy announced he had to go. They all exchanged phone numbers, and Matthew invited Jeremy to join his team for Jeopardy Pursuit Night the following week.

"What's Jeopardy Pursuit?"

"A cross between Jeopardy and Trivial Pursuit," Ryan said. "We use the Trivial Pursuit board, plus all the pieces, rules, and categories, but we write our own trivia in the style of Jeopardy. All answers must be phrased in the form of a question."

"So you don't use cards from the game?" Jeremy asked.

"Nope. It's all original content."

"I need someone to cover Science & Nature," Matthew said. "You're probably good at Geography and History too, right?"

"I can hold my own."

"Awesome. You interested, then?"

"Definitely. When is it?"

"Second Thursday of the month," Ryan said. He glanced at the calendar on the wall, then reached over to flip the page and look at May. "That would be the eighth. It starts at seven o'clock."

"But I'll text you beforehand," Matthew added.

"Sounds like fun. Are you on the team too, Ryan?"

"No, I have to take Uncle Ian's place as master of ceremonies. I'll be asking the questions. Or giving the answers, depending on how you look at it."

"Cool. I'll see you both later, then. Thanks for the latte."

Ryan and Matthew watched as Jeremy exited La Tazza. When the door closed, Ryan said, "That was nice of you, inviting him to join your team. He said he's having trouble meeting people."

"I'm a good guy, Ryan. And I believe you'll prove to be a good guy too. Jeremy's frigging adorable. We have to find him a boyfriend."

"Not interested yourself?"

"What? You're calling me white trash, now?"

"That's not what I meant."

"No," Matthew said. "He's not the right guy for me."

RYAN CLOSED La Tazza at ten o'clock and went home to call Mark. It took him a few minutes to decompress and slip back into being Ian.

"I think Matthew likes me."

"He's a piece of work, that one," Mark said. "Bizarre but fascinating discussion this morning. And I hate to disagree with you, but I think Matthew likes *Ryan*."

"That's what I meant."

A pause.

"This is weird," Mark said.

"I know."

"Let's talk about something else."

"Ryan has a date with Bartley on Friday. Bess Bistro and tour afterward. Maybe walking, maybe driving. He's going to give it some thought and come up with something. Mark, I haven't been this excited about a date in over five years."

"I'm happy for you. Really. It's sad, that's all."

"What's sad?"

"Ian is slowly disappearing. Don't get me wrong. I'm not blaming you. You have to do it. You have to become Ryan. But it feels like my friend is slipping away, and a part of me doesn't like it."

"I'm sorry. I'll try to be Ian when we talk."

"No. That's not smart. I can be friends with Ryan. I think he can even help keep me young. But it's never going to be the same, and we both know it. Your life is beginning all over again, and mine… well, mine isn't."

CHAPTER NINE

THREE DAYS later, on the last morning of April, Ryan and Matthew opened La Tazza together. Matthew had taken Monday and Tuesday off but then asked for a double shift on Wednesday to recoup the lost income. They were standing behind the bar at 8:35 when Bartley James walked through the north door. Ryan could feel Matthew tense up next to him.

Bartley smiled as he approached the counter. "Good morning, boys."

"Hi, Bartley," Ryan said.

Matthew cleared his throat. "Hey, Monte."

"Excuse me?" Bartley said.

Ryan kicked Matthew under the bar. "Ignore him." A young woman entered through the west door. Ryan switched places with Matthew and said, "Would you get her order, please?" Matthew stepped up to the register while Ryan and Bartley moved down the bar and out of his way. "I'm looking forward to dinner on Friday."

"Me too," Bartley said. "Have you heard from Ian?"

"I…. He's doing good. I talked to him last night."

"How's your grandma?"

"She's doing better, but I think Uncle Ian is going to be there awhile."

Bartley turned his head, like he was distracted.

"Are you okay?" Ryan asked.

Bartley looked back and blinked. "I'm fine."

"Would you like a double-skim latte, like last time?"

"Thank you. That would be great. Sorry, I spaced out there for a moment. I haven't been sleeping well lately. A double skim to go, please."

Ryan made the drink, and Matthew rang up his order. "Here's your change."

"Thanks," Bartley said as he deposited the three quarters into the tip jar. "Matthew, good luck with finals. And Ryan, I'll see you Friday night, if not before."

"Have a good day," Ryan said.

"The next time you talk to your uncle, tell him I said hi, will you?"

"Sure. I'll do that."

Matthew began to say something as Bartley walked away, but Ryan turned and slapped his hand over Matthew's mouth. Matthew's eyes bulged out, and they both started laughing. Ryan removed his hand and said, "I don't want to hear any of your lip right now, okay?"

"I still say you're going to change your mind before Friday."

AS AFTERNOON approached Ryan regretted setting up his date with Sam at La Tazza. He had done it to throw Matthew off the scent, a moot point now that Ryan had admitted to the entire scheme. He thought about texting Sam and changing the location, or even canceling altogether, but then he remembered he could only text Sam from Ian's phone.

At five o'clock, Sam arrived and waved at Ryan. Matthew stood next to him behind the bar and muttered, "Do you realize your life has turned into a season of *The Bachelor*?"

Ryan elbowed him in the ribs. "Why don't you try helping me for a change, instead of causing trouble?"

"Trouble? When did I cause trouble?"

"Calling Bartley Monte?"

"Oh. That. You didn't think it was funny?"

"Not the point. At all. I have to figure out a way to let Sam down easy."

"So no rose for the pizza boy?" Matthew asked.

"What?"

"On *The Bachelor*. The dude gives a rose when he wants to keep someone around."

"Are you telling me you've actually watched that show?"

"No, but I've watched *The Bachelorette*. Same concept, better eye candy."

Sam walked up to the bar. "Howdy, Ryan. This is a cool hangout. Never been here before. How'd you get a job so fast?"

"My uncle owns the place. I'm covering for him while he's out of town."

"Right on. House-sitting and free coffee. Good deal."

"Would you like a sandwich? Or something to drink?"

"Well, I'm starving, but I doubt I can afford your sandwiches. Maybe just a cup of regular coffee. Nothing fancy."

Ryan picked up a menu and handed it to Sam. "The sandwich is on the house. Whatever you want."

Sam looked awed. "Really?"

"Really. This is Matthew, by the way."

"Sam White."

The two young men shook hands.

Sam scanned the menu. "I'll take the roast beef, then, but can you make it with white bread?"

"Sorry," Matthew said, "but we don't even stock white bread. How about a light whole wheat?"

Sam handed the menu to Matthew. "Okay. I reckon beggars can't be choosers."

"It comes with a cup of tomato soup too," Ryan said.

"Can you add a bag of chips?"

"Sure," Matthew said. "You want one, Ryan?"

"I'll take a half. Keep mine on a French roll, though. And no chips."

"You old enough for a beer, Sam?"

"Just turned twenty-one, but I'm not much of a drinker."

"A coke, then?"

"Please," Sam said.

"What kind?"

"Dr Pepper."

Matthew nodded. "You two grab a table, and I'll bring everything out when it's ready."

Ryan took a seat with Sam, who looked around La Tazza with excitement. "This is so cool, going out and meeting people. Who knew asking for your number would lead to a free sandwich?"

"Free sandwiches are my specialty," Ryan said. "Do you do that a lot? Ask for numbers, I mean."

"No. You're the only one. Most of the customers are gross. But when you told me you liked boys too, I reckoned I should pounce on the chance to make a gay friend."

"So you're not looking at this as a date?"

Sam lowered his head. "No. The spark's just not there. Is that okay?"

Ryan sighed with relief. "It's more than okay. I'm actually interested in someone else right now."

"Right on. I'd love to meet a nice guy, but all I've done since I moved to Austin is work."

"When was that?"

"Three weeks ago," Sam said. "I found my job on the second day, but I got to get me another one. I'm barely scraping by."

"Maybe you can work here."

"Well," Sam said. "That's nice of you, but I wasn't trying to turn this into a job interview."

"I know that. We're losing a few baristas next month when school lets out. You should think about it."

"Well, I'll definitely fill out an application, if you think your uncle would hire me."

"I'm doing the hiring while he's gone, so it's up to me."

"Wow. Okay, then. I guess it's settled."

Matthew appeared at their table with a tray of sandwiches and drinks. He set down the tray and said, "Anything else I can get you?"

"Why don't you join us?" Ryan said.

Matthew shook his head. "I don't want to barge in on your date."

Sam took a bite of his sandwich. "It's not a date," he said with his mouth full. "Pull up a chair and take a load off."

Matthew turned around and checked the register. "Okay, but just until someone comes in." He grabbed a stool from the adjacent table and sat down.

"Sam is looking for another job," Ryan said. "So I suggested he work here."

"You deliver pizza, right?" Matthew asked.

Sam nodded. "Papa John's. Better ingredients. Better pizza. Better bullshit."

"You don't like it there?" Ryan said.

"What's to like? It's a below-minimum-wage job, and most people tip for crap. But my education ended in high school, so hoping for something better just makes me feel like a goddamned fool."

"Talk about better bullshit," Matthew said. "I'm sorry, but delivering pizza is not the best you can hope for. Even if all you have is a high-school diploma, you could at least aspire to work at a place like this."

Ryan threw a couple of death stares in Matthew's direction. "Take a Xanax or something, would you?"

"No, he's right," Sam said. "I have a tendency to get down on myself, and it's good to hear someone tell me otherwise. But I never said I have a high-school diploma." He took another bite of his sandwich and a spoonful of soup.

It looked to Ryan as if this might have been Sam's first meal of the day. "What brought you to Austin?" Ryan asked.

"I had to get out of my current situation at the time. I was living with my mom and her boyfriend in a double-wide east of town and working at a seed factory in Bastrop. My mom's boyfriend was a drunk and spent some time in prison. One night he and I got into a scuffle. Now you've got to understand, I've been fighting off drunks since I was knee-high to a grasshopper. I may be small, but I'm fast, and I got a mean left hook that no one sees coming. So I laid him out. And then I had about five minutes to pack everything and get the hell gone. I slept the first few nights in my truck. I quit my job in Bastrop and drove around Austin looking for a new one. I finally got hired at Papa John's, and then I did a Craigslist search for rentals under two hundred bucks a month. All I could find was a room in some creepy guy's house. My door doesn't even have a lock on it."

Matthew nudged Ryan. "We've got to help this kid."

"No," Sam said. "That's not why I told you all that. I don't need anyone to rescue me. I can take care of myself, thank you. Now, if you want to set me up with one of your cute friends, well, I wouldn't turn that down."

"What kind of guys do you like?" Matthew said.

"Smart." Sam ate several spoonfuls of soup and then continued. "Brains are sexy as hell and a huge turn-on. I like 'em a little older too, but no one past thirty. A nice body don't hurt, but no big muscle fags."

Ryan looked at Matthew and silently mouthed, "Jeremy."

Matthew nodded. "Do you know anything about sports?"

Sam wiped his face with a napkin. "I know a lot of things about sports. Why?"

"I'm putting together a team for Jeopardy Pursuit Night. It's a trivia thing we do here, and I need someone to cover sports. Do you think you can do that?"

"No problemo, as long as I don't have to be responsible for any of the other categories. When is it?"

Ryan swallowed a bite of his sandwich and answered, "A week from Thursday." Then he turned to Matthew. "Uncle Ian told me Quentin and his brothers are virtually unbeatable."

"The guy who calls me Harry? That little prick? Oh, I'm going to enjoy wiping the floor with his face. Unbeatable, my ass."

"Why does he call you Harry?" Sam asked.

Before Matthew could answer, a customer walked through the east door and Matthew jumped off his stool. "I gotta head back to work, but make sure to give me your number before you leave, Sam." He moved his stool to the side and ducked behind the bar.

Sam ate the last bite of his sandwich and emptied the crumbs from his bag of chips directly into his mouth. "You two make a cute couple."

"Who?" Ryan said.

"You and Matthew. You said you were interested in someone else. It's him, right?"

"No."

Sam looked surprised. "Oh. Okay. You seem like a smart guy, Ryan."

"I am."

Sam took a swig of his Dr Pepper and said, "Then why can't you see what's right in front of your face?"

CHAPTER TEN

TWO DAYS later, Ryan opened La Tazza well after sunrise. An unusually slow Friday morning gave way to a brisk lunch rush, and as things wound down around two, Ryan's phone vibrated in his pocket. He pulled it out and answered.

"Hey, Uncle Mark. What's up?"

"Admit it. There's a part of you that relishes calling me that."

"Don't be so sensitive."

"Easy for you to say."

"What's up?" Ian said.

"Are you nervous about your date?"

"No. I'm more nervous about seeing Matthew when our shifts overlap."

"Why?"

"Because he expects me to come around to his way of thinking and cancel my plans with Bartley."

"But you have Ian's blessing," Mark said.

"It doesn't matter. Matthew thinks Ryan should back off and give Ian a chance with Bartley. And he's right. That's what sucks about this. Matthew is right, except for the tiny detail that Ian and Ryan are the same person. Oops. I forgot to mention that to him."

"Is the train starting to fly off the tracks?"

"We'll see. I like Matthew, but there's no way I'm canceling my date with Bartley James."

SHORTLY BEFORE four o'clock, Matthew walked through the north door. He didn't make eye contact with Ryan as he stepped behind the bar and said, "Hey."

"Hey," Ryan grunted.

"Your shift is over now, right?"

"Right."

"So?" Matthew asked. "Any chance you canceled your plans with Bartley?"

"No. I'm sorry. I think you're making way too much out of one dinner and expecting way too much from me. So I like the guy? That doesn't make me a bad person. If Uncle Ian were here, and I thought for even one second that he liked Bartley, I would back off. I swear I would. But he said he wasn't interested. He told me to go for it."

"Read between the lines, dude."

"I'm not canceling my plans. I'm sorry you have a problem with that."

The chill between them felt like an Eskimo winter. With as little enthusiasm as possible, Matthew said, "Excellent. Have a nice evening, then."

"Don't forget to reserve the corner table for the freshman study group."

"I won't forget. I got everything covered. You can go out and relax and forget all about this place. And me, for that matter."

"So I was right," Ryan said. "That's what this is about."

Matthew huffed. "Of course that's what this is about. I thought if I gave you enough time, you'd figure it out on your own, but it looks like that's not going to happen. I like you, Parker. There, I said it. When I came in today, I was hoping you'd ask *me* to show you around the city. But you'd rather chase after someone who doesn't give a rat's ass about you."

"You don't know that."

"Don't I? Bartley comes in here sometimes when you're not working. Does he ever ask about you? No, never. But do you know who he does ask about? Your uncle. Every. Single. Time. On Wednesday, I could hear your entire conversation. What was the first thing he asked you about?"

"Had I talked to Ian."

"And what was the last thing he said to you?" Matthew asked.

"Tell Ian he said hi."

"Doesn't that send up a red flag? Wake up, Ryan. If you're not into me, just say so, even though I know you'd be lying. But don't go running after some douchebag who has the hots for your uncle. It's embarrassing, for both of you."

Ryan picked up his bag. "Thanks for the advice."

"You asked for it. You said that if I liked someone, I should tell him. I'm sorry the timing is inconvenient for you."

"Good night. If something comes up, call Colleen. I don't want to hear from you this evening."

RYAN LEFT La Tazza, shaken and confused. He rode his bike back to the house and took a shower. Afterward, he smoked a joint and got into the Jacuzzi. He tried to unwind, but he kept playing the confrontation with Matthew over and over in his head.

He got dressed around six and poured himself a glass of milk. Bartley arrived about five minutes early. He wore loafers, jeans, and a short-sleeved polo shirt. It didn't matter whether he was Ryan or Ian—Bartley always took his breath away.

"Come on in."

Bartley crossed the threshold and gazed at the vaulted ceilings. "This is Ian's house, right?"

"Correct. You like it?"

"Like it? I love it. Look at the sweep these arches give the room. It almost has a Roman feel. Do you know who designed it?"

Ian knew, of course, but he didn't think Ryan would. "Sorry. I wouldn't remember even if he told me. Would you like to come in for a glass of milk?"

"Milk? No, I think I'm good. We should head downtown, anyway. We have to park, and it's Friday. Traffic is going to be insane."

"You're right. Let's get going, then."

Bartley drove an old Jeep Wrangler with the top down. Ryan found it difficult to hold a conversation because of the noise, so he just nodded when Bartley pointed out a building along the way.

When they arrived at the restaurant, they were immediately seated at a two-top in one of the interior rooms.

"Have you been here before?"

"A few times," Bartley said as he perused the menu.

"Any recommendations?"

"I usually get the Grilled Skin-On Salmon, but I've heard the Seared Diver Scallops and the Bess Wagyu Burger are excellent as well."

"I do like scallops."

"This is my treat," Bartley said. "So don't worry about the prices."

"No," Ryan insisted. "It's the other way around. This is my treat. I asked you, remember?"

"Look, I remember what it was like at your age. My mom used to say I had champagne taste on a beer budget."

"Used to?" Ryan said.

"She passed away two years ago."

"Oh. I'm sorry to hear that."

"It was pretty tough at the time, but now it seems like the least of my worries."

"I can't imagine you have many of those."

"Worries? You'd be surprised, then."

The waiter arrived, and Bartley ordered the salmon. Ryan vacillated between the burger and the Shrimp and Grits but decided on the shrimp at the last minute.

"Have you talked to your uncle recently?" Bartley asked.

Maybe Matthew had a point.

"I talked to him at work today. He sounded good. My grandma seems to be improving, but my grandpa is getting used to the help. When it's time to come back, Ian said it's going to be harder on Gramps than it will be on Grams."

"He's probably right. I miss seeing him every day at La Tazza. Oh, by the way, before I forget—are you free Sunday afternoon?"

"I'm working nine to four."

"Perfect. Do you remember that guy I told you about, the one who makes furniture? He's having an open house from six to eight on Sunday. We can go, if you'd like to meet and talk with him."

Ryan lit up inside. The entrees hadn't even arrived, and Bartley was already planning their second date. "I would love to go. Where does he live?"

"Just south of the river, in Travis Heights. He's a real 04er."

Ian knew exactly what Bartley meant, but since Ryan didn't, he asked, "What's an 04er?"

"The zip code of the south central area of Austin is 78704."

"Ah, I see."

"There's a bumper sticker that reads, '78704... more than a zip code, a way of life.' Luke's got that going on in spades."

"How do you know him?" Ryan asked.

"He's one of the interior designers we work with at my firm."

"Is he an old flame?"

"God, no. His wife owns and operates three restaurants here in town. I'm afraid my track record with old flames isn't very good."

"How many do you have?"

"Only two," Bartley answered. "Reggie and Mason."

"What happened?"

"Reggie died in a car accident. He was driving home one night when a drunk driver swerved into his lane and hit him head on."

"How old were you?"

"Twenty-four."

"That must have been tough," Ryan said.

"Excruciating. He was fifteen years older than me and wasn't out to his family. We'd been together for almost two years, and they didn't even know I existed. At the funeral, I had to hide in the back. I was practically the only white person there."

"He was black?"

Bartley nodded. "I was living in Houston at the time."

"You were in grad school at Rice?"

"That's right. Everyone reacts differently to those kinds of extreme situations. Me, I poured myself into work. I designed a

119

whole slew of nonexistent projects—office buildings, museums, vacation homes, shopping malls—even a water park."

"No way."

Bartley took out his phone and showed Ryan a picture of a sketch. "See. It's got this cool double slide. They sit side by side and face each other, so the slides form a giant X. When two friends go down together, they can high-five each other as they pass in the middle, where the two slides cross paths."

Ryan smiled. "That's really fun. Do you still have all those designs?"

"You bet. I plan to build them too. Someday."

"Who was the second flame?"

Bartley pulled his napkin from under the silverware and placed it on his lap. "I don't like to talk about Mason."

"Why not?"

"I just don't."

"Do you still keep in contact with him?"

"No," Bartley said.

"Okay." Ryan decided to lighten the mood. "Are you taking applications for flame number three?"

Bartley spread some butter onto a piece of bread. "Can I be honest with you?"

"Sure. About what?"

"Ian told me I'm your type. Is that true?"

Ryan blushed. "Maybe."

"I want to be upfront with you. I get the impression you're thinking of this as a date, and I don't want to lead you on in that direction. You're cute and enthusiastic and very charming. I really do like you a lot."

"But?"

"But there are reasons why it would never work out."

"What reasons?"

"It's a long story," Bartley said.

"So? We have all night, and I'm a good listener. Is it because of what happened with Mason?"

"Kind of, but—"

"Did he break your heart?"

"He broke a lot more than that."

"Like what?"

"I'm sorry, Ryan, but Mason is a painful subject. I don't know you well enough to open up about that. Besides, I said reasons. This isn't all about Mason. I'm... I'm kind of interested in someone else."

"Oh." Ryan died a little inside. "You could have told me you had a boyfriend when I asked you to dinner. What does he think about—?"

"I don't have a boyfriend. We haven't even gone on our first date yet. In fact, he doesn't even know.... Shit, I might as well just tell you. I'm interested in your uncle. I have been for several months now. I've been working up the courage to ask him out, and then when I finally did, he disappeared. Don't get me wrong. I know his going to Arizona had nothing to do with me. At least I hope it didn't."

"But you told me you two were just friends. I asked you both if it was a date, and you both said no."

"That's because I was scared to just straight out ask him. He runs La Tazza. What if our connection was all in my head? What if he was just being nice to me because I'm a good customer? I figured, once I got him alone, I could gauge his real interest and see if he felt the same way. He had no idea I was hoping it would turn into a date, and I didn't want to say anything until it had. I'm sorry if I misled you."

Ryan felt sucker punched by the irony of it all. His chest hurt, and he wanted to hit something. "Uncle Ian has no idea you're interested in him. Trust me, that's something he would have wanted to know. Are you even aware he has some pretty big insecurity issues? He's probably had a crush on you for months too but figured he didn't stand a chance, you being Bartley James, and all."

"What does that mean?"

"Oh, come on. Look at you. You have 'winner' written all over your face. Uncle Ian doesn't see himself as husband material for golden boys like you."

"Why not? Your uncle is one of the sexiest men I've ever met, and if you knew my story, you wouldn't be calling me a winner or a golden boy."

Ian couldn't help but react. *He thinks I'm sexy?* But what did it matter? He wasn't Ian anymore—he was Ryan. His whole second chance now seemed royally screwed up. "Do you know where the restroom is?"

"Right behind you," Bartley said as he indicated the direction with his hand. "Down that hallway."

"Will you excuse me for a minute?"

"Sure. Are you okay?"

"I'm fine. I just need to use the john."

Ryan went into the men's room and locked himself in one of the stalls. He took out his phone and called Mark.

"I thought you were on a date tonight."

"I am. He's at the table."

"Where are you?"

"In one of the bathroom stalls."

"Good Lord," Mark said. "What happened?"

"He likes Ian. *Bartley likes Ian.* He likes the forty-year-old version of me. I think I'm going to throw up."

"Don't do that, especially not while I'm on the phone with you. If you start to gag, I'll start to gag."

"Didn't you hear me? He likes Ian. I'm totally fucked, Mark. Some quirk of the universe made me twenty years younger, and now that same quirk is exacting some kind of sick revenge. Do you know, we haven't even started our meal yet? He shut me down before the entrees arrived. He doesn't want to lead me on. He's totally into Ian. Fuck, how did this happen?"

"Calm down. What are you going to do?"

"Admit defeat. What else can I do? Except...."

"What?"

Ryan stood up in the stall. "Bartley doesn't know Ian's HIV positive."

"Maybe Ryan should accidentally lay that card on the table tonight."

Ian paused to consider how terrible that sounded. "Ryan could let it slip to Bartley that Ian is HIV positive."

"If it's the deal breaker you think it's going to be—if you believe HIV will put an end to Bartley's interest in Ian—then do it. Once Ian is out of the picture, maybe Bartley will see Ryan as potential boyfriend material."

"I feel like I would be throwing myself under the bus."

"You would be, at least a little. But like you said, Ian and Ryan are the same person. You just have to find a way to do it without sounding like an asshole."

"I'll think of something. Thanks, I'll let you know how it turns out."

"Wait a minute," Mark said. "If Bartley is so shallow that he'd reject Ian because of his HIV status, then why would Ryan want to be with him?"

"Because I… I don't know. I'll talk to you later."

Ryan ended the call and returned to the table, where he found his shrimp waiting for him. "Sorry about that," he said as he sat down. He took a bite of the grits. "These are delicious. Do you want to try a forkful?"

"No," Bartley said. "I'm good. You want to try the salmon?"

"No, that's okay. I'm not a big fan of fish."

Bartley ate a bite and then took a drink of water. "Is it okay that I told you all that about your uncle?"

"Totally."

"I feel like I should have said it to him first. And I would have, if he were here."

"I'm not going to lie to you, Bartley. You're exactly my type, and I *was* hoping this would turn into a date. I had no idea you had feelings for my uncle, so it came as a shock, that's all. I think it'll come as a shock to him too."

"So what do you think my chances are? Do you know what kind of guys he likes?"

Ryan tried to eat one of the shrimp, but he had lost his appetite. "I don't think you have to worry about whether or not he's going to be into you. But maybe you shouldn't get your hopes up quite so high."

"Why not?"

"Because your feelings may change when you find out certain things."

"What are you talking about?" Bartley asked. "What certain things?"

"It's not my place to say. Look, I know it's none of my business, but at the same time, I don't want to see my uncle get hurt again. Like I said, there are things you don't know about him, and I'm afraid once you find out…. Forget it. I should shut my mouth. Some things only Uncle Ian can tell you."

"You can't lay a teaser like that on the table and then shut up. What is it? Does he have a kid somewhere?"

"No. Nothing like that."

"A boyfriend?"

Ryan shook his head. "You asked me that question before and I told you no."

"Is he an ex-con or a serial killer?"

"Ian? A serial killer? Get real."

"Then what is it? I mean, he's a perfectly normal, healthy—" Bartley stopped talking and set down his fork. "Is he…? Is Ian…? HIV positive?"

Ryan didn't speak, but no response was a response.

"Oh my God," Bartley said. "I…. For how long?"

"About ten years. See what I mean now? It's great you like my uncle. Really, it is. But do you understand now why I brought this up? If you had told Uncle Ian you liked him, only to take it back once you found out about his status, then that would be way worse than not telling him at all."

"I see what you're saying. Still, it wasn't your place to tell me something like that."

"I'm sorry. You're right. I'm protective of my uncle. He's had terrible luck with men, and I don't know if he could take another disappointment right now. Life has been throwing a lot of curve balls at him lately."

"I know how he feels."

"Then please, don't tell him you like him. Just let him think you guys are friends, and move on. I'm sure there are plenty of negative guys in this town who would love to go out with you. Like me, for instance."

Bartley wiped his mouth and laid the napkin on the table. "I'm sorry, Ryan, but I'm not feeling well. Do you mind if we cut this short? I think there's something wrong with the salmon."

"Should we tell the waiter?"

"No, I just want to go home and lie down."

"Did I upset you?"

"Not at all."

"I should never have brought it up. I ruined everything, didn't I? Believe me, I wasn't trying to sour you on my uncle so that you'd date me."

"That's not—"

"I don't want to see him get hurt again."

"He's a grown man, Ryan. He doesn't need your protection. Besides, I'm not going to hurt him. Look, I'll make it up to you another time, but right now I need to take you home. Please."

Ryan sighed in resignation. "Okay, fine. Why don't I take care of the check and you go get your Jeep and bring it around."

"Thank you." Bartley bolted from the restaurant and returned five minutes later with the Jeep. Ryan hopped into the passenger side, and Bartley drove them up Guadalupe in silence. When they pulled into Ian's driveway, Ryan undid his seat belt and got out. "I hope I didn't screw everything up."

"You didn't. I'm sorry about this, really."

"Don't sweat it. I'm sorry I told you about Ian. It was a total invasion of privacy. I feel like shit."

"It's okay. You were just looking out for your uncle."

"Thanks for understanding. Can we still go to the open house on Sunday, so I can meet this Luke guy?"

"Of course. I'll call you tomorrow and we'll sort it. Good night, Ryan."

Bartley pulled out of the driveway, and Ryan walked up to the porch. He heard a horn honk once and turned around. Bartley smiled and said, "By the way, in case you haven't figured it out yet, Matthew likes you." Then he drove off.

Ryan went into the house and checked the time. Eight thirty. He dialed Mark's number, and when he answered, Ian heard loud voices in the background.

"Where are you?"

"Happy hour," Mark said. "Or at least the end of happy hour. I met some friends, and we're going to a party later. What happened?"

"I played the HIV card."

"And?"

"It didn't work. I went with the whole, 'I don't want to see my uncle get hurt' angle. He still seemed to think it was a douchey move on Ryan's part. Whatever. He's not into Ryan because Ryan's not Ian, and he's not into Ian because Ian's poz. No matter who I am, it's over before it even began. I thought Ryan would be a fresh start. I thought things would be different, but absolutely nothing has changed. I'm still making the same bad choices."

"I think you're being a little hard on yourself. Do you want to come out and join us?"

"Is everyone in their forties?"

Ian heard Mark gasp. "Are you being ageist all of a sudden?"

"Sorry, but I don't want to hang out with a bunch of old people tonight."

"Listen, young man, do I need to remind you that you're an old person inside?"

"You know I love you, Uncle Mark, but I'm going to walk over to La Tazza and see if they need any help."

"Oh, for Christ's sake. If you want to change something, why don't you change the way you escape into that coffee shop every time life disappoints you? There will be young people at this party, or younger at least. Come out and meet some of them."

"Thanks, but not tonight. I need to be somewhere familiar. I'll talk to you tomorrow. Don't worry. I'm fine."

"You sound like you're about to do something stupid," Mark said. "What is it?"

"You're wrong. I need to run. Have fun at your party tonight."

Ryan ended the call and looked at the clock. He still had several hours before La Tazza closed, so he decided to get stoned and clean the house. He put on some dance music from Ian's circuit-party days, and with a bottle of 409 in one hand and a roll of paper towels in the other, Ryan scrubbed the kitchen, living room, and bathroom from top to bottom, all in less than three hours. The amount of energy he had astounded him, not to mention the fact that he could eat twice as much as Ian without gaining an ounce.

Around eleven thirty, Ryan grabbed a handful of condoms and a small bottle of lube from the nightstand. He checked Ian's phone and saw a missed call from Bartley, which he ignored. He went out to Ian's truck, put the condoms and lube into the glove compartment, and then drove to La Tazza. He parked at Mr. Gatti's Pizza across the street and watched the last stragglers leave the coffee shop. He knew Quentin and his freshman study group would stay until last call, but Ryan didn't want to deal with them or any other customers. At about five minutes before midnight, the final two patrons left the building. Ryan looked through the large windows and saw Matthew standing by himself behind the bar. Then he disappeared into the back, and Ryan got out of the truck. He crossed the street, walked up to the north door, and stepped inside.

"Sorry, we're closed," Matthew yelled.

Ryan didn't move. "I'm not here for a latte." He waited, and after a moment, Matthew came into view. Without any music playing, La Tazza was eerily quiet. Ryan heard a car pass on the street, the honk of a horn, and then a cyclist curse in response.

"Hey," Matthew said.

"Hey."

"How did your date go?"

"It was over by eight thirty. You were right. Bartley likes my uncle."

Ryan watched as a series of mixed emotions played out across Matthew's face.

"Are you okay?" Matthew asked.

Ryan nodded once. "Did you mean it? What you said earlier. About me."

"You know I meant it. But I'm not a consolation prize, Ryan. If you're still hung up on him—"

"I'm not. I promise. Sometimes I get fixated on someone and don't even realize he's not the right person for me. I was being stubborn. I don't like people telling me who I can ask out."

Matthew looked dismayed. "I'm sorry if it came across that way."

"No. I'm sorry I didn't figure it out sooner—but I did figure it out. That's got to count for something, doesn't it?"

"I don't know. Maybe I believe you, and maybe I don't. It's gonna take more than words."

"That's fair," Ryan said. "Do you have plans?"

"When?"

"Now."

Matthew gathered a couple of stray coffee cups and set them into a tub. "I don't know. I was probably going to head home and call some friends."

"Would you like to learn how to drive a stick?"

Matthew laughed. "Are you serious? It's after midnight."

"So? You turn into a pumpkin or something, old man?"

"Watch it, Parker. Where would we go?"

"There's that big parking lot up near the DMV, just north of Koenig."

Matthew smiled and shrugged. "Okay, sure. I've always wanted to learn. Everything's done here, so we just need to lock up. Why don't you get the doors, and I'll kill the lights?"

Ryan crossed through the seating area and locked the east and west doors. The lights went out, and Matthew joined him. "Where did you park?"

"Across the street," Ryan said.

Matthew looked out the window. They stood in the dark, about a foot away from each other. Ryan wanted to kiss him, but Matthew kept his distance and avoided eye contact. "Let's go, then."

They exited through the north door, and Ryan locked it behind them. They got into Ian's truck, and Ryan pulled onto Guadalupe Street.

"Quentin asked where you were tonight," Matthew said.

"Really?"

"He said he needed to ask you about something, so I told him you'd be in tomorrow."

"Thanks. Did he call you Harry again?"

"No. I asked him if he'd downloaded the new One Direction album yet, just to let him know I didn't appreciate it."

"What was his reaction?"

Matthew rolled down his window. "He apologized. He's actually not a bad guy, once you get past the snark. I told him about the team I'm putting together for Jeopardy Pursuit Night. Boy, you should have seen his chest puff out when he heard that. Did you know he and his brothers have won three months in a row?"

"I guess that's what Uncle Ian meant by 'virtually unbeatable.'"

"And did you also know he's friends with all the guys in Dime Box?"

"What's Dime Box?"

Out of the corner of his eye, Ryan could see Matthew do a double take. "It's a band. They had a monster hit two summers ago called 'Homesick.'"

"Oh, I've heard that song," Ryan said. "I just never knew who sang it. Whoever it is has an amazing voice."

"Topher Manning. He's one of the first openly gay pop stars of our generation. He and his bandmates are from a little town east of here, called Dime Box."

"Hence the name of the band, I suppose. Do they live in Austin?"

"Austin and New York. I read they inherited this sweet apartment in Manhattan. Their second album dropped last month, so they're doing two shows next week at Stubb's. They're already sold out, but Quentin said he'd look into getting tickets."

"For you?"

"Isn't it crazy? He asked about my major, and so we started talking about music. He mentioned he was going to the show at Stubb's, and I said 'I hate you.' So he said he'd look into an extra set of VIP passes."

"That's pretty cool."

"Tell me about it. He's stopping by tomorrow afternoon to talk to you. He said he'd let me know about the tickets then."

"Look at you. Besties with one of the Walsh brothers."

"Has your uncle ever told you what their story is?"

Ryan stopped the truck at a red light. "Supposedly their parents were killed in a car accident. The oldest brother, Ben, was living in New York at the time. He's gay. He moved back to take care of the other three. Quentin is the next oldest. Then there's a middle one who's also gay. I can't remember his name. The youngest is about fifteen now."

"That's only four. Who are the other two members of their team?"

"I don't know," Ryan lied. "I think Ben has a boyfriend, so I suppose he's number five. No idea who their sixth person is."

Matthew pointed up at the light. "It's green."

Ryan looked forward and drove. A half mile down the road, he pulled into a vast parking lot and stopped under one of the lights. "We're here." He killed the ignition, got out of the truck, and walked around to the passenger side. He opened the door and motioned with his hand. "Go on. Get behind the wheel."

"Aren't you going to explain it first?"

"Just get your ass over there, will you, Butler?"

Matthew got out and walked around to the driver's seat. Ryan climbed in and fastened his seat belt.

"You think you're going to need that in a parking lot?"

"Better safe than sorry," Ryan said. "Have you ever driven anything with a clutch before?"

"Nope. Never."

"Okay," Ryan began. "See that extra pedal next to the brake? That's the clutch. There's no 'park' or 'drive' on a manual. Right now the truck is in neutral. Put your hand on the stick." Matthew did as instructed, and Ryan laid his hand on top of Matthew's. "Wiggle it around a little. That's it. Feel neutral. Nothing is engaged. Now, you can't put her into gear without engaging the clutch."

"Her?"

"What's wrong?" Ryan said. "Traditionally, cars are referred to with feminine pronouns."

"That's because straight men started the tradition."

"Fine. You can't put *him* into gear without engaging the clutch."

"Did Uncle Ian ever give this fine truck a name?"

"No. It's a truck, not a—"

"I've always liked the name Max," Matthew said. "Max the truck. What do you think?"

"Max it is, then. Now, with your left foot, press the clutch to the floor."

"Does he have a last name? Or would it be Max Parker? Do trucks take the last names of their owners?"

"Oh my God, would you just put the clutch to the floor, please?"

Matthew laughed and did as instructed.

"Good," Ryan said. "Now, if we move left and up, that's first gear. Down is second. Each gear has a limit to its maximum speed. Up, right to the middle, and up is third. Every time you shift, you increase the upper limit of your velocity. Down is fourth. And up, far right, and up again is fifth."

"What happens in fifth?"

"You can go as fast as you want."

Matthew laughed. "Be careful what you ask for."

"It wasn't a question. I don't know what gutter your mind is in, but I'm talking about driving a truck here."

"So what's with the clutch? You just lift your foot up and go?"

"No," Ryan said. "Not exactly. There's an engagement point— a spot as you lift up your foot. You need to ease through that spot and apply gas at the same time."

"I don't understand."

"You will soon enough." Ryan removed his hand from Matthew's. "Put it into neutral, press down on the clutch, and start the engine." Matthew followed his instructions. "Release the emergency brake. With the clutch pressed to the floor, put it into first gear. Then gently lift off on the clutch while you give it a little bit of gas."

Matthew made his first attempt, and the truck sputtered and stalled. "What happened?"

"Failure is always the best instructor. You didn't ease through the spot. Try again. Neutral, clutch, start the engine, put it into first, ease up on the clutch, a little bit of gas, then go. The hardest part is getting from zero to five miles per hour. After that it's a piece of cake."

Matthew's second attempt also ended in a fast stall, as did his third, fourth, and fifth. But by number six, he began to grasp the concept. "I get it now. There's a spot in the clutching motion where I'm actually engaging the engine."

"Correct. But you can't think about it."

"What do you mean?"

"You can't approach it intellectually. You have to feel it in your body."

Matthew turned his head and smiled. "Like sex?"

"That's a good analogy."

"Well fuck, Parker. Why didn't you just say so? Okay. I can do this. Neutral, down on the clutch, start the engine, into first, up on the clutch, a little bit of gas, then go."

On the next attempt, Matthew worked through the engagement point perfectly and sailed across the parking lot. He hollered and jumped in his seat until he realized his speed topped out at ten miles an hour. "What's wrong?"

"You need to change gears," Ryan said. "Press your foot on the clutch, shift down to second, then lift to engage. You don't need to worry about easing through the spot, though. That's only when you're going into first gear."

Matthew successfully shifted into second. He raised his fist and whooped. "This is awesome."

"Stop and start again. You have to press down on the clutch when you stop."

Matthew brought the truck to a halt and put it into neutral. Then he shifted into first and started off again. He drove around the parking lot, shifting and downshifting and having a ball.

"That's it," Ryan said. "You're a natural at this. It took me forever to catch on."

Matthew drove around to the back of the DMV building and parked in one of the dark spots hidden from the street. He turned off the engine and set the emergency brake. The night breeze passed through the open windows of the truck. The siren from an ambulance wailed past them and then faded, replaced by the hoot of a nearby owl. Ryan could hear Matthew's steady breathing and feel the tension in the small cab.

"I like you too," Ryan said.

Matthew leaned over and kissed him. Ryan wrapped his arms around Matthew's neck and pulled him close. He tasted like espresso and chocolate.

Matthew ran his hand under Ryan's T-shirt and tugged on his nipple. "You want to go somewhere else?"

"Eventually, but this is kind of hot, don't you think?" Ryan grabbed Matthew's hand and moved it to his crotch.

"Hot and hard," Matthew said.

"All the better to fuck you with."

"Are you negative?"

"You bet," Ryan said. "Just got tested last week. You?"

"Two months, but nothing even remotely risky since then. You want to…?"

"What?"

"Go raw?" Matthew asked.

Ian tried to protest, but Ryan shut him down. "Are you sure?"

"If you say you're negative, I believe you."

"Uncle Ian tells me to use a condom every time, even with people I'm dating."

"But if we're both negative, what does it matter? We can't give each other something we don't have. Do you think I'm lying to you?"

"No."

"I don't do random hookups, Ryan. I told you I like you, and I meant it. I get a hard-on whenever we work together. You're my boss's hot nephew, and you're here with *me*. I want to spend all night with your bare dick up my ass, and in the morning, I want to fall asleep with your come inside me. I don't see what's wrong with that if we're both clean."

Ryan cringed. "Don't use that word."

"I'm sorry, you're right. It's a bad habit. Look, if you want to use a condom, I under—"

"No. I don't want to use a condom. Take off your pants and get over here."

Matthew slipped off his shoes and jeans. Ryan undid his fly and pulled out his stiff dick. He spit on his hand and covered his cock with saliva. Matthew straddled Ryan, and they kissed. Then Matthew eased himself onto Ryan's dick. Ryan looked up in time to see Matthew's eyes roll into the back of his head.

Matthew moaned. "It's just like a clutch. You have to ease through that engagement point. And once we get to second gear, you won't have to worry about taking it easy anymore."

"I can slam you all the way to fifth?" Ryan reached between them to feel Matthew's dick. "Nice. I like a bottom who can stay hard while he's getting fucked."

"Are you kidding? A cock up my ass is what gets me that way." Matthew increased the pace of their fucking.

"Be careful. I'll come fast if you—"

"But you can come more than once, right?"

"Sure. Several times."

"Then shoot your load, Parker. Shoot it right up my ass, and then use your spunk for lube in the next round."

Ryan found the whole scene so hot that he immediately started coming. Matthew's cock swelled in his hand, and Ryan felt a warm liquid dripping down his knuckles. Matthew slowly came to a stop and lifted himself off Ryan. He moved back into the driver's seat and laid his head against the rest.

"Jesus, I hope that was just a preview."

Ryan tucked his dick back into his briefs. "You want to drive home?"

"Absolutely. Can we go to my place, though? I have three roommates, but we each have our own room."

"Why? I have a whole house to myself."

"I know, but it would be too weird, sleeping in my boss's bed."

"Okay," Ryan said as he leaned over and kissed Matthew. "I didn't even think about that. Your place is fine. But I hope your roommates don't complain about the fucking noises."

CHAPTER ELEVEN

RYAN HAD to be at La Tazza the next morning at eight. At seven, he left Matthew sound asleep and content. He drove home, took a shower, and changed his clothes. He checked Ian's phone. In addition to another missed call, there was a new voice mail from Bartley. He tapped through and listened.

Hey, Ian. Can you give me a ring? I really need to talk to you. Anytime this weekend, but the sooner the better. Thanks.

Ian thought about calling him back, but he already knew what Bartley was going to say. Something about maybe them having dinner together wasn't such a good idea, and frankly Ryan didn't want to hear it. He stuffed the phone into his pocket and left the house.

He met Teresa at La Tazza and went into the office. He planned on texting Matthew a big "*Good Morning*" with a smiley emoticon so it would be waiting for him when he woke up, but then Ryan realized he had the wrong phone. He reached for a pile of invoices and turned on his laptop. Ian's phone buzzed. Ryan looked at the caller ID. *Bartley*. He might as well get this over with. Ryan cleared his throat, lowered his voice, and answered the call.

"Hey, Bartley."

"Hi, Ian."

"I got your message. I was going to call you back."

"It's okay. I'm sorry to bug you, but I've been up all night going crazy. Have you talked to Ryan since yesterday?"

"No. Why? What's wrong?"

"Do you have a minute to talk?"

"Can you hold on a second?"

"Sure."

Ryan put the phone on mute and went out front to check on Teresa. She gave him a thumbs-up to indicate she had the situation under control, and then Ian returned to the office. He took the phone off mute and dropped his voice again. "Sorry, I had to check on my dad and make sure he was settled. We can talk now. What happened with Ryan?"

"I don't know, really. I've played it over and over in my head, trying to figure it out. I wanted to be upfront with him. I got the impression he had a little crush on me, and I didn't want to lead him on. I thought I was doing the right thing. But then I ended up telling him a lot of stuff that I should have told you first. And he said some things I would rather have heard from—"

"Bartley, you're not making any sense. In fact, I don't have a clue what you're talking about."

Ian heard Bartley take a deep breath. "I told Ryan I couldn't date him because I'm hoping to date you instead. I know I asked you to dinner as friends, but that was just me not wanting to make you uncomfortable, in case you weren't interested. I like you, Ian, and I was afraid you were only being nice to me because I'm a customer. But then Ryan told me something that changed everything. Something about you."

"What did he say?"

"He told me you're HIV positive."

"Oh." Ian played with a paper clip on his desk. "Well, it's not exactly a dirty little secret."

"I understand that. But I wanted to—"

"Let me guess. Once you heard I'm poz, you changed your mind about the date. Why are you calling me, Bartley? Do you feel the need to rub it in or something?"

"Ian, let me—"

"Do you know how many times I've been rejected by negative guys? Neither do I, because I've lost count. Why couldn't you just leave me alone? I'm in Arizona, for Christ's sake, taking care of my sick mom. Is this a sympathy call? Do you have any idea how offensive that is? Think about it. Did I really need to hear that you wanted to go on a date with me until you found out—"

"So am I."

Ian stopped talking. He stood up, stunned. He closed his eyes and took a deep breath. "What?"

"I'm HIV positive too."

Ian silently mouthed, "Fuck" and then said, "Since when?"

"Seven months and thirteen days."

Ian counted back to September—the month Bartley broke up with Mason. Did Bartley cheat on his boyfriend and get HIV in the process?

"I'm sorry," Ian said. "I don't know why I assumed…. Shit. I feel like a total dick. You're just not the kind of guy I expected to be—"

"But you are?"

Ian sat back down. "I'm sorry. I'm a little defensive when it comes to that. I'm so sick and tired of explaining my status, I sometimes fly off the handle. Please, forgive me."

"Forget about it. I didn't call you for an apology."

Ian smiled. "How are you doing? Do you have a doctor?"

"I'm okay. All that's taken care of, but I don't want to burden you with my stuff right now. You have your mom to think about."

"Please, I'd be grateful if you took me away from that for five minutes. I've been where you are."

"Well, I doubt you've been quite where I am."

"What does that mean?" Ian said.

"Nothing. I'd rather skip the gory details for now, if that's okay. I called because I got excited. I've been wanting to ask you out for months, but I was scared that you wouldn't want anything to do with me once you found out. And then when Ryan told me you're—am I crazy, Ian? Tell me I'm not crazy."

"You're not crazy. I've wanted to ask you out for months too, but I never did, and for the exact same reason."

"When are you coming back to Austin?" Bartley asked.

"I don't know yet."

"Can I visit you in Phoenix?"

"No," Ian said. "That's not a good idea."

"Why not? Your parents will love me. I can help out."

"No, really. I'm sure they'd love you, but now's not a good time. Please, trust me, Bartley. Don't get on a plane and surprise me."

"Okay. But I want to see you."

"I'll try to talk to my brother about an exit strategy next week." Ian needed to change the subject. "How did the groundbreaking go on your project?"

"Wow, you remembered. It went great, thanks. The couple is happy, and the contractor's already ahead of schedule. And that's not even the best part."

"What's the best part?"

"The wife recommended me to one of her friends, and now I'm designing house number two."

"Bartley, that's awesome news. You're really on your way."

"I feel like things are finally turning around. It was the worst winter of my life. I felt like dying, but do you know what kept me going?"

"No. What?"

"La Tazza."

"Are you serious?"

"There's something about that place," Bartley said. "I can't put my finger on it, but I feel like I'm under a magic spell when I walk through the door. No matter how bad things got, La Tazza was always there for me—constant and dependable. It saved my life."

"I don't know what to say."

"And the guy who owns it is really hot too. Oh, I almost forgot. I watched Elias and Lari on YouTube while you were in Denver."

"You did not," Ian said.

"I'm serious. At first I couldn't get past the bad acting, but then I got sucked in by the story. And the scenes in the sauna were hysterical."

"Which one do you think is cuter? Elias or Lari?"

"Neither. The boys do nothing for me, but Elias's father? I think his name is Sebastian. Wow, what a stud. He reminds me of you. I wouldn't mind seeing his towel slip in the steam room, one of these days."

Ian laughed. "I can't believe you watched that."

"I tried out *Hollyoaks* too, and I see what you mean about those Roscoe brothers, but I couldn't follow what was going on. Now I need something else to watch, though. Is there another story that's more self-contained?"

"Christian and Oliver, from *Verbotene Liebe*. But stop once they get married the first time. After that, it's just an exercise in frustration. Or, if your heart can take it, check out Lenny and Carsten. Their story is very dark and very German but so worth it in the end. Those two couples can really stand up to Brian and Justin or Will and Sonny in the legendary department."

"Who are Will and Sonny?"

"They're from *Days of Our Lives*. They just got married. You can also check out Ian and Mickey from *Shameless*. They're the best written and acted gay couple I've ever seen on television. I'll text you the link to their YouTube trims. There are only six of them, so it's not a huge commitment. Watch them first, and don't bail at any point. Things get brutal in season three, but push past it."

"Okay," Bartley said. "Enough about me and my new YouTube addiction. How are you doing?"

"I'm making the best of a difficult situation."

"I bet. What do you do all day while you're there?"

"We have a routine with my mom, getting her out of bed and cooking all the meals. The rest of the time, I watch baseball games with my dad and brother."

"No way. I love baseball. Can you believe the Brewers this season?"

"They won't be able to keep that up," Ian said. "They're going to be a streaky team, mark my words."

"We have to go to Houston when you get back, and see an Astros game."

"You're kidding, right? They're the worst team in baseball."

"So? I embraced them when I was at Rice, and I'm not one of those fair-weather fans. Besides, I have a soft spot for the underdogs. It'll be fun. Maybe they'll even put us on the kiss cam."

"This is surreal."

"Why?" Bartley asked.

"Because I've had a crush on you for so long, and now we're suddenly talking about trips to Houston and kiss cams."

"I guess we have Ryan to thank. If he hadn't told me you're positive, I might have chickened out on the whole thing and never said a word."

"I thought I was too old for you."

Bartley laughed. "Too old? Boy, did you have me pegged wrong. I like men, not boys. I can't tell you how many times I've wanted to jump across that bar and make out with you."

"Well, you wouldn't have encountered any resistance."

"I'm glad to hear that. You're one sexy motherfucker, Ian Parker. I can't wait until you fuck me." Bartley took a brief pause and then laughed. "Sorry, did I just say that? I hope you know my intentions are more—"

"Has there been anyone since…?"

"No, but you're the perfect person to break the dry spell. Do we have to use condoms?"

"I'm fine without them. 'Membership has its privileges' and all that."

"Nice. Oh, before I forget, I need to run something by you. Ryan mentioned that he wanted to take a carpentry class while he was here, so I invited him to a party tomorrow afternoon. It's a friend of mine who makes his own furniture. You should see his house. He and his wife are doing a wine and cheese thing in the afternoon. I thought it'd be a good chance for Ryan to meet him. What do you think?"

"Sounds like a great idea. You don't have to do that, though."

"I want to. He's your nephew. Look, I know he wanted our dinner to turn into a date—he even admitted it—but at his age, he'll move on after ten minutes. Besides, once he figures out that Matthew is the one he belongs with, he'll forget all about me. You should see those two together. They're frigging adorable."

"Hmm. I never would have guessed Ryan would go for someone like Matthew." Ian knew he should stop talking, but he couldn't help himself. Then someone knocked on the office door, and Ryan hung up the phone in a panic. He jumped out of his chair and said, "Come in." Teresa opened the door and told him she needed help. "I'll be right there."

He redialed Bartley. "I'm sorry, I hung up by mistake. My dad needs some help with the washing machine, so I gotta run."

"I understand. We'll talk soon?"

"You can count on it."

"I'm glad you picked up the phone this time," Bartley said.

"Me too."

"Okay, I'll let you go. Come home soon. I miss your smiling face."

Ian hung up the phone and said, "What on earth have I done?"

RYAN LEFT the office and stepped behind the counter to help Teresa. Once the wave of customers passed, he went outside and dialed Mark.

"Why are you calling me from Ian's number? Are you at home?"

"No," Ian said. "I'm on the patio at La Tazza. I was in a rush this morning and grabbed the wrong phone."

"What could you possibly have to tell me at eight thirty on a Saturday morning?"

"I thought everything was fucked up last night. Turns out that was just a curtain raiser."

"How much damage could you have done in twelve hours?"

"Ryan spent the night with Matthew, but then this morning Bartley told Ian he's HIV positive too and has wanted to ask him out for months." Mark didn't respond. "Hello?"

"I heard you. It's a lot to take in before I've had my first cup of coffee. Give me a minute, will you? Did you at least play safe with Matthew?" Ryan didn't respond. "Are you kidding me? What happened to the biggest mistake of your life? Are you going to repeat it all over again?"

"It's not the same thing."

"It's exactly the same thing," Mark said.

"I didn't know the guy in Honolulu. I was on vacation, and he was so much hotter than me, and we were both doing coke. Matthew's not anonymous. He's not lying to me. He's negative. I'm negative. We can't give each other something we don't have."

"You don't even sound like Ian anymore."

"We all take risks, Mark. We just draw the line about what's acceptable at different places. I'm okay with what I did."

"You're okay, or Ryan is?"

"We're getting off track. We haven't even talked about the fact that Bartley likes me."

"Correction—Bartley likes Ian. You're not Ian anymore, remember?"

"I know that. Shit, this is so screwed up."

"Is it time to call Enchantmints and talk to Tad?" Mark asked. "Maybe Mrs. Brown knows of a way to reverse this. You could go back to being Ian and live happily ever after with Bartley."

Ian looked up into one of the trees and saw a robin building a nest in the branches. "I think that's a good idea. Can you meet me at my house around six?"

"I'll be there."

"Thank you. I appreciate everything you're doing for me, Mark. I really do. I'll talk to you later."

AT FOUR o'clock, Teresa's shift ended and Matthew came bouncing into La Tazza. Ryan was stacking glasses at the counter when Matthew walked up behind him. He kissed Ryan on the neck and said, "Thanks for last night."

Ryan turned around and grinned. "You're welcome."

"Are you okay?"

"What do you mean?"

Matthew grabbed some glasses and helped with the stacking. "I don't know. You could have said you had a good time, or something. Are you having second thoughts?"

"No. Are you?"

"Nope. It isn't going to be awkward or anything, is it? Working together?"

"I hope not. Uncle Ian is your boss, not me."

"Was it a one-off?" Matthew asked.

"No. Why would you think that?"

"I don't know. Haven't you ever slept with a guy who did a complete one-eighty the next morning? Hell, I've done a complete one-eighty the next morning."

Ryan grabbed Matthew by the shoulders and kissed him. "That's not what's going on, okay? I had a great time. But I also don't rush into things. Is that cool?"

"Absolutely."

Ryan couldn't tell if his casual attitude worked on Matthew, but fortunately he didn't have to think about it for long, because the east door opened and Quentin walked in.

Matthew looked excited. "Hey, Walsh."

"Hey, Matthew. Ryan." Quentin had a small yellow envelope in his hand. He placed it on the bar and pushed it toward Matthew.

"Is this...?"

"Two VIP passes for Tuesday night. They'll get you backstage after the concert."

"Are you fucking with me?"

"No. Even I'm not that big of a dick."

"Dude, I have no idea how to thank you. This is just...." Matthew opened the envelope and took out the laminated passes. He handed one of them to Ryan.

"You're inviting me?"

"Duh. Who else would I take? Teresa and Timothy can work that night. Or Colleen. It's going to be a great concert."

"Ryan," Quentin said. "Can you take a break? There's something I want to ask you."

"Sure. Can you cover the counter, Matthew?"

"Go, sit down. Take as much time as you want. We have VIP passes to the Dime Box concert Tuesday night. Does this mean we don't have to stand in line?"

143

Quentin nodded. "That's what it means. There's a VIP entrance next to the Will Call window. They also rope off a small section where we can watch the concert. Look for me when you get there, or just flash your badge around and pretend you're a big shot. That always works."

"Thanks again. I owe you big time."

"Forget about it," Quentin said. "I was happy to do it."

"How about an espresso?" Matthew said. "On the house."

"Sure. That sounds good."

"Okay. You go talk to Ryan, and I'll bring it out."

Ryan walked into the seating area, and he and Quentin took one of the smaller tables against the wall.

"What's up?" Ryan asked.

"I noticed you didn't work last night."

"No, I had a date. Well, I thought it was a date at least. Turns out it wasn't."

Matthew came up and set Quentin's espresso on the table. "You want anything, Ryan?"

"No, I'm good. Thanks."

"Okay, cool. Let me know if there's anything I can get you guys."

Matthew left them alone, and Quentin took a sip of the espresso. "Best rocket fuel in town."

"What did you want to ask me?" Ryan said.

"I don't know quite how to start this conversation. I just hope you haven't hurt Ian or something like that."

"What are you talking about?"

"I know you're not who you say you are."

Ryan's throat went dry. "Excuse me?"

"Ian has a nephew named Ryan, but I looked his parents up on Facebook. Ryan is ten years old."

"Why would you do that?"

"Because you told me you worked here three summers ago, and I've been coming to La Tazza since it opened. I've met every barista who ever walked through those doors."

"Fuck," Ryan muttered. "I didn't even think about that."

"Who are you?"

"Even if I tried to explain it, you'd never believe me."

"Will you answer one question, then? Do you have Ian tied up in a basement somewhere?"

"God, no. You think I kidnapped him in order to take over his life?"

"What else am I supposed to think?"

"Trust me, Quentin. That's not what's going on here."

"Look, Ian's gone and you're running the place, but I have no idea who you are. All I know is, you're not Ryan Parker. I could have come in today with my brother and the cops, because you're probably in major felony territory here."

"Then why didn't you?"

"I don't know," Quentin said. "There's something familiar about you, so I figured I'd at least let you explain first. But before we get to that, I want to talk to Ian."

Ryan had no backup plan should someone blow his cover. He couldn't excuse himself to call Mark, because that would only prompt Quentin to call the police.

"You are," Ian said.

"I am what?"

"Talking to Ian."

Quentin rolled his eyes in frustration. "Jesus. Come on, dude. Enough with the moronic riddles. Who in the fuck are you?"

"You'll never believe me."

"You might be surprised. I've heard some crazy shit in my short life."

Ian turned around to make sure Matthew wasn't listening. "The night before I went to Denver, I made a wish on a cupcake. It was my birthday. I wished I could go back and do it all over again. Then I bought this chocolate kiss made with Manick Butter, which is an anagram for 'turn back time.' It made my wish come true. I woke up on the plane ride back to Austin and I was two decades younger." Ian pointed to himself. "This is me. I'm Ian."

Quentin stared at him for a long minute, then took out his cell phone and said, "Okay, that's it. I'm calling Ben and getting the police over here, stat."

"Wait." Ian reached out and grabbed Quentin's arm.

"Don't touch me."

Ian quickly pulled away. "I'm sorry, but look at me. Look into my eyes. Why do you think there's something familiar? It's because I've known you for five years."

"That's not possible."

"Then ask me something that only Ian would know. Some detail from all the times you've come into La Tazza."

Quentin fidgeted with his spoon. "I can't think of anything off the top of my head."

"Try. If I'm not Ian Parker, then stump me. I know how the Walsh brothers love a challenge."

Quentin stared at him. "Okay. The week after my parents died, I came in here with my girlfriend at the time."

"I remember her. Dakota."

"Anyone could know that. Ian said he was sorry for my loss, but then he also put on some special music for me. What was it?"

Ian didn't hesitate. "James Taylor. *Sweet Baby James*."

Quentin looked stunned.

"That's my go-to album for moments like that," Ian said. "I remember you started crying during 'Fire and Rain.' I forgot that song was on there. I'm sorry."

Quentin drank the remainder of his espresso. "It's moments like this that make me want a cigarette, and I don't even smoke." He stood up and said, "I need some air." He exited through the east door and onto the patio.

Ryan looked at Matthew and shrugged. Then he followed Quentin outside. "I know this is a lot to take in."

"You have no idea. Just give me a minute to…. How is it even possible?"

"I don't know."

"Why are you pretending to be Ian's nephew?" Quentin asked.

"It's a cover story. My friend Mark came up with it. I woke up on a plane twenty years younger. What was I supposed to do?"

"Are you dating Matthew?"

"Kind of."

146

"Does he know you're really Ian?"

"No."

Quentin took a step back. "That is totally twisted. You're lying to him?"

"I'm lying to everybody," Ian said. "That's the premise of a cover story. It's not like I can tell the truth. Look at you—you're reacting like you've seen an alien. People will think I'm crazy—or worse—they'll cut me open to figure out how I did it."

"But how are you going to live like this? I mean, forever?"

"I'm meeting Mark at six to call the guy who sold me the chocolate kiss. It might be possible to reverse it. If I go back to being Ian, I stand a real chance at love. But being young again? I don't know if I can give this up for anybody."

Quentin looked distracted and pulled out his phone. "Maybe that's the point. Are you coming to the concert on Tuesday with Matthew?"

"I suppose. It sounds like fun."

"Good. I gotta run now, but there's someone I want you to talk to."

"Who?" Ian asked.

"Never mind." Quentin turned and started to walk away but then yelled over his shoulder, "Just make sure you're at the concert on Tuesday."

RYAN LEFT La Tazza shortly before six to meet Mark. They went into Ian's kitchen, and Mark sat his phone in the middle of the island. He tapped the screen and put it on speaker. It rang three times, and then Tad answered.

"Hello, you've reached Enchantmints, home of the Rocky Mountain high."

"Hello, Tad. My name is Mark Sterling. I was in your shop a couple of weeks ago with my friend Ian. He's the one who bought the chocolate kiss made with Manick Butter."

"Oh, yeah," Tad said. "I remember you guys. Did you enjoy the product?"

"Well," Mark said. "That's why we're calling. Ian is here too. I have you on speaker."

"Hi, Tad," Ian said.

"Hello. What's this about?"

"After Ian ate the chocolate kiss, he woke up on the plane twenty years younger."

No one spoke for a moment, and then Tad said, "Okay.... Have you guys been smoking this evening?"

"No," Ian said. "We're serious. I ate the kiss before I got on the plane. I fell asleep, and when I woke up, I went to the bathroom and saw my face. I was forty when I left Austin and twenty-one when I came back. Did you know Manick Butter is an anagram for 'turn back time'?"

"No. I didn't know that. But—"

"You told us Mrs. Brown's special editions are magical," Mark said. "Can you ask her if it can be reversed? You don't have to admit to any liability or even believe us. We just want to know if there's a remedy. That's all."

Ian and Mark waited for an answer.

"Okay," Tad said. "I'll ask her and get back to you. Might be a few days, though. In the meantime, maybe you two should seriously think about laying off the bong."

CHAPTER TWELVE

THE NEXT day, Sunday morning, Ryan and Matthew opened La Tazza together.

"Was it busy last night?" Ryan asked as they prepped the counter.

"Insane. Every single seat was filled until we closed. The full-court press of finals has begun. Did you get some sleep?"

"About ten hours. I needed it after you kept me up all night Friday. Not like I'm complaining."

"You better not be. We're both off at four today. You want to do something? Maybe go see a movie?"

"I can't. I'm going to a party with Bartley."

Matthew froze. "Excuse me? I thought you were done with him."

"It's not like that. He's going to introduce me to a friend of his who makes furniture and owns a shop in South Austin. I'm looking for a carpentry class while I'm here."

"I didn't know you wanted to be a carpenter."

"There's a lot you don't know about me."

"Okay. That's true I suppose. Can I come along?"

"Matthew, don't get that way."

"What way?"

"Jealous and possessive. It doesn't suit you."

"Sorry. I just know how much you like him."

"Liked. Past tense. I can tell you right now, with 100 percent certainty, that Ryan Parker is never going to date Bartley James. And speaking of finals, when is your first one?"

"Tomorrow," Matthew said.

"Then focus on school right now, not me. We'll have plenty of time to hang out and see where this goes after the semester ends. Have you finished your porn paper yet?"

"No. But that can—"

"It can't wait," Ryan insisted. "Besides, I told you, I don't like to rush into things. We're going to the concert on Tuesday, and I'm really looking forward to it."

"Me too."

"Good. Then let's have fun. Don't spoil it by turning into a clingy chick."

"Ouch. That was uncalled for. Since when did you turn into a misogynistic douchebag?"

"You're right. I'm sorry." The first customer had yet to arrive, so Ryan put his arms around Matthew and kissed him. "I don't know what's wrong with me. Taking over La Tazza has been.... I'm on edge. Can you just trust that I like you?"

"I'll try, but it's hard when you call me a clingy chick."

"I'm sorry. Really." Ryan kissed him again. Matthew wrapped his arms around Ryan's waist and tightened his grip. Ryan pressed his forehead against Matthew's and said, "Are we good now?"

"We're good. And you might be a little right. I do this when I like someone. I'm impulsive. I rush in and fall hard. But I need to focus on school. This is my last semester, and I don't want to fail anything."

"You're not in danger of that, are you?"

"No, but if I start blowing things off, I could be."

"I'm not going to let that happen."

"Thank you. I appreciate it." The first customer of the day walked in, and Matthew stepped out of their embrace. "I'll get this one. Did you notice I'm getting better with the machine since you taught me how to drive a stick?"

"I noticed."

"Your uncle said that would happen."

BUSINESS PICKED up quickly after that. Matthew put on the new Dime Box album, and they served a steady stream of customers throughout the morning. Then, around ten o'clock, Bartley walked in. He had a bounce to his step and a thousand-watt smile—both of which made him look like a kid again. He waltzed up to the bar and slapped his hand on the counter. "Good morning, boys. And what a fine one it is."

"What's gotten into you today?" Matthew asked.

"I am in love."

"Really?" Ryan said. "Did you talk to Uncle Ian?"

"I did. Yesterday. I finally got up the courage to tell him how I feel, and turns out, he feels the same way."

Matthew elbowed Ryan in the ribs. "I told you."

"So when he gets back to Austin, I'm going to lock him in a room, jump his bones, and not let him out for a week. Ryan, the next time you talk to your grandmother, please ask her to get well soon. Very soon."

Ryan knew he had to feign ignorance of Bartley's conversation with Ian. "But what about…?"

"That's not an issue. Let's just say your uncle and I are in the same boat."

"Why didn't you say something Friday night? You let me blabber on like an idiot."

"Because I wanted to tell him first."

"What are you two talking about?" Matthew asked.

"Nothing," Ryan said.

Bartley hesitated for a moment but then said, "Your uncle was right. It's not a dirty little secret. Matthew, Ian and I are both HIV positive."

"Oh. Okay." He turned to Ryan. "What's the big deal? I dated a guy who was poz once."

"You did?"

"Sure. I know some dudes are total assholes about it, but not me. Especially these days, with Truvada and all that. Michael Lucas is on PrEP, and his boyfriend is poz. They don't even use condoms. Of course, since Lucas is a total top, that reduces his risk, but still."

"Well," Bartley said. "He's a total top in front of the camera. Who knows what he does behind it."

Matthew put his arm around Ryan and grinned. "That's fantastic news, Bartley. There must be something in the air."

"Are you two…?"

"After you blew Ryan off Friday night, he realized I'm much better looking and practically threw himself at me."

"I did not throw myself. Well, maybe a little."

"I knew it," Bartley said. "I told Ian you two were adorable together. We should go on a double date when he gets back."

Matthew squeezed tighter. "That sounds like fun. What do you think?"

Ryan feigned a grin. "Sounds like a blast. Can't wait."

Bartley's smile grew even wider. "I stopped in to check about the party this afternoon. Matthew, you don't mind if I borrow him for a few hours, do you? I'm going to introduce him to my carpenter friend, Luke."

"I don't mind at all."

"You're welcome to join us."

"No," Matthew said, removing his arm from Ryan's shoulder. "Finals start next week, and I have a paper to finish. Thanks for the invitation, though."

"Can I get a double skim to go, please?"

"Sure," Ryan said as he turned toward the machine. "Coming right up."

"Are you any good at trivia?" Matthew asked Bartley.

"I'm not bad. I have a lot of facts stored in my head. Why?"

"I'm putting together a team for Jeopardy Pursuit Night on Thursday. I need six people, and I only have five. Would you like to join us?"

"Sure," Bartley said. "I've always wanted to do that. Who's all on the team?"

"Me, Ian's friend Mark, two friends of Ryan's, Jeremy and Sam—who we're kind of setting up on a blind date—and my best friend, Cecilia. She's the smartest person I know."

"I would love to join you."

Ryan set the latte on the counter. "That's four twenty-five."

Bartley pulled out two five dollar bills. He handed one to Ryan and put the other in the tip jar. "You can add the change to that as well. Ryan, how about I pick you up at Ian's house around six?"

"That works. I'll see you then."

"Fantastic. Matthew, if I don't see you before Thursday, good luck with your paper and finals."

"Thanks. Tell Ian I said hi the next time you talk to him."

"I'll do that. I'll probably call him tonight, though he never answers his phone. He must leave it on vibrate or something. Anyway, I'll see you both later."

AT NOON, Sam came in for his first training shift. Matthew and Ryan greeted him with bro hugs. Then Ryan took him into the office to sign some tax forms. He gave Sam a general tour of La Tazza, and Matthew walked him through the menu. He proved to be a quick study and made an excellent cup of espresso on his first attempt.

"I hate you," Matthew grumbled.

While Matthew and Sam worked the counter, Ryan spent the afternoon catching up on some bookkeeping. At four o'clock, he left Sam in Timothy's hands and walked out to the parking lot with Matthew. "What's the plan for Tuesday night?"

"Can you drive?" Matthew asked.

"Sure. Or I'll pick you up and you can drive. How did Sam do?"

"Fantastic. We have a lot in common. The girls love him. He could do this job with one hand tied behind his back, but he's got no filter on his mouth."

"He should fit right in," Ryan said. "Hopefully he can upgrade his living arrangement soon."

"He said that's his first priority. Now that he's got a second income, it shouldn't be hard to find something. I'm off tomorrow, so I'm gonna take your advice and spend the day studying and working on my paper. Then I have my final in the evening."

"Good luck."

Matthew kissed him. "Thanks. Enjoy your boring party with Bartley."

"I'm glad you're okay with that now."

"Well, he's clearly not into you, and you're clearly into me, so...."

Ryan laughed. "There's nothing more attractive than a man with confidence."

TWO HOURS later, Ryan was sitting in the kitchen eating a bowl of cereal when the doorbell rang. He crossed to the foyer and opened the front door. "Come on in. I'm just finishing up dinner."

Bartley still had his smile set to megawatt. He followed Ryan into the kitchen and gestured toward the cereal box. "That's dinner?"

Ryan sat down on his stool and pushed the box across the island countertop. "See for yourself. Five whole grains and ten essential vitamins. Cereal is health food now."

"Don't you know bullshit when you see it?"

Ryan ate another spoonful and swallowed. "I just got off the phone with Uncle Ian about ten minutes ago."

"Really? How's he doing?"

"Good. He was pretty excited about your phone call yesterday. You'd better not break his heart, or you'll have me to answer to."

"Don't worry. I'm glad you listened to me about Matthew."

"He's a great guy."

Bartley took a seat on the other stool. "You don't sound very enthusiastic."

"Well, he wasn't my first choice."

Bartley looked uncomfortable.

"Sorry. I didn't mean that the way it came out. I'm happy for you and Uncle Ian. You guys will make a great couple. I hope."

"Well, we haven't even gone on a date yet, so it's a little premature."

"Maybe. But I can see it in your smile, and I could hear it in his voice. You two are into each other—that much is clear. Besides, you've probably had hundreds of five-minute conversations over the past year that add up to more than you realize. Uncle Ian doesn't give free sandwiches to just anybody."

"How did you know about that?" Bartley asked.

"Hmm, I… I don't remember. Matthew must have told me about it. I think he saw the whole thing."

"I have to admit, it feels good—having something to look forward to. My life has been pretty grim these past few months."

"Do you want to talk about it?"

"No. I haven't been able to talk to anyone yet, but I want Ian to be the first."

"He's a good listener and super supportive. He helped me a lot when I came out to my parents." Ryan spooned the last of the Cheerios into his mouth and then drank the remaining milk straight from the bowl. He got up, set the bowl in the sink, and said, "Okay, I'm ready to go."

THEY GOT into Bartley's Jeep and headed to South Austin. When they arrived at the party, a hundred guests already filled the house. The entrance off the porch led to a long central hallway. There was a drawing room on each side in front. On the right, the drawing room preceded a dining room and the kitchen, and on the left, a library and small guest bedroom. Luke and his wife managed to blend contemporary design with Colonial décor, mixing paintings from the eighteenth and nineteenth centuries with modern sketches and random portraits, all to spectacular effect.

"Bartley!"

A towering man approached them and wrapped Bartley in a bear hug. Ryan figured he stood at least six foot five and maybe even taller, with a full beard and a jovial, booming voice. When the man released him, Bartley turned to Ryan and introduced them.

"Luke, this is the young man I was telling you about, Ryan Parker."

The next thing he knew, Luke swept Ryan up until his feet left the floor. When he set him back down, he held Ryan at arm's length and looked him over. "So, Ryan Parker, Bartley tells me you want to be a carpenter."

"I think so. I'd like to check it out, at least. I think I'd be good with my hands."

"Let me see." Luke took Ryan's hands into his own, which were almost twice as big. He turned them palm up and inspected the fingers. "They look a little pretty to me. We'll need to rough them up a bit. Look at mine." Ryan stared down at Luke's hands and touched them. There were scars and protruding knuckles, and the skin felt like sandpaper. "Those are the hands of a carpenter. I host a workshop on Thursday afternoons in the store. Only three students at the moment, but that means you get lots of personal attention. And I only charge thirty-five bucks a lesson, plus the wood for your projects. Sound like something you'd be interested in?"

"It sure does," Ryan said. "That's exactly what I'm looking for."

"Everyone works at their own pace, but you'll learn a lot from the other students too." He pulled a card out of his shirt pocket. "Here's my number and the address of the shop. Two o'clock on Thursday. You only have to pay for one week at a time."

"Thank you. I'll be there on Thursday, for sure."

"Excellent. Now, walk around and enjoy the house. There's wine and cheese and other snacks in the dining room on the right. My wife is a chef, so make sure you try everything. I can't pronounce most of it, but that's because I was raised in a trailer park. Bartley, don't forget to show him the upstairs."

"I won't. Thanks for everything."

Luke turned to a tiny female guest and picked her up in a hug. Bartley led them to the food table, where he introduced Ryan to Mrs. Luke, a gorgeous black woman with long cornrows pulled into a ponytail. She gave them an introduction to the hors d'oeuvres, distinctive for their fusion of classic French and soul food cuisine.

Bartley and Ryan strolled through the rooms and took in the extensive art collection. Ian wanted to hold Bartley's hand and tell him how handsome he looked in his blue shirt. He wanted to continue their conversation from the day before, when Bartley told Ian that he missed his smiling face. But he knew Ryan couldn't do that.

In the east drawing room, a large black-and-white drawing caught Ryan's eye. With a thick charcoal pencil, someone had sketched the portrait of a stunning young woman in a spring dress. In the bottom left corner was an inscription.

Dallas, 1992

Ryan stared at the young woman. He guessed she was a debutante and this was her coming-out portrait. Her eyes were bright and awake, her smile sly and playful, if not exactly innocent. Ryan wondered if she had been sleeping with the artist when he drew her. She represented all the aspects Ryan associated with youth—hope, beauty, and endless possibility. And then the inscription—*Dallas*—the towering, larger-than-life symbol of Texas. J. R. Ewing and Southfork ranch. Oil, power, and wealth. Ryan didn't remember 1992, but Ian certainly did, and this drawing captured the moment perfectly. It marked the beginning of a decade filled with prosperity and optimism—before 9/11, global warming, texting, and the collapse of the American economy.

"This is my favorite piece in the whole house," Ryan said to Bartley, who stood beside him and appeared to be equally enthralled.

"I can see why. Would you like to check out the upstairs?"

"Sure."

Bartley led him to the back of the house, where a stairway took them to the second floor. At the top, they stepped through a doorway and into the master bedroom. It must have been the original attic, because it had a high, vaulted ceiling and a giant four-poster bed against the far wall. A fireplace stood opposite the bed, with two chairs facing it. An elegant blonde woman in her forties sat in one of the chairs with a slightly younger man beside her. Luke stood talking in front of them.

"Bartley. You made it up here."

"Wow," Ryan said. "This is something." Luke introduced them to the two sitting guests, but Ryan couldn't forget the drawing downstairs. "You have an amazing house," he said to Luke, "but if I could take home one piece, it would be the portrait of the debutante in the front room. The one with the inscription that reads *Dallas, 1992.*"

The woman sat up in her chair and smiled. Luke gestured and said, "That's her, sitting right there."

"No way." Ryan felt goose bumps run up and down his arms. "You're absolutely gorgeous," he said to her. "And the portrait is almost... magical. It should be hanging in a museum somewhere."

"Why, thank you," the woman said. "You are too kind."

And she was, in fact, correct. Ryan had been too kind, because he never would have recognized her from the picture. Her face was lined now, and her hair had grown thin. Her eyes were muted by the intervening years, and all the aspects of youth that had drawn Ryan to the portrait were gone. She was not the symbol of an era, frozen in time, but a real person who aged and sagged like everybody else.

The experience unnerved Ryan. He listened to Bartley talk about the house he had designed, but then two more guests came into the room, and Luke's focus shifted to them. Bartley and Ryan excused themselves and returned to the first floor. They chatted with a few more people and eventually made their exit.

When Bartley pulled into Ian's driveway, Ryan thanked him again, said good night, and went inside. He walked into the bedroom and lay down. As he stared at the ceiling, his thoughts were still consumed with the portrait of the debutante and the woman in front of the fireplace. He closed his eyes and heard a buzzing sound.

Ryan lifted his head and looked beside him. Ian's phone sat on the nightstand, still plugged into the charger. He picked it up, looked at the caller ID, and smiled. Then he tapped the answer button and lowered his voice.

"Hey, Bartley. How was your day?"

CHAPTER THIRTEEN

ON TUESDAY morning, Ryan was serving lattes at La Tazza when Matthew texted him about the concert. Instead of texting him back, Ryan waited for a break between customers and then dialed his number.

"A voice call?" Matthew said. "Did we flash back to 2007?"

"I'm old-fashioned. I prefer calling over texting and face time over Facebook."

"I was teasing you. I'll take some face time, please."

"How did your final go last night?"

"Not bad. I think I got a B, maybe a B plus."

"Congratulations," Ryan said. "What time is the concert tonight?"

"The VIP passes say nine, but no self-respecting rock band would go on before ten o'clock."

"How about I pick you up at nine, then? That will get us there around nine thirty. We don't want to be too late."

"Sounds good."

"Have you finished your paper yet?" Ryan asked.

"Almost. It'll be done before you get here, so I'll be able to forget about school for one night and enjoy myself. I'm really looking forward to this. I hope we get to meet Topher Manning afterward."

"I wouldn't be surprised. Quentin must know somebody, the way he pulled those tickets out of his ass at the last minute."

Matthew chuckled. "Are you working today?"

"Just until four. I pulled a double yesterday. Teresa and Timothy keep asking for time off to study, but Colleen is covering for me tonight. The place has been packed all day. We should consider staying open 24/7 during finals."

"Maybe, but then you wouldn't have a life."

"I think Jeopardy Pursuit Night will be a good stress reliever for everyone."

"How many teams have signed up?"

"Five," Ryan said. "So we have room for one more, but I doubt we'll get anyone else at this point. Hey, I gotta run. Someone just walked in."

"Thanks for calling, Parker. I'll see you tonight."

WHEN THEY arrived at Stubb's, the long line wrapped around the block, but their passes allowed them to skip the wait. A young man wearing a Stubb's T-shirt led them into a large outdoor space with no seating. The usher directed them to the roped-off VIP area to the right of the stage. It held about twenty people, Quentin among them. He came over and greeted them.

"Hey, guys."

"Hey, Q," Matthew said as he stared past him. "Are those your brothers?"

Quentin turned around and checked. "How could you tell? Pretty formidable bunch, aren't we?"

"Dude, I heard you guys look alike, but that's outrageous. Still, my team is gonna kick your ass on Thursday."

"You're welcome to try," Quentin said. "You ever been here, Ryan?"

"No, first time." He sniffed the air. "I could get high off the second-hand pot smoke. And we're outside."

Quentin laughed. "I know. It's nice to see Austin living up to its reputation."

"I'm not complaining. I would have brought a joint, had I known."

"Just stand next to Stanton and Marvin. They'll pull one out eventually. Don't let Jason and Cade see, though. We have to hide the weed from them."

"Do you smoke?" Ryan asked.

Quentin shook his head. "No. Never."

Matthew looked around the VIP area. "Which one is Stanton Porter?"

"The tall guy in the corner, next to the short Jewish dude. That's Marvin."

"Who are they?" Ryan asked.

Quentin started to answer, but Matthew cut him off. "Stanton is Topher Manning's husband. He's a music critic for NPR. And Marvin is Marvin Goldstein, the classical music critic for the *New York Times* and also Topher's writing partner. He can make or break the career of a classical musician with one stroke of his keyboard. I didn't know they would be here, though. Now I'm nervous as shit. Do you know them?"

"Of course," Quentin said. "How do you think I got those tickets? Why, you want me to introduce you?"

"Would you? You've already done so much."

"No problem. Let's go."

Ryan took his hand and squeezed it. "Just be your usual charming self, and you'll do fine."

"Okay." He kissed Ryan. "You gonna stay here?"

"I think so. But if they spark one up, come and get me."

"Will do."

Quentin and Matthew walked away, and Ian noticed Jason Walsh and his boyfriend, Jake, were staring at Ryan. He quickly reminded himself that they'd never met, even though Ian knew everything about them. They walked over and said hello.

"I'm Jason."

"I'm Jake."

"Hi. I'm Ryan."

"You're Ian's nephew, right?" Jake said.

"That's right."

Jason nodded. "My brother told us he's in Phoenix taking care of his mom. How's she doing?"

"Better."

"So who's running Jeopardy Pursuit Night on Thursday?" Jake asked.

"Me. I heard you guys are three-time returning champions."

"That's right," Jason said. "The key is intellectual diversity. And Ben is our secret weapon. His mind is like a trap for useless information."

"Are you two in high school?"

Jason's smile disappeared. "I am."

"What's wrong? Is that a sore subject?"

"Kind of," Jake said. "I graduate in a couple of weeks, and then I'm going to NYU film school in the fall." He took Jason's hand and kissed him. "Don't worry. It's only for a year."

"Film school?" Ryan said. "I think that takes more than a year."

"No," Jake said. "Jason graduates next year, and he's going to Columbia."

"If I get in."

"Oh, please. There's no way you won't get in. After that, we'll be together again."

"NYU," Ryan said. "That's a big change from Austin. Do you know anyone there?"

Jake looked surprised. "The whole band lives there half the year."

"Plus Colin and David," Jason added. "And Colin's mom and dad."

"I'm an only child," Jake said. "I don't have a lot of relatives, but dating Jason has given me an entire extended family."

"So you guys know the band too?"

Jason nodded. "We've worked on all their music videos. See the redhead over there? That's Travis, my brother Ben's boyfriend. Travis and Topher are kind of like best friends. They used to work together, back when Topher was a mechanic."

Ryan saw Matthew waving his hand, motioning Ryan to join him. "Will you two excuse me? My date is summoning me."

Jason and Jake turned around. "Where did he come from?" Jake asked.

"He's the newest barista at La Tazza," Ryan said.

"Nice work," Jason said. "He's a total hottie."

Jake nodded enthusiastically and added, "He's like a hunky version of Ben Whishaw."

162

"Why does everyone compare him to an English dude?" Jason and Jake looked confused. "Never mind. I'm going to… it was great meeting you." Ryan walked to the other side of the VIP area. Matthew had a joint in his hand and offered it to him. Ryan took it and said, "I see you found the party."

"Just be discreet."

Matthew introduced him to Stanton and Marvin, who both looked a little stoned. Matthew put his arm around Ryan and said, "I was just telling them we were listening to the new Dime Box album at La Tazza the other day."

Ryan glanced around and took a hit. "That's right. It's really good."

"Shotgun," Matthew said.

Ryan kissed him and blew out the smoke as Matthew inhaled. "I still can't get over Topher's voice," Ryan said. "Where did that come from?"

Stanton laughed. "It's a very long story."

Ryan considered Stanton's age, and it made him realize that maybe Ian had overreacted a little about turning forty. Stanton was at least ten years older than that and married to a young rock star. Ben Walsh entered their circle and whispered something into Stanton's ear. Stanton pointed to Ryan.

"You have the joint?" Ben asked. "Who the hell are you, anyway?"

"I'm Ryan Parker."

"Oh, right. Ian's nephew. Quentin told me about you. Sorry, I didn't mean to be a dick. Things like that just fall out of my mouth."

Ryan handed him the joint.

"Is Jason or Cade watching?"

Stanton put his arm around Ben to hide what they were doing. "You're good now. But it's funny that you think your brothers don't know you smoke pot."

"Shut up, Porter. I have to at least keep up the appearances of being a good guardian."

"Please," Stanton said. "They couldn't ask for a better brother than you."

"Aw, you're so sweet. I love you."

"And I love you too."

Ben and Stanton hugged each other, and Ryan whispered to Marvin, "I thought they each had partners."

"They do, but they're friends from a previous life. It's a special bond." Matthew laughed, and Marvin said, "You think I'm joking?"

The lights went dark, and a hush fell over the yard. Ryan and Matthew turned toward the stage and waited. Ryan could see four people walk out, and then a spotlight illuminated a young man with a guitar, standing in front of a microphone.

"That's Topher," Matthew whispered.

He stepped up to the mic and said, "This is a song I wrote for my husband, Stanton. It's called 'Play the Long Game.'" He strummed an intro and began to sing. His voice defied description— a soaring tenor to which no recording could do justice. The audience held up their phones, taking pictures and recording videos. The new Dime Box album had only been out for a few weeks, but everyone in the crowd knew the words. They sang along with Topher as he told the story of two lovers, separated by time and space but ultimately rewarded for their perseverance with a lifetime of happiness. The standard rock concert usually opened with an up-tempo number, but Dime Box subverted that expectation and began with a ballad instead. Everyone, men and women alike, listened to the melody with tears in their eyes. Topher had them in the palm of his hand from the very first note. Ryan looked over at Stanton, who laughed and cried at the same time. Marvin put his arm around Stanton and hugged him.

When Topher finished, the crowd cheered, and the stage lit up. Ryan could see the other three members of the band, and he didn't need Matthew to tell him which ones were the Ackerman twins and which was Peter Moses. A group of girls standing next to the VIP area counted to three and then screamed in unison, "We love you, Topher."

"I love you too. It's great to be back in Austin. We've been in New York for a while, recording our second album, but this next song was our very first single back in 2012. It's called 'Beaches on the Moon.'"

They launched into one of the band's most popular songs. The girls next to them cheered and twirled around. A bolt of energy surged through the room, and Ryan started to dance. It was the kind of joyful moment Ian hadn't experienced in years.

The concert continued in that vein for a full two hours and then closed with the band's biggest hit, "Homesick." The resident string quartet at UT joined them onstage for the final number, which prompted Matthew to say, "I'd kill to be one of those violinists right now." At one point, Topher stopped singing and let the crowd carry the signature line of the song.

Afterward the band left the stage and the audience stomped their feet. Matthew put his arm around Ryan. "They only do one encore, and it's always a cover. I read they keep it a secret from everyone, even Stanton and Marvin."

When the four members of Dime Box returned, Topher stepped up to the mic and said, "You might recognize this next one." He pulled a harmonica out of his back pocket, and the riff he played sent a wave of hysteria through the yard. Everyone in the VIP area looked at each other in shock.

"They're not…?" Matthew asked.

Ryan recognized the tune immediately, and the members of Dime Box threw themselves into the opening bars of Bruce Springsteen's "Thunder Road." Topher's voice had worn out just enough to lend it a rough edge. The four musicians attacked the rock classic like a band who had never left their garage. For this one song, they were just four kids from a tiny Texas town, playing the music of a man they no doubt considered to be a god, and to hell with what anyone thought.

A thunderous ovation followed the closing bars. The audience would have stood all night listening to the band, but Topher waved and blew them a kiss. "I gotta get home and check on my kids. Thanks for coming out. We love you. Good night, y'all."

When the lights came up, Quentin walked over to Matthew and Ryan and put his arms around them. "You're invited back to the house, if you're free."

"What house?" Ryan asked.

"The band's. They have a big place just east of here."

Matthew's eyes almost popped out of his head. "You mean you're inviting us to Topher Manning's house? The one he lives in?"

"Can you both make it?"

"Definitely. Both of us. Right, Ryan?"

Ryan nodded. "Don't worry. We can make it."

"Good," Quentin said. "I'll text you the address and then see you over there in a few."

He walked away, and Matthew turned to Ryan. "Can you believe this?"

"No, I can't. But I think your dream of meeting Topher Manning is about to come true."

SINCE THEY didn't want to be the first ones there, they hung out for a while and got a drink. Ryan and Matthew left Stubb's around one o'clock and drove to the address Quentin provided. Their GPS led them to a huge two-story house in East Austin with a sign in front.

← *PARTY IN BACK*

They walked up the driveway and found everyone gathered inside the garage apartment. The small group included the members of Dime Box, Stanton and Marvin, the Walsh family, the UT string quartet, and what were probably a few stagehands.

Moments after they arrived, the Ackerman twins made a beeline across the room and said, in unison, "Is one of you Matthew?"

"That's me. I'm Matthew."

"I'm Robin, and this is my brother Maurice. We hear you play the violin."

"How do you know that?"

"Quentin told us," Maurice said. "You ever hit the bong?"

"Sure," Matthew said.

"Let's go out on the patio and smoke a bowl." Then Maurice turned to Ryan and asked, "Do you mind if we borrow him for a little while?"

"Not at all. You just made his night."

The twins put their arms around Matthew and escorted him out of the room. Ryan felt uncomfortable for a second, but then he saw Quentin near the kitchen, standing next to Topher. Quentin whispered something into Topher's ear, and then Topher looked at Ryan.

He smiled, crossed the room, and offered his hand. "Hi. I'm Topher Manning."

"I...." Ryan felt a little starstruck but shook it. "I know who you are. I'm Ryan Parker."

"I know who you are too. Would you like to see the house?"

"Sure. I'd love to."

"Groovy. Follow me, then." Topher led them out of the garage apartment. As soon as they closed the door behind them, a peaceful, late-night silence replaced the loud clamor of the party. "The kids are asleep, so we have to keep the celebration confined to Marvin and Ty's place."

"They live in the garage apartment?"

Topher started down the steps. "When they're in town. Ty couldn't get away from work this week."

Ryan followed him. "That's Marvin's boyfriend?"

"Husband."

"How many kids do you have?"

"Two for now. I like to check on them after a show, just to remind me of what's important."

Ryan followed Topher across the backyard and through the kitchen door. They cut through the living room and then climbed a set of stairs to the second floor.

"Are they up here alone?"

"No," Topher said. "The nanny is across the hall." He opened the first door on the right and stepped inside. Ryan stood in the doorway and watched as Topher crossed to the first crib. He leaned over and gave its inhabitant a kiss. Then he motioned to Ryan and whispered, "Come on in. This here is Gracie." Ryan stepped into the room and looked down into the sleeping face of a little girl who looked about a year old. Topher crossed to the second crib. "And this is William. You can see he's gonna be a soccer player from the way he kicks his covers off." Topher replaced the blanket and sang a verse of "The Cradle Song." Ryan listened in rapt wonder.

They stepped back into the hallway, and Topher shut the door. They went downstairs and returned to the kitchen.

"You want a beer or something?"

"Can I have a glass of milk?" Ryan said.

"Sure." Topher went to the fridge and pulled a carton of milk from the top shelf and a bottle of Shiner from the door. He poured some milk into a glass and handed it to Ryan, then twisted off the cap of his beer. "Have a seat." Topher returned the milk to the fridge, and they sat at the big table in the center of the kitchen.

"Did you adopt?"

"No," Topher said, "we used a surrogate. I was so excited when we found out we were having twins. Being around Robin and Maurice my whole life, it just seemed natural. Stanton was a little resistant to the idea. Of having kids, I mean. But you should see him now. Gracie has him wrapped around her little finger."

Ryan took a drink of milk and wiped his mouth with the back of his hand. He wasn't quite sure how he got there—sitting in the dark kitchen of a rock star at two o'clock in the morning—but he wanted to find out. "Why am I here?"

Topher laughed. "Quentin asked me to talk to you. He told me about your, um… situation."

Ryan panicked. "What situation?"

"Relax. I know everything. But it's okay, I promise. I've had some otherworldly experiences myself."

"Really? Like what?"

"It's a long story. Stanton even wrote a book about it. Let's just say I know my way around unexplained phenomena. Ben and I both talk to dead people."

"You're kidding, right?"

Topher looked at him suspiciously. "You woke up one day twenty years younger, and you think I'm the crazy one?"

"Sorry. I see your point."

"Do you mind if I ask how it works? Are you young on the inside too?"

"Physically, I'm twenty-one. But I have forty years of memories."

"Hmm," Topher said. "There is only one of us."

"What does that mean?"

"Nothing. Just something someone said to me once. So your name's not really Ryan?"

Ian fidgeted with his glass. "No, it's Ian. Ryan is a cover story. It was my friend Mark's idea. I don't really know what I'm doing. Mostly I'm just making it up as I go along."

"I've been there."

"Any advice?"

"You've probably forgotten something."

"Like what?"

"I can't say since I don't know you. Were you happy at forty?"

Ian shrugged. "Not really. I owned a coffee shop, which made me look successful. But I didn't feel successful when I went home to an empty house. My one true love never materialized. I wasted most of my life. I tested positive ten years ago, which has been a convenient scapegoat for every mistake I've ever made."

"Are you still…? I mean, have you been tested since…?"

"I'm negative again."

"Wow," Topher said. "How are you dealing with that?"

"I'm not sure. It feels like a cheat. The whole thing feels like a cheat."

"So when you turned forty, you weren't in a good place?"

"No, I wasn't. I made a wish on my birthday cupcake. I wanted to go back and do it all over again."

"Oh, I see. So this isn't something that's happening to you. This is something you're choosing. Tell me, what was it like when you were twenty-one?"

Ian thought back to those days. "Amazing. Everything was a possibility, and I had so many dreams. Who doesn't love their early twenties?"

"A lot of people," Topher said. "Myself included. I was still reeling from my dad's death, at that age. I'd never want to be twenty-one again. But you're different. My guess is, you left a part

169

of yourself back there. You forgot something, and this is your way of remembering what it is."

"It's an awfully extreme way to jog my memory."

"There are more things in Heaven and Earth, Horatio, than are dreamt of in your philosophy."

Ian grinned. "I never expected you to quote *Hamlet*."

"I have a very smart husband."

"Well, he's a lucky guy." Ian took a drink of milk. "You were great up there tonight."

"Thanks. It still feels like a fantasy most of the time."

"I know how that goes. Why does your guitar strap say 'Hutch'?"

Topher smiled. "Read Stanton's book."

"Okay, I'll put it on my Kindle. I'm glad Quentin said something to you."

"Well, I'm glad you're not mad about that. You have to trust Quentin. We all do. He'll stick his nose right into your business, but if he ever gets that crazy look in his eyes and tells you to do something? Do it."

"Okay, I promise I'll listen to him. Should we go back to the party?"

"That's probably a good idea. Who's the guy you're hanging out with?"

"His name is Matthew. He's an awesome guy, really…."

"But?"

"But I'm in love with someone else, just not as this version of me."

"Shit, that's a tough one. Well, you know what the Backstreet Boys said."

"What?"

"Quit Playing Games with My Heart."

"I hear you."

"Sorry," Topher said. "Stanton listens to the boy band station on Pandora, and a few weeks ago, he started quoting song titles. Then I started doing it. Last week we were in bed, and he looked at me all serious and shit and said, 'God Must Have Spent a Little More Time on You.'"

"Were you able to keep a straight face?"

"Hell, no. I burst out laughing, but that was the point. He loves to crack me up in bed. Do you sing, by any chance?"

"No," Ian said.

"Play an instrument?"

"No."

"Dance? Paint?"

"No and no."

Topher sat forward. "Have you ever seen a play called *Love's Labor's Lost*?"

"No."

"You love that word, don't you? No. Maybe you've forgotten how to say...." Topher took a drink from his bottle of beer. "Let me tell you a story. *Love's Labor's Lost* is a play by William Shakespeare. I happen to be partial to the name William, for obvious reasons. Anyway I had to read *Romeo and Juliet* in high school, but I didn't understand a word of it, to be honest. Then Stanton took me to see *R&J* live in Central Park, and I loved it. Even if I didn't get the meaning of every word, it didn't matter, because I got the feeling of it. So I told Stanton I wanted to see more, and we started going to all these little productions downtown. We saw a version of *The Tempest* in a SoHo loft and a woman playing *Hamlet*. And then, a few weeks ago, we went to an NYU student production of *Love's Labor's Lost*. It's about these four guys who swear off women, and you can imagine how far that gets them. The ringleader's name is Biron. He's a real hardass, let me tell you.

"After the production, the director took questions from the audience. An old man raised his hand and said, 'I noticed this credit in the program for something called a dramaturg. What's that?' And the director explained that a dramaturg helps with research and historical context and such. The old man asked for an example, and the director told us about this thing called a concordance, which counts the number of times any word appears in one of Shakespeare's plays. You can find out, for instance, that Juliet says the word 'love' thirty-two times and Romeo says it forty-four times. So one day the dramaturg comes to the director and says he knows something interesting about Biron, the real hardass character I told you about."

"The ringleader?"

"That's the one," Topher confirmed. "The dramaturg says he was playing around with an online concordance. The whole thing is searchable now, he says. So he types in the following question: How many times does Biron say the word 'no'?"

"How many?"

"Twenty-one. He says the word 'no' twenty-one times."

Ian sat up and took a drink of milk. "Okay. So how many times does he say the word—?"

"Once. He only says it once, and it's the turning point of the play. It's the moment when he wakes up to love."

The back door opened, and Stanton walked in. "Oops. Am I interrupting something?"

"Of course not," Topher said. "Have you met Ian?"

"I thought your name was Ryan."

"It is. Kind of."

Stanton crossed behind Topher and leaned over to kiss him. "Did you look in on the kids?"

"What do you think?"

Stanton took a swig of Topher's beer. "Was Grace still sniffling?"

"No, she's better. I could use some attention, though. I haven't seen you all night. What did you think of 'Thunder Road'?"

Stanton placed the beer bottle on the table and rubbed Topher's shoulders. "It took balls, that's for sure."

"You didn't like it," Topher said.

"I thought it was a fun idea. The crowd loved it. But musically, it wasn't your finest moment. I used to think you could sing anything, but tonight you proved me wrong."

Ian put his hand over his mouth and mumbled, "Oh my God, that was so harsh."

Topher laughed. "You think that was harsh? Trust me, he's just getting warmed up. But that's one of the reasons I love him. He never sugarcoats it with me."

"Your hair looked good."

"That's what he says when he hates something."

Stanton grinned. "Let's hope it doesn't go viral on YouTube."

"Should we go back to the party?" Topher said.

Ian stood up. "Good idea."

Stanton leaned down and whispered into Topher's ear, "Or we could go upstairs, and I could show you some attention."

Topher bit his lip and grinned like a schoolboy, clearly defenseless against Stanton's charms. "Will you give me a back rub?"

"As Long As You Love Me."

"Ian," Topher said. "Can you find your way back on your own?"

"Don't worry, boys, I gotcha covered. I'm about to disappear. Topher, thanks for the talk."

"You're welcome. It's gonna work out. I promise."

Ryan left the kitchen and crossed the backyard. He started up the stairs to the garage apartment but then paused when he heard the first note. The party had gone silent, except for the sound of someone playing the violin. Ryan continued up the steps and slipped through the door unnoticed. Matthew stood in the middle of the room, surrounded by the other partygoers, giving a command performance. Ryan didn't know enough about classical music to recognize the piece, but he knew enough to recognize Matthew's skill—not to mention that his frenetic and emotional style only added to his already considerable sex appeal.

Matthew finished to wild applause. Robin and Maurice came to his side and put their arms around him. "You're playing on our next album," one of them said, though Ryan didn't know which one. "Marvin, can you write something for Matthew?"

"How about a duet for violin and tenor?"

Matthew saw Ryan next to the door and mouthed, "Can you believe this?" He handed the violin to one of the quartet members and crossed the room. "Where did you go?"

"I was in the house, talking to Topher," Ryan said. "I met the kids."

"No way. Where is he now?"

"Having sex with his husband. What happened to you?"

Matthew threw up his hands. "I have no idea. Robin and Maurice got me stoned—really good shit, by the way—then they said I had to play something. And I was like, okay, but I don't have my instrument. So one of the violinists from the quartet lent me his, and the next thing I know, I'm standing in front of Marvin Goldstein playing the opening Allegro moderato from Tchaikovsky's Concerto in D Major."

"Is that a hard one?" Ryan asked.

"It's very challenging technically, but I think I knocked it out of the park."

"It sounded amazing, at least the part I heard."

"What did you and Topher talk about?"

"A little bit of everything. Boy bands, Shakespeare plays, and his kids, of course. They're really cute. Did you meet Peter?"

"No," Matthew said. "He's been talking to Marvin all night. But Robin and Maurice are off the hook. I might actually get to record something with them. Can you believe that? And to think all this happened because your uncle gave me a job. I would never have met Quentin otherwise. You know, before he went to Denver, Ian told me he always wanted to open an enchanted coffee shop. He thought it was stupid, but maybe that's exactly what he did."

"You might be right."

Matthew introduced Ryan to Robin and Maurice, and the four of them spent the rest of the night on the small patio outside the bedroom. Some of the stories the twins told about their childhood were terrifying, but they seemed to take it all in stride. Topher eventually came back to the party, and Matthew got to meet him. Around five in the morning, Matthew began nodding off, so they said good night, and Ryan helped him into the truck.

"I pulled an all-nighter to finish my paper," Matthew said. "I haven't slept in two days."

"Why didn't you tell me? Good thing you don't have to work until four. I have to be there in two hours."

"I'm sorry. I wasn't even thinking."

"Don't apologize. I wouldn't have missed this for the world. One night without sleep isn't going to kill me."

They arrived at Matthew's house, and Ryan carried him to his room. He sat on the edge of the bed and watched him sleep. He had planned to tell Matthew they couldn't have sex anymore, but now that would have to wait. Instead he turned off the lights, slipped out of the house, and drove home.

CHAPTER FOURTEEN

THE NEXT afternoon at four o'clock, Ryan and Matthew passed each other, as their shifts overlapped at La Tazza.

"Thanks for putting me to bed this morning."

"You're welcome," Ryan said. "I'd love to stick around and talk, but I need to hit the sack. Do you mind?"

"Not at all. Last night was epic. Do you think they were serious about writing a song for me and Topher?"

"They don't strike me as the bullshitting type. I'll see you tomorrow night for Jeopardy Pursuit?"

"You bet. I need Friday and Saturday off to study, though."

"You too?"

Matthew winked. "Do you want me to fail?"

Ryan turned and walked to the door. "No, I don't. Ask Sam if he can cover for you. He's working from seven to close."

"Will do, Parker. Get some sleep."

WHEN HE got home, Ryan took a shower and thought about how to break up with Matthew. He should have known an office romance would never work out. After he dried off, Ian crawled into bed and called Mark.

"How was the concert last night?"

"Fun," Ian said. "I met Topher Manning."

"Who's that?"

"It doesn't matter. Have you heard from Tad?"

"Not yet. He said it would be a few days."

"I need to end things with Matthew," Ian said. "But I'm going to wait until after tomorrow night. You haven't forgotten about Jeopardy Pursuit, have you?"

"No, I haven't forgotten."

"It starts at seven. Don't be late."

Ian ended the call and pushed his head into the pillow. A minute later, the phone on the nightstand vibrated. He grinned, pressed the screen, and lowered his voice.

"Hey, Bartley."

"Hey, stud. Were you sleeping? Your voice sounds a little groggy."

"No, I was just resting. Are you at work?"

"I'm at home. I took the afternoon off."

"Is everything okay?"

Ian sat up and waited for an answer.

"It will be," Bartley said. "Do you have a minute?"

"Sure. I'm right here."

"It's just…. Something happened to me, and I haven't told anyone the whole story yet. You said the other day that being HIV positive wasn't a dirty little secret. I've been thinking about that a lot."

"What am I missing here? You already told me you're poz."

"I know," Bartley said. "But I haven't told you how I got it."

"It doesn't matter. Really."

"It does to me. I think it's a piece of information you might need in the future—to explain my crazy thoughts and all my trust issues."

"What's this about, Bartley?"

"Before Saturday, there were only three people who knew about my HIV status—my doctor, my dentist, and a social worker I talked to for ten minutes."

"You mean you haven't told your family?" Ian asked.

"No."

"Or even a friend?"

"No. It's been my dirty little secret."

"I didn't mean it that way, Bartley. We all go through a denial stage at the beginning."

"I know, but I got stuck there. When I dropped by La Tazza on Sunday, I told Ryan and Matthew that I'm positive—and it felt amazing. It was like coming out of the closet all over again. I realized I need to do more of that. I need to tell someone what happened, and I'd like that someone to be you."

"Okay. I'm listening."

"Mason and I were in a monogamous relationship. We didn't use condoms. Last summer, he started working on the weekends. He said it was a special project, but he never picked up his phone when I called him. Then after Labor Day, I went in for a routine HIV test. It came back positive. I had them redo it, but the second one came back positive too."

"Oh, no."

"You see where this is going?"

"He cheated and then gave you HIV?"

"I've never been deceived like that before, Ian. At least, not with those kinds of consequences. It shattered everything. My mind, my heart, my whole life. And it wasn't really the HIV. It was the betrayal. I told my friends that Mason and I broke up, but I didn't give them any explanation why. I eventually stopped socializing to avoid their questions. I worked and slept—and that was about it. I told you, it was the worst winter of my life. Then spring came, and I found myself looking forward to seeing you at La Tazza, and to our chats about sandwiches and soap operas."

"Bartley, I would give anything to be there right now. I would kiss you, and hold you in my arms, and tell you everything's going to be okay. And it will be. I wish I could turn back time and wipe away all the damage Mason caused, but I can't. All I can do is help you put the pieces back together, if you'll let me."

Ian heard sobs, and Bartley said, "I know what you're thinking. How could I have been such a fool, right?"

"That's not what I'm thinking."

"I'm so pissed off. I have these moments of blind rage, when all I can think about is ripping his throat out. I feel so ashamed and stupid for trusting him."

"Please," Ian said. "Don't feel ashamed and stupid. I know that's easy for me to say, but he's the one who should feel that way, not you. You did everything right. You loved someone and believed in him. What's the alternative?"

YES

"I don't know. I'm sorry. I didn't mean to be such a downer."

"You're not being a downer, and besides, now the secret is out. You told me. It's time to turn the corner and move on."

Bartley laughed and sniffed. "That's what Rachel said."

"Who's Rachel?"

"The woman who did my tattoo."

Ian stood up. "Are you ready to tell me what it means?"

"Do you mind?"

"Mind? I'd be honored."

"Okay." Bartley cleared his throat. "A few weeks back, I was having lunch with two of the women I work with. One of them reads tarot cards, so she took out her deck and told me to pick one. I pulled the reversed Five of Cups, which she said signifies acceptance and resolution. Then she added, 'Very interesting.' An hour later, she texted me the address for a tattoo parlor and a name. Rachel. I texted her back a question mark, and she replied simply, 'Go.' This was just before you went to Denver."

"I remember."

"So that evening, I grabbed some dinner at Julio's and drove over to the tattoo parlor. When I walked in the door, this small woman with black hair and a black tank top said, 'Are you Bartley?' She introduced herself as Rachel, gestured to a chair, and I sat down. She just stood there and looked right through me. I'm talking straight into my soul. After about a minute, she tapped the inside of my right forearm and said, 'How about right there?' I didn't know what to do. She hadn't even asked me what kind of tattoo I wanted. She must have seen the doubt on my face, because she said, 'You're afraid to trust your instincts because they failed you once.' I kind of laughed and nodded and said, 'Right there would be fine.' An hour later, she finished the work and covered it with a bandage. She asked for my phone number and then texted me a picture of two Chinese symbols, which she explained represented the central struggle of my life. I asked her why I only got a tattoo of one of the symbols, and she said, 'People will always do shitty things to us, Bartley, but it's our ability to turn the corner and move on that matters. Remind yourself of that every day, and show a little gratitude that you're still alive to feel the pain.'"

"Whoa," Ian said. "Rachel is totally hardcore badass. Did she ever tell you what the symbols mean?"

"It was on the picture. Hold on. I'll send it to you."

Ian waited a few seconds and then opened Bartley's text messages. He tapped on the picture.

宽恕
Forgiveness

Ian smiled and sat back down. "Of course. She only gave you one of the symbols because forgiveness is never finished."

"Every morning," Bartley said, "for the rest of my life, it'll remind me there's only one way forward. I'm done being angry. I'm done feeling sorry for myself. And most of all, I'm done being celibate. When are you coming home?"

"Soon. I promise." Ian lay back down and nestled under the covers. "Do you feel better now?"

"Much. I don't know how to thank you."

"Well, you can start by telling me about your day. What did you work on this morning? I want to hear all about the design for the second house."

"You won't believe the idea I had yesterday for the kitchen."

"What's the idea?"

"A fireplace," Bartley said.

"In the kitchen?"

"What do you think?"

"Well, I would love to have a fireplace in my kitchen."

"But no one ever puts one there."

"It's a very cool idea."

"How's your mom?"

"A lot better," Ian said. "I told you, I'm going to be coming home soon."

YES

ON THURSDAY, Ryan worked the day shift and left early for his first carpentry class. It consisted mostly of introductions to the other students plus an overview of the different tools and what they were used for. Luke helped him sketch out his first project—a birdhouse for Ian's backyard.

Ryan returned to La Tazza at six thirty. Matthew and his friend Cecilia were already there. Mark, Bartley, and Jeremy arrived ten minutes later. Ryan got the board set up as the other teams arrived. Shortly before seven, Ben Walsh and his family burst through the west door and caused a wild commotion, which involved Matthew and Quentin engaging in some good-natured trash talk.

Ryan looked into the parking lot and saw Sam smoking a cigarette. He stepped outside. "We're about to start."

"I was just fixin' to head in," Sam said as he indicated the cigarette. "I'm trying to quit, but these group things make me nervous. I'm always afraid I'm gonna say something idiotic, and usually I do."

"Don't worry about that. Matthew's put together a good team. Everyone's going to like you."

"I trust him." Sam shoved his free hand into his jean pocket. "Hey, before we go back in, I wanted to say thank you. Things have really started to turn around for me, and I can pretty much trace that back to meeting you. Matthew feels like a brother already and.... Well, I really like this job."

"You're good at it. Better than I am."

"Your uncle's created something special here. I'm looking forward to meeting him." Sam extinguished the cigarette against the bottom of his work boot and then threw the butt into the trash can. "Okay, I'm ready. Let's go."

Ryan led them inside and over to Matthew's table. Matthew stood up, kissed Ryan on the cheek, and whispered, "I made sure to save him a seat next to Jeremy."

"Hey, everybody," Ryan said. "This is our friend Sam. He's new in town and just started working at La Tazza on Sunday, so be nice to him. He's going to be your sports guy."

Bartley slapped Sam on the back and said welcome. "There's an empty chair next to Jeremy."

Ryan and Matthew watched as Sam walked around the table and sat down. He smiled and offered his hand to Jeremy, who turned red as he shook it. They started talking, and Matthew said, "Parker, our work here is done."

The east door opened, and several of the younger women screamed. Ryan looked up and saw Topher Manning, accompanied by all three of his bandmates, plus Stanton and Marvin.

"What the hell…."

"Surprise," Matthew said. "I signed them up for the last open slot." He walked over and greeted the Ackerman twins.

Ryan followed and welcomed Topher with a warm hug. "Thanks for coming."

"How are you doing?"

"I'm good. Are you ready for some Jeopardy Pursuit?"

"You bet, though I hear the Walsh brothers are gonna kick our asses. We know a lot about music but not much else."

"Speak for yourself," Stanton said.

Ryan laughed. "You guys can have the sofas in the corner."

It took about fifteen minutes to settle everyone down and explain the rules, but once it started, the evening turned into a raucous affair. They played the variant rule, which ended a team's turn whenever it collected a wedge, preventing any single team from running the board.

All of the teams were strong and quickly went about collecting wedges. In the third round, Quentin rolled the die and moved his team's game piece. Ryan turned to the Walsh family and read the answer. "In what has been called her defining moment, Joey Potter sings this song in the eleventh episode of the WB teen-angst series, *Dawson's Creek*."

"I know this one," Travis said. "I used to love that show. What is 'On My Own,' from Les Miz?"

"You are correct, for a wedge."

Ben showered his boyfriend with kisses.

Ryan turned to Topher, who rolled the die for his team. Ryan pulled an Arts & Literature answer. "The date and location of the now legendary final performance by the Beatles, which came to an abrupt end when the police shut it down."

Topher and Stanton turned to Marvin, who said, "What is January 30, 1969, on the rooftop of the Apple headquarters in London?"

"Correct."

Maurice rolled the die again and moved their piece four spaces.

"If they get this one right," Ryan said, "it will give Dime Box a wedge. The category is History. The country with the highest number of fatalities during World War II, it lost more than twice as many lives as the country with the second highest number."

"What is the Soviet Union?" Stanton said.

"Correct. Twenty-seven million dead. China had eleven million."

Robin grabbed a history wedge and added it to their collection.

"Team Matthew, you're up next." Cecilia rolled the die, and Ryan read an Entertainment answer. "This 1990s television series starring Matthew Fox told the story of a family of siblings who struggled to stay together after the death of their parents in a car accident."

Cecilia turned to her team.

"What is *Party of Five*?" Mark said.

"Congratulations. You may continue." Bartley stepped up and took a turn. Ryan smiled, and Ian longed to hold him. He remembered Bartley's confession from the day before and wanted to tell him again that everything would be okay. Bartley landed on Geography, and Ryan read the answer. "The names of the five Great Lakes, created by retreating glaciers ten thousand years ago, in order of size, from largest to smallest."

Matthew stood up. "Are you kidding me?"

"Anyone can name the five lakes," Ryan said. "We needed to make it challenging."

Bartley put his hand up. "I can do this. Superior, Huron—"

Ryan cleared his throat.

"Oh, sorry. What are Superior, Huron, Michigan, Erie, and Ontario?"

"Correct. Keep going." Sam stepped forward, rolled, and moved the piece. "Science & Nature," Ryan said. "For a wedge. After recanting his belief that the Earth revolves around the Sun, Galileo supposedly uttered these famous four words as he rose to his feet, though scholars highly doubt the story's authenticity."

Sam looked at Jeremy. "I hope you know this."

"What is 'And yet it moves'?"

Ryan took a dramatic pause and then said, "Congratulations. You have successfully loaded another wedge."

Ryan cycled through the three remaining teams and then circled around to the Walsh family. Ben rolled and moved. "Entertainment. In the motion picture *Psycho*, Alfred Hitchcock used this substance in place of stage blood, because it looked better on black-and-white film."

Ben looked at Jake, who said, "What is Bosco chocolate syrup?"

"Nice job," Ryan said. "I didn't expect anyone to know the actual brand. Jake, do you want to come up here and go again?" Jake rolled a three and moved the piece into the wedge position for Sports & Leisure. "This Boston Red Sox player, who hit the three-run homer that tied up game six of the 1975 World Series, admitted in 2010 that he was high on drugs and alcohol at the time."

Cade raised his hand. "Who is Bernie Carbo?"

"And the Walsh family has their fifth wedge. Dime Box, it's your turn." Peter rolled the die and moved. "Arts & Literature. The closing chapter of this American classic contains the line, 'I left the woods for as good a reason as I went there.'"

"What is *Walden*?" Maurice said.

"Correct. Peter, roll again." The die came up a six, and their piece landed on the Geography hub. "For a wedge. Although there are currently three hundred plus cities with a population of over one million people, this city was the first to reach that milestone."

"Oh, that's tough," Stanton said. "It's either Rome, London, or New York. You pick, Peter."

"What is Rome?"

"You are correct. The Italians did it in 133 B.C. Collect your wedge. Jeremy, have you rolled for your team yet?"

"Nope." He got up from his chair, and Ryan put his arm around him. "Jeremy here teaches calculus at one of the local high schools and is a real gamer."

"No kidding?" Topher said. "You play D&D?"

"I do."

"Talk to me afterward. Maybe you can hook me up with a game."

"Okay, I'd be happy to." Jeremy rolled the die and moved three spaces.

"Sports & Leisure," Ryan said. "Not exactly your strong suit."

Jeremy shrugged. "Maybe not, but that's why we have Sam."

"Here is your answer," Ryan said. "In Texas hold'em, it's the name given to the three face-up cards dealt after the initial round of betting."

Travis slumped in his chair and mumbled, "I know this one."

"So do we," said the twins.

Ryan smiled. "Unfortunately, it's not your turn."

Jeremy looked at Sam, who answered, "What is the flop?"

"Are you sure?" Matthew asked.

Sam chuckled. "Where I come from, every night was poker night. Trust me, I'm sure."

"You should listen to him more often," Ryan said, "because he is correct."

Jeremy raised his fists and cheered.

The game continued for three more rounds, and despite everyone's valiant efforts, team Walsh collected all six wedges and entered the hexagonal victory hub first. The other teams agreed that their question should come from the Geography category.

Ryan looked down at the card. "Colleen wrote this one, and I thought it was pretty good. For the win. This northernmost US city is the setting for the vampire comic book series *30 Days of Night*."

The entire Walsh clan erupted into cheers.

"Not fair," Stanton said.

Ryan turned to face him. "Why not?"

"Because Travis has been there."

Ryan turned back to the Walsh team. "That's perfectly fair. Travis, would you like to give us the question?"

"What is Barrow, Alaska?"

"And for the fourth month in a row…. You. Are. Correct."

Ben and his brothers jumped up and threw their arms around Travis. As the other teams congratulated them, Ryan noticed Mark answer his phone. He nodded toward the door, and Ryan followed him onto the patio.

"I'm going to put you on speaker, Tad." Mark tapped the screen. "Ian is here too."

"Hey, Tad. Did you talk to Mrs. Brown?"

"She just left the shop."

"And?" Mark asked.

"She didn't seem surprised when I told her about your claim, but she almost fell off her chair when I told her you want to reverse it. She said she can do it, though."

Ian smiled. "That's great news. Thank you. What do I need to do?"

"She has to steep the butter for three days. It will be a white chocolate kiss, but you'll have to come back to Denver. We can't send marijuana-laced candy through the mail."

"I'll fly in on Sunday, then."

"Great. Just come by the shop when you get here. We're open every day until midnight."

Mark ended the call. Ian turned away and looked through the window. He saw Bartley talking to Ben and Travis. "I knew it."

"Are you okay?"

"I don't know." Ian took a few steps toward the street and watched the cars go by. Then he turned back to Mark and said, "Something's not right."

"What are you talking about?"

"Didn't you notice? During the game. No one got any of the answers wrong."

CHAPTER FIFTEEN

THE NEXT night at seven, Quentin's freshman study group came into La Tazza and claimed their Friday table. Quentin approached the bar and said hello.

"First round is on the house," Ryan said. "As a way to say thanks for Tuesday night. It was very cool of you to invite us to the after-party."

"You made quite an impression on Topher."

"He's not what I expected at all." Ryan leaned on the bar and lowered his voice. "We got a call from Denver last night. They have a remedy."

"What are you going to do?"

"I booked my flight this morning. I'm in love with Bartley, but he's in love with Ian, not Ryan. So I'm going to reverse what happened to me, and when I get back, I plan on dating Bartley. But do I keep everything that's happened over the past two weeks a secret for the rest of my life? I told him my mom had emergency surgery, and now I hope he'll meet her someday. I've systematically deceived him, which is exactly why his last relationship ended."

Quentin took a deep breath, and Ian could read the concerned look on his face. "You have to tell him everything. Now, before you go to Denver."

"Why would he believe me? And even if he does believe me, how can I ask him to forgive all the lies?"

"Maybe that's the point."

"Why do you keep saying that?"

"He needs to know someone will be honest with him," Quentin said. "And you need to know someone will forgive you when you screw up. I'm not saying it's all going to be hunky-dory if you tell him. I would never blow smoke up your ass like that. But if you don't tell him, there's no way in hell you two stand a chance."

"But you know how he's going to react. He'll probably think I have Ian in a basement somewhere and then call the police, just like you threatened to do."

"Hmm." Quentin thought for a moment. "You need someone there who he trusts. Someone whose reputation is irreproachable. Someone like Ben."

"I saw them talking last night. Do they know each other?"

"I think they worked together on some fundraising event for one of the gay groups in town."

"Would Ben do it?"

"He will if I ask him," Quentin said. "Call Bartley and set something up for tomorrow afternoon. Do it here at La Tazza. Once you have a time, let me know, and I'll talk to my brother."

"Okay, thanks. Are you sure this is the right thing?"

"It's the only thing. How are you going to explain never seeing Ryan again? Or the surgery your mom never had? You can't start a relationship based on lies. You have to come clean."

"Okay. I get it. Join your friends, and I'll bring the drinks out."

Quentin walked away, and Ryan pulled out his phone. He dialed Bartley's number and waited. He picked up after three rings, and Ryan asked if he was free the next day. Ryan explained that he wanted Bartley's advice on something, and they arranged to meet at two in the afternoon. Ryan relayed the time to Quentin, who exited to the patio to call Ben. A few minutes later, Quentin returned with a thumbs-up.

THE NEXT morning, Ian called Mark and told him about the plan to spill his guts to Bartley. Mark warned that he should be prepared for the worst, but Ian explained he had no other choice. Ryan tried to stay busy at La Tazza during the day. Finally, at a few minutes before two o'clock, Bartley walked through the north door and waved at him. Timothy covered the counter while Ryan took two drinks out to Bartley's table.

"A double skim, right?"

"Correct," Bartley said, imitating Ryan's Jeopardy Pursuit MC Voice.

Ryan sat down. "Very funny. Ben Walsh is going to be joining us soon."

"Ben? What for?"

"There are some things I need to tell you, and they're going to sound a little crazy. Well, actually, they're going to sound a lot crazy."

"What things?"

Ryan spooned some milk froth into his mouth. "There's no other way to do this except straightforward. When Ian went to Denver for his fortieth birthday, he bought a chocolate kiss laced with a special kind of pot called Manick Butter. He ate the kiss before he boarded the plane back to Austin. While he was on the plane, he took a nap and woke up twenty years younger. In other words, me. He woke up as me. I'm Ian."

Bartley blinked. "I don't understand. Your uncle was on a plane, and you body swapped with him?"

"No, it wasn't a body swap. The real Ryan Parker is ten years old. I've just been playing him because.... Well, because I didn't know how else to explain my circumstances."

"But Ian's in Phoenix. I've been talking to him on the phone."

"No, you've been talking to me." Ian dropped his voice. "Sound familiar?"

Bartley scooted his chair back. Ian knew he couldn't absorb this kind of information in the span of a few seconds. Bartley shook his head and said, "Why would you play such a sick joke on me?"

"It's not a joke," Ian insisted. "I woke up on a plane twenty years younger, and I had no idea what to do."

"Did you hit your head or something?"

"No, I'm not crazy. This is really happening."

After a long pause, Bartley pushed his latte away, stood up, and turned toward the door.

A voice behind them said, "Don't go yet."

Ian swiveled in his seat. Bartley stopped and said, "What are you doing here?"

Ben Walsh stepped up to their table. "Sit down and hear me out. Please."

"What do you have to do with—?"

"I'll explain everything. Why don't the three of us have a seat together?" Bartley hesitated for a second but then returned to his chair. Ben pulled up a stool and joined them. He turned to Ian. "What have you told him?"

"Everything." Ian looked at Bartley. "I don't blame you for wanting to leave. I would leave too."

"What have you done with Ian?" Bartley asked.

"Nothing. I told you, I'm Ian."

"And you expect me to believe that? Chocolate makes you younger? That's your explanation? It's the craziest thing I've ever heard. And you, Ben? Are you going to tell me you believe him?"

"No, I'm not. Look, I've had some bizarre conversations in my life, but this one takes the cake. Ryan or Ian or whatever your name is, I don't believe you, and I'm not going to advise Bartley to believe you either."

"Thank you," Bartley said.

"But for some unknown, godforsaken reason, my brother Quentin does believe you. Bartley, that's something I can't ignore. So I'm going to ask you, if it turned out that Ryan or Ian was telling the truth, would that change anything?"

"There's no way you could ever convince me of that."

"What if I told you there's a remedy?" Ben said. "Ryan is flying to Denver tomorrow, and when he comes back, he claims he's going to be Ian again."

"So what's the con here?" Bartley asked, turning to Ryan. "You get on a plane, and two days later, Ian shows up? Do you think I'm an idiot?"

"No," Ben said. "That's why you need to go with him."

Bartley and Ian both looked at Ben and asked, "What?"

"That's the solution. It's the only way to prove whether or not Ryan's telling the truth. Bartley, go with him to Denver. Be there when he eats the kiss, be there when he falls asleep, but most importantly, be there when he wakes up. I would never suggest this if my brother hadn't vouched for him. But Quentin can see things the rest of us can't, and just because I don't believe Ryan doesn't mean he's not telling the truth. I had a conversation with my dead father once. There's more to the world than we know, Bartley, and if you don't go with him to Denver, you may end up regretting it in ways you can't even imagine."

Bartley paused. He stared at Ian, then turned to Ben and said, "You're both nuts. Ben, I didn't expect this from you."

Bartley got up and walked out the door.

"Go after him," Ben said.

"He doesn't want to talk to me."

"You're wrong. I've been where you are right now. Trust me. This is the most important moment of your life. Plead your case. Tell him how you feel. Hurry, before he gets away."

Ian ran out of La Tazza and into the parking lot. Bartley had just reached his Jeep.

"Please," Ian said. "I made a wish, and it came true." Bartley stopped, so Ian continued. "I wanted to go back and do it all over again. I thought being twenty-one and HIV negative would make you want me. So I didn't say anything."

Bartley turned around. "You're negative?"

"As Ryan I am, but that's not me anymore. After I eat the white kiss, I'll be poz again. And forty. I'll be who I really am."

"White kiss? Do you even hear yourself? And what about Matthew? The whole time you've been talking to me on the phone, you've been sleeping with him?"

"No, I haven't. I slept with him once, the night before you told Ian how you felt. And if you're going to beat me up over every guy I had sex with before that conversation, then I won't try to stop you. I've had more than my share of sexual partners, and some of them were mistakes. But I'm not the man I was yesterday. I wouldn't even advise you to date that man. But this guy—the one inside the guy standing in front of you—I'm worth it. I know what you're thinking. You're wondering, what's the difference between me and

191

Mason? I don't know. Maybe I'm a monster too, except telling the truth was more important than holding onto you, and that's got to count for something. These past few days, every time we talked on the phone, I had trouble breathing afterward. That's how much I love you, Bartley. If you can find a way to forgive me, I'll spend the rest of my life earning your trust. And I'll never, ever lie to you again. I promise."

Bartley didn't say anything. Instead he shook his head, jumped into his Jeep, and drove away.

THE NEXT morning, Ian packed an overnight bag for his trip to Denver. He had no doubts about his decision, but Ryan owed one person a good-bye at least. Before lunch, he drove to La Tazza and went inside. Matthew smiled at first, but then his expression changed when he saw the serious look on Ryan's face.

"What's wrong?"

"You've been off for two days, and I didn't want to bother you. My grandmother is better. Ian's coming home, and I'm heading to the airport soon."

"Soon? What do you mean, soon?"

"In about an hour," Ryan said.

"You're joking, right? Why didn't you call or text me?"

"I'm sorry, it happened so fast. That's why I'm here. To say good-bye."

Matthew's eyes filled with panic. "Where are you going?"

"Thailand. I have some friends who are island hopping, and they want me to join them. It's a once-in-a-lifetime opportunity. I'm not ready to settle in one place yet."

"You've been here for two weeks. I'd hardly call that putting down roots."

"I'm not the right guy for you, Matthew. I think deep down you know that. I really want to say good-bye as friends, but if you can't, I understand. You're an amazing guy, and I'll never forget you for as long as I live."

Matthew didn't respond, and Ryan added, "Would you say good-bye to Sam for me?"

Matthew nodded, and Ryan turned to go. He was halfway out the door when Matthew said, "Wait."

Ryan stopped.

"I can say good-bye as friends," Matthew continued. "And you never know—maybe our paths will cross again someday. Thanks for teaching me how to drive a stick. I'll never forget you either."

Ryan turned his head and smiled. Then he left La Tazza for the last time.

IAN WENT home, and as he waited for his cab to the airport, the doorbell rang. When he answered it, he found Bartley standing on the front porch.

"Let me get this clear," Bartley said. "You went to Denver as Ian, where you bought a chocolate kiss, and you ate it before you boarded the plane home. You took a nap, and when you woke up, you were twenty years younger and HIV negative?"

"That's pretty much the long and short of it."

"And now they have a white chocolate kiss that will put you back the way you were?"

Ian nodded.

"But you don't have to take it, right?"

"No."

Bartley rubbed his forehead. "Is someone forcing you to be HIV positive again?"

"No. No one's forcing me to do anything."

Bartley had tears in his eyes. "So you have this chance to start over—to go back and be young a second time. To have a clean slate. Nothing but endless possibilities. And you're going to give all that up? For me?"

Ian was done being a "no" man.

He smiled and said, "Yes."

CHAPTER SIXTEEN

IAN WOKE up when a flight attendant brushed his arm with the beverage cart. He looked down and saw age spots.

He turned to Mark and shook him. "Wake up."

Mark jumped and lifted his face mask. "Why? What's wrong?"

"I just had the trippiest dream ever. I was twenty-one years old and HIV negative again. Oh my God, it was so real, but you won't believe how badly I fucked it up."

"Was I in it?"

"Of course. You told me it wasn't a hallucination because I could read from a book."

"Where did I get that idea from?"

"You said you saw it on *Teen Wolf*."

Mark laughed. "That should have been your first clue, right there. I don't watch *Teen Wolf*. You do."

"I became my nephew Ryan and…. Oh, no. I had sex with Matthew, my newest employee. Oh my God. I'm such a perv. And the three of us had the most random conversation about porn. You and I created an elaborate backstory about my mom having surgery, and I talked to Bartley on the phone, pretending to be Ian in Phoenix."

"Who's Bartley?"

"The architect. He blew off Ryan because he was into me. Can you believe that? He told me he's poz too and that he likes older guys. He wanted to have sex with *me*, not a negative twink. The whole thing was total fantasy fulfillment."

"That Manick Butter sounds like some good shit."

"It's an anagram," Ian said.

"What is?"

"Manick Butter. It's an anagram for 'turn back time.' You're the one who figured it out."

"What else happened?"

"I met a rock star named Topher Manning, and I had a glass of milk in his kitchen at two o'clock in the morning. It was one of the coolest moments of my life, even if I made it up. He introduced me to his kids and told me this story about some Shakespeare play. That's when I started thinking, 'None of this is real.' Then, when no one answered anything wrong during Jeopardy Pursuit, I knew something was off. In hindsight, it makes perfect sense. If I was dreaming, why would I make up questions I didn't know the answers to?"

"How did it end?" Mark asked.

"The plotting got very bizarre. Ben Walsh showed up and tried to help."

"Ben Walsh? The lawyer?"

"Don't ask. It had something to do with his brother, Quentin. At that point, the whole thing was just one big narrative mess. Except...."

"What?"

"I liked myself again," Ian said. "I told Bartley the truth and put my heart on the line and it felt good. Just before the dream ended, he showed up on my porch. I was heading to the airport, and I think he was going to forgive me."

"I haven't seen you this happy in a long time."

Ian thought about it. "You're right."

"Worth the hundred bucks, then?"

"Every penny. I feel more awake than ever. And so thrilled I didn't actually sleep with Matthew. Can you imagine the sexual harassment suit?"

Mark put away his pillow and eye mask. "Not to mention your spot on the sex offender's registry."

"But the best part is, I never actually lied to Bartley. It's like another clean slate. I will never lie to him. Ever."

"Well, I wouldn't get my hopes up if I were you. Remember, it was just a fantasy. Chances are, he *is* into negative twinks."

"I know," Ian said. "You're right. Still, it was nice to live in an alternate reality for a while."

THE NEXT day, Ian opened La Tazza and worked the morning shift alone. Shortly before ten, Timothy called and asked for a few days off in May. Ian went to the calendar behind the bar and lifted up the April page. Timothy said something, but Ian just stared at the calendar. On Friday, May 16, someone had written:

> *Architect Happy Hour*
> *A. Marlow*

"Ian? You there?"

"Do you know who scheduled this event for May 16?"

"I did," Timothy said. "I was going to tell you about it. The dude came in Saturday night when I was working by myself. Alexander Marlow was his name. He wanted to book La Tazza for a student happy hour. He mentioned Bartley James, so I took his information and put it on the calendar. I told him he had to confirm with you, though. He should be dropping by with Bartley this afternoon."

"Are you sure he said this afternoon? With Bartley?"

"I'm sure. Trust me, this guy didn't hold back on the details."

"Okay. Thanks. What days did you want off again?"

AFTER HE ended the call, Ian went into the seating area to bus tables. He was so distracted, he didn't hear one of the customers say hello.

"Excuse me? Ian?"

"Oh. Hey, Dean. Sorry, I was off in la-la land. How's the writing going?"

"Great, thank you. I took your advice and sent my manuscript to one of the smaller presses. They only publish historical fiction. Nothing else. Guess what? I got an acceptance e-mail yesterday."

"Congratulations," Ian said. "That's amazing news."

"They have editors and a cover art department. It's going to be on Amazon and everything."

"I'm so proud of you, Dean. Will you tell Terry Gross you wrote it at La Tazza when she has you on *Fresh Air*?"

Dean blushed. "You bet. Thanks for letting me sit here and write all day."

"I'd be offended if you went anywhere else." Ian carried the tub of glasses back to the bar and took out his phone. The morning had taken a very interesting turn. He Googled the neighborhood location and dialed the number.

A young woman answered. "Papa John's, can I take your order?"

"May I speak to Sam White, please?"

"Sam's not working today. I'd take a message, but I'm not his secretary."

"Thank you." Ian ended the call. He Googled "Harvest Island Academy" and scrolled through to their faculty page. When he saw a picture of Jeremy under the math department heading, he quickly thumbed over to his contacts and dialed Mark's number.

"I had a lovely weekend too," Mark answered. "You're welcome."

"Something weird is going on," Ian said.

"What do you mean by weird?"

"That dream I told you about? The one I had on the plane? I'm not saying it happened, but some of the people I met in the dream are turning out to be real."

"You must have met them and not remembered. That's what dreams do. They tap into your subconscious."

"No," Ian said. "Dean got a book deal in the dream, and now he has a book deal in real life. As Ryan, I talked to a guy named Alexander Marlow. He booked a student happy hour in May. This morning I saw his event on the calendar. Mark, it wasn't there before I went to Denver. What if everything I learned is true? What if everything I learned about Bartley is true?"

"You can't be serious."

"What if the kiss was magic?"

"I can't believe we're even having—"

"I promise you, I'm not making this up for attention. There's something going on here. You have to believe me."

"Okay," Mark said. "Let's pretend, for argument's sake, that the kiss was… magic. You lived out some fantasies, and some people you met and things you learned turned out to be real. So what? Magic is supposed to grant you a wish or turn your enemy into a toad or make someone fall in love with you. Who cares if Alexander Marlow is real?"

"I haven't told you about Sam and Jeremy."

"Can you keep it high level? I'm at work."

"Sam was the pizza boy, and Jeremy was a Grindr hookup. Matthew and I figured out they're each other's type, so we invited them to join the same Jeopardy Pursuit team. They totally hit it off, but there's no way they'll ever meet in real life."

"Maybe Jeremy will order a pizza," Mark said.

"Even if he did, he'd be too embarrassed to ask for Sam's number."

"So, this is about matchmaking?"

"It's about showing two people an off-ramp to happiness. What if they're made for each other, but I'm the only one who knows it? Mark, I'm about to do something completely off the hook. Do you want to be a part of it or not?"

After a moment, Mark answered, "I can get off work early and be there by four."

"Perfect. That's when Matthew starts his shift. I'm going to ask him to help too. And Quentin Walsh."

Ian ended the call and dialed Quentin's number.

"Hey, Ian. Is something wrong?"

"No. Sorry to bother you, Q, but I need your help. I think you'll want to be in on this. Can you stop by La Tazza around four?"

"Umm, sure. What's it about?"

"I'd rather give you the details in person."

"Okay," Quentin said. "You definitely have my curiosity piqued."

Colleen arrived at noon and worked the lunch crowd with Ian. When the rush ended, Ian told her he had to step out for an hour or two. He drove to the tattoo parlor on Airport and Forty-Fifth Street and asked for Rachel. A young woman matching Bartley's description appeared from the back and introduced herself.

"This is going to sound bizarre," Ian said. "But I think you did a tattoo for a friend of mine last week. It was one of the Chinese symbols for 'forgiveness.'"

Rachel smiled and gestured toward her chair. "I've been waiting for you."

AT FOUR o'clock in the afternoon, Ian returned to La Tazza Magica, where he was soon joined by Mark and Quentin. Matthew arrived as well and took his place behind the bar next to Ian. He nodded awkwardly toward Quentin and said hello. In the alternate dimension, they were all friends, but here the three of them had never met, so Ian introduced them.

"What's going on, boss?" Matthew asked. "Did I miss something?"

"No," Ian said. "Let me explain. Some of this is going to sound a little crazy, but try to look past that aspect and focus on my proposal."

Mark pointed at Ian's bandaged forearm. "Did you burn yourself?"

The north door opened, and instead of answering, Ian turned and grinned. Matthew nudged him and said, "Who's the hottie with Bartley?"

"His name is Alexander Marlow."

"Introduce me to him. *Please*."

Ian walked around the bar and met them in the middle of the main aisle. The smile on Bartley's face confirmed what Ian already suspected. He wrapped his arms around Bartley and pulled him close. If he was surprised, Bartley didn't show it. He buried his face in Ian's chest and hugged him back.

"How did you know I missed you?" Bartley said.

"I'll explain everything."

Bartley pulled away and noticed the bandage on the inside of Ian's left arm. "What did you do?"

"I'll explain that as well." Ian kept his arm around Bartley's shoulder as he turned to Alexander Marlow.

"Who's your friend?"

"This is Alexander," Bartley said. "He's one of the UT architecture students I'm mentoring this semester." Bartley wrapped his arm around Ian's waist and tightened his grip. He introduced himself to Mark and Quentin. "Is this some kind of secret meeting?"

"We're hatching a plan," Ian said.

Alexander Marlow stepped forward, and Ian heard the voice again, exactly as he remembered it. "May I inquire as to what type of plan you are in the process of hatching?"

Ian could feel Matthew swoon from across the counter.

"Let's get everybody drinks first," Ian said. He reluctantly released Bartley, and their fingers intertwined for a moment as Ian slipped behind the bar. Matthew took their orders, and Ian knocked them out—a cappuccino, an espresso, a double-skim latte, and a bottle of filtered water. Ian made a soy latte for himself and went back out front so he could sit next to Bartley. As Ian handed Bartley his double skim, they looked at each other and laughed. This felt more unreal than the Manick Butter trip.

"What's going on?" Bartley said as he sat next to Ian. "We just came in to put a special event on your calendar."

Ian put his arm around the back of Bartley's chair. "I know that, but then Alexander inquired as to what type of plan we are in the process of hatching, so do you want to hear it or not?"

Alexander Marlow sat his bag down on one of the nearby tables but remained standing. "I would like to hear it. Please, if you do not object, Mr. James."

Bartley took a sip of his latte. "Absolutely. I'm dying to find out what happens next, because this is turning out to be one hell of a day." He leaned into Ian, and their legs brushed.

Then everyone gathered around, and Ian began his story: "When Mark and I were in Denver, I bought a chocolate kiss laced with THC. I have a feeling I don't need to explain what that means, even if you've never done it yourself. I ate it right before the trip back to Austin. On the plane, I fell asleep and had a dream that I was twenty-one again. Crazy, I know. But what happened in the dream is

YES

almost inconsequential. The important thing is what happened when I woke up. People I met in the dream turned out to be real."

"Like who?" Alexander said.

"Like you."

Alexander Marlow looked unfazed.

"I met you in my dream," Ian continued. "Your mother is a private detective, and you're going to work for her in September."

"You are correct, Mr. Parker."

"Your father's from Argentina, and you're going to recreate *The Motorcycle Diaries*."

"You are no longer correct. My father runs a chain of dry cleaners in Odessa."

"Really?" Ian said. "Okay. So that means some of the things I learned are true and some aren't. This should be interesting, then. Matthew, did you move to Austin after your father died? When you were fifteen?"

"How did you know that?"

"Are you writing a paper about gay porn for a Performance Studies class?"

Matthew laughed from behind the bar. "I wish."

"Quentin, do you know Topher Manning, the lead singer of Dime Box?"

"Very well. I've known him for a couple of years."

"Have you ever been to San Diego?"

"Nope. Never."

Matthew raised his hand. "What does this have to do with a plan, boss?"

"Hey," Bartley said as he put his hand on Ian's leg. "What about me?"

Ian felt himself turn red and took Bartley's hand. "I'll get to you in a minute. But right now, we need to focus on Sam and Jeremy."

"What you two need to do is get a room," Matthew said. "And who are Sam and Jeremy?"

"Two guys I met in my dream. They exist in real life. They're made for each other, and they don't even know it, and they're never going to meet unless we do something. That's what this is about.

Matthew, you and Sam are like brothers in my dream dimension. He's this twenty-one-year-old struggling kid who delivers pizza, and Jeremy is an adorkable math teacher from a wealthy Dallas family. I need to figure out a way they can meet naturally, without any pressure. Whatever we do has to be completely invisible. That's the mission I place in front of you today, gentlemen. Design a blueprint to bring Sam and Jeremy together without them knowing about it."

There was a long pause.

"Will we ever tell them?" Mark asked.

"I haven't thought that far ahead," Ian said. "I guess we can play it by ear."

Bartley took another sip of his drink. "I don't know about the rest of you, but count me in."

"Me as well," Alexander said. "If, in fact, I have been formally invited to participate."

"You have," Ian said as he looked at Quentin for an answer.

"Are you kidding? I live for this kind of shit."

Ian turned to Matthew, who nodded and said, "Of course. I can't wait to meet this Sam dude. And where does Jeremy teach high school?"

"Harvest Island Academy," Ian said.

"No way," Matthew said. "That's where I went."

"My little brother, Cade, just finished his sophomore year there."

"That may prove useful," Alexander said.

Matthew smiled and nodded. "We should use La Tazza as the meeting place."

"Just have a pizza delivered here," Mark suggested.

"But how do we make sure Sam's the one who delivers it?" Quentin asked.

Alexander pulled up a stool and sat down. "We call ahead and inform the pizza parlor management that we are sponsoring a surprise birthday party for Sam, and would it be possible to assign a certain order to him."

"You're good at this," Matthew said.

"But how do we get Jeremy here?" Quentin asked.

"That's where your brother will come into play," Alexander said. "But the setup cannot be dependent on a single meeting. We must design a plan that will bring them together over a sustained period of time."

"In my dream," Ian said, "we got them on the same Jeopardy Pursuit team."

Alexander Marlow looked puzzled. "I have no idea what that is."

"I'll explain it to you," Matthew said.

Ian tapped Bartley on the shoulder and nodded toward the patio. "I think they can get the ball rolling. Can we talk for a minute in private?"

"Sure," Bartley said as he followed Ian outside.

"It's a beautiful day," Ian said.

"Sure is." Bartley chuckled.

"What?"

Bartley shook his head and grinned. "You're a real character, you know that? What you did in there?"

"What harm can come of it? If Sam and Jeremy don't like each other, then at least we tried, right? At least we did everything we could."

"I'm not being critical. It's just the more I get to know you, the more…. Okay, no more stalling. What exactly did you learn about me in your dream?"

"I learned a lot, but I don't know which parts are true and which parts were my imagination. So let's pretend I don't know anything. I'm just going to say what I have to say, no games. I'm really into—"

"Wait," Bartley said. "I'm sorry, but I have to stop you. Obviously something happened in that dream of yours, and you finally figured out I've been flirting with you for weeks. You were about to say you're really into me, I know that, and I want nothing more than to hear those words. God, you have no idea. But this will all come crashing down when I tell you that I'm—I'm sorry. Can you give me one more minute to enjoy this feeling? Please, before you take it all away."

"Don't be afraid," Ian said. "Say it."

"I can't."

"Bartley, I'm HIV positive, and I've made a lot of mistakes. I won't judge you for yours if you don't judge me for mine."

Bartley's face registered a rapid series of emotions. Then he threw his arms around Ian and kissed him. Ian almost fell backward, but he recovered and stood solid. He held Bartley in his arms, and their kiss lingered. Ian reached around and cupped Bartley's ass.

"So am I," Bartley said. "HIV positive. Is it wrong that I'm happy about that?"

"No. Not at all. I understand it's weird—being happy someone is positive. But we're compatible. For us, that's a good thing."

Bartley kissed him again. "How long?"

"Ten years," Ian said.

"Oh, you know your way around this thing. Maybe you can give me some pointers. It happened to me last September, and I know what you're thinking. But I didn't cheat on Mason and get HIV in the process."

"That's not what I was thinking. At all."

"I would really like to have sex with you. And I'm talking about the kind of sex where we disappear for two days, and Colleen will have to run La Tazza. Do you understand what I'm talking about?"

"I do."

Bartley reached down and squeezed the bulge in Ian's pants. "I was actually asking you out on a date last week, before you went to Denver. But when you looked at me with that blank expression, I panicked and added the 'as friends' part."

"I understand. By the way, I know what your tattoo means."

Bartley stepped back. "Are you serious?"

"I went to see Rachel earlier today. Yours is one of the Chinese symbols for 'forgiveness.'"

"Did she tell you that?"

"No, you did. In my dream."

"Ian, come on." Bartley looked away. "This is getting a little *Twilight Zone*-ish, don't you think?"

"I know. I'm sorry. But something good is happening to us. Are we just supposed to ignore that?"

Bartley paused but then stepped forward and kissed Ian again. "No. But you got something wrong with everyone else. I wonder what you got wrong about me."

"Hmm, let's see. Do you like baseball?"

"Love it. Big Astros fan."

"Did you watch Elias and Lari on YouTube?"

"Who?"

Ian laughed. "One of the European soap opera trims I told you about. You told me you watched it."

"Sorry, that never happened. I vaguely remember the conversation before you went to Denver, but sometimes I pretend to pay attention just because I want to sleep with you. I used to watch you talk and wonder what your lips tasted like."

"Now you know."

Bartley kissed him and licked his lips. "Espresso and chocolate. We should take a road trip to Houston for a ball game."

"Maybe they'll put us on the kiss cam."

Bartley grinned. "I'm so glad to see you again. So what tattoo did you get?"

"At first I thought I'd get the other symbol for 'forgiveness.' You know, so we'd have a complete set between us. But Rachel didn't ask me what I wanted. She just pointed to my left arm and said, 'How about right there'?" Ian peeled off the bandage and showed the tattoo to Bartley. In simple block letters was an English word.

Yes

"When I was dreaming, this is what woke me up," Ian said. "Every day, for the rest of my life, it'll remind me there's only one way forward. I'm done being angry. I'm done feeling sorry for myself. I'm done with regrets and living on the sidelines. From now on, if life is a question, then this is the answer."

"I don't know if I can do that," Bartley said. "At least not by myself."

"Then let's do it together. Look, I know you've been hurt. You said you didn't cheat on Mason, which means there's only one way you could have gotten HIV—and of all the ways to get it, that one sucks the most. I understand why Rachel gave you that tattoo. Every morning, when you wake up, you'll need to forgive him just to get out of bed. You think the idea of ever trusting someone again is impossible. But now imagine you roll over and I'm there, next to you. And I'm there tomorrow too, and the day after, and the tomorrow after that. Every morning, I'm there—day after day, week after week—a constant reminder that someone puts you first. After a while, those weeks will roll into months. And then one day, a few years from now, you'll look at me and be sure. Because every time I get frustrated and ask myself if I should stay, I'm going to look down at my arm for the answer—and that answer will never change. If I've learned anything from doing it all over again, it's that I need to stop thinking of my life as a series of mistakes. Nothing that led me to this moment with you could be a mistake. I'm going to be a good boyfriend, Bartley. I'm going to treat you well and tell you the truth and never betray you."

Bartley ran his hands through his lush hair. "I swear to God, La Tazza must have some kind of magic spell cast over it. It's just...."

"What?" Ian said.

"You're the one dream I thought would never come true."

Ian put his arms around Bartley and kissed him. "This isn't a dream."

"Okay," Bartley said. "I'm all in. Nothing would make me happier than to wake up next to you every morning. But at the risk of sounding fast and easy, can I ask you a favor? I haven't had sex in over seven months, and all this kissing and touching has flipped every crank and lever in my body. So can we just skip the first date and go straight to bed? Please."

Ian held out his arm and pointed to his tattoo in response. "Come on," he said as he took Bartley by the hand. "Let's go ask Colleen if she can run La Tazza for a couple more days. I've got a feeling we're going to need it."

Quentin opened the east door and stepped onto the patio. "Hey guys. Sorry to interrupt, but you'll never guess who just called me."

"Who?" Bartley said.

"Topher Manning. He asked if I knew someone named Ian Parker. He had a dream about you last night. Something to do with his kitchen, a late-night conversation, and a glass of milk?"

BRAD BONEY lives in Austin, Texas, the seventh gayest city in America. He grew up in the Midwest and went to school at NYU. He lived in Washington, DC, and Houston before settling in Austin. He blames his background in the theater for his writing style, which he calls "dialogue and stage directions." His first book was named a Lambda Literary Award finalist. He believes the greatest romantic comedy of all time is *50 First Dates*. His favorite gay film of the last ten years is *Strapped*. And he has never met a boy band he didn't like.

Website: http://www.bradboney.com
Facebook: https://www.facebook.com/BradBoneyBooks
Twitter: @BradBoney

The Eskimo Slugger

By Brad Boney

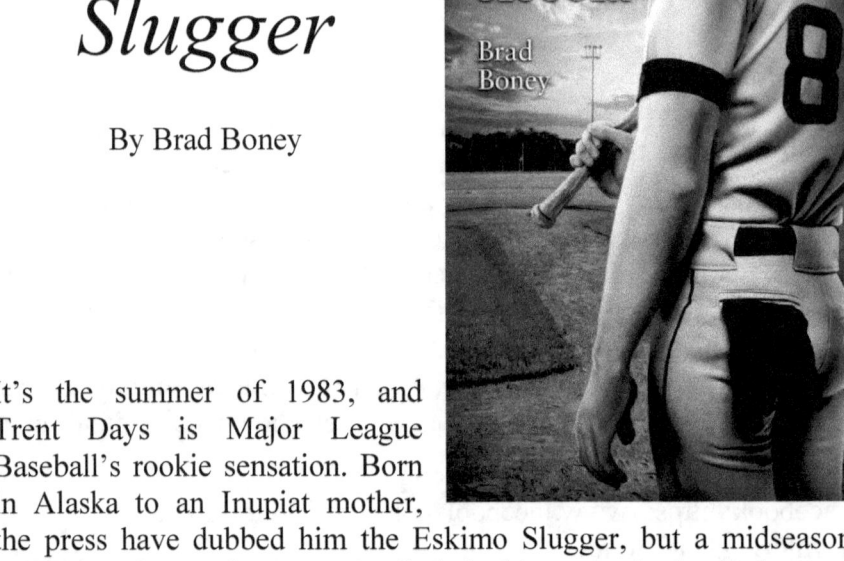

It's the summer of 1983, and Trent Days is Major League Baseball's rookie sensation. Born in Alaska to an Inupiat mother, the press have dubbed him the Eskimo Slugger, but a midseason collision at home plate temporarily halts his meteoric rise to the top.

Sent back to Austin to recuperate, Trent visits his favorite record store, Inner Sanctum, where he meets amiable law student Brendan Baxter. A skip in the vinyl of New Order's "Blue Monday" drives Trent back to Brendan, and their romance takes them into uncharted territory.

As Trent's feelings move from casual to serious, he's faced with an impossible dilemma. Does he abandon any hope of a future with Brendan and return to the shadows and secrets of professional sports? Or does he embrace the possibility of real love and leave baseball behind him forever? As he struggles with his decision, Trent embarks on a journey of self-discovery—to figure out who he really is and what matters most.

http://www.dreamspinnerpress.com

The Nothingness of Ben

By Brad Boney

Ben Walsh is well on his way to becoming one of Manhattan's top litigators, with a gorgeous boyfriend and friends on the A-list. His life is perfect until he gets a phone call that brings it all crashing down: a car accident takes his parents, and now he must return to Austin to raise three teenage brothers he barely knows.

During the funeral, Ben meets Travis Atwood, the redneck neighbor with a huge heart. Their relationship initially runs hot and cold, from contentious to flirtatious, but when the weight of responsibility starts wearing on Ben, he turns to Travis, and the pressure shapes their friendship into something that feels a lot like love. Ben thinks he's found a way to have his old life, his new life, and Travis too, but love isn't always easy. Will he learn to recognize that sometimes the worst thing imaginable can lead him to the place he was meant to be?

http://www.dreamspinnerpress.com

The Return

By Brad Boney

THE RETURN

BRAD BONEY

Music. Topher Manning rarely thinks about anything else, but his day job as a mechanic doesn't exactly mesh with his rock star ambitions. Unless he can find a way to unlock all the songs in his head, his band will soon be on the fast track to obscurity.

Then the South by Southwest music festival and a broken-down car drop New York critic Stanton Porter into his life. Stanton offers Topher a ticket to the Bruce Springsteen concert, where a hesitant kiss and phantom vibrations from Topher's cell phone kick off a love story that promises to transcend ordinary possibility.

http://www.dreamspinnerpress.com

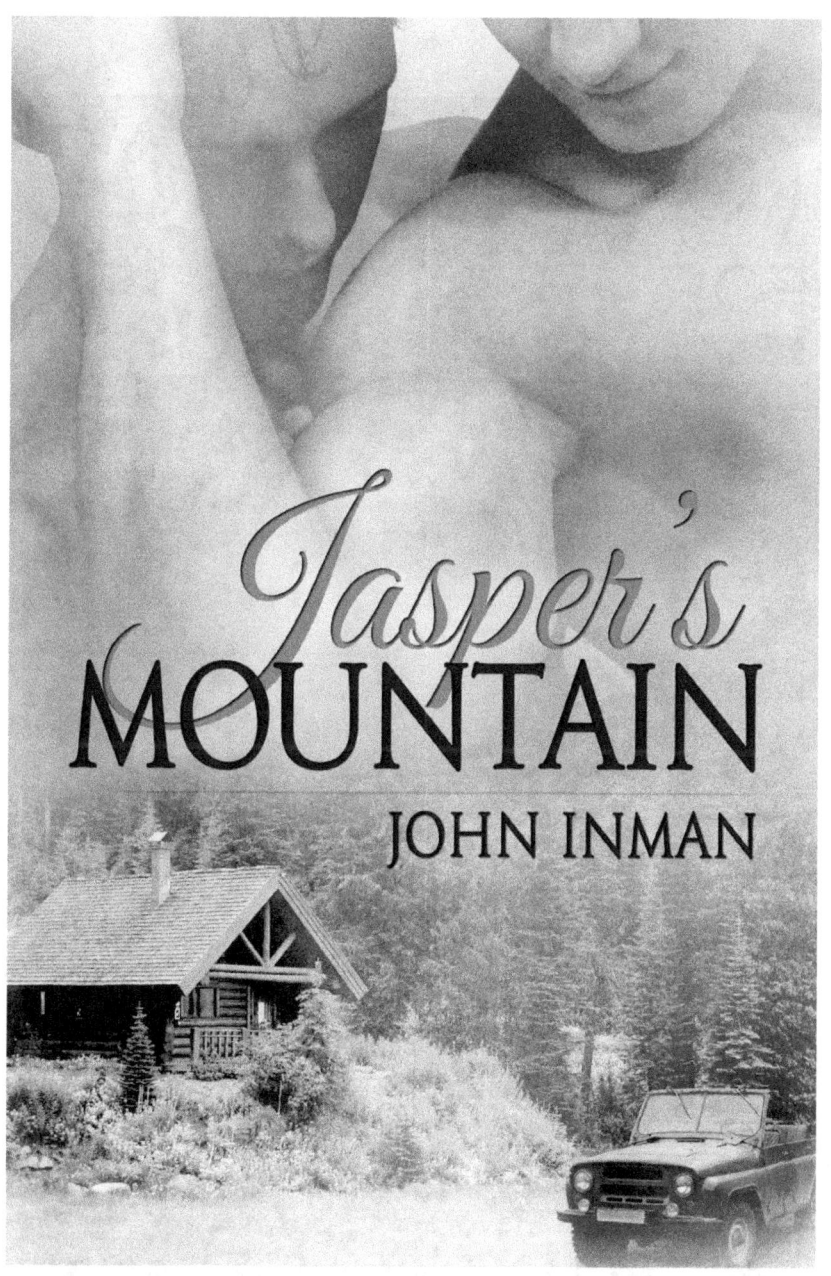

Jasper's MOUNTAIN

JOHN INMAN

http://www.dreamspinnerpress.com